TRUE STATUS

ENDORSEMENTS

True Status is a spiritual page-turner that pulls back the curtain to reveal the cosmic battle between God and Satan over the salvation of humanity. It brings us on the fascinating journey of one man's search for meaning and redemption. From the first paragraph until the story's conclusion, Chuck Richardson reminds us of the power of faith, the boundlessness of God's love, and the infinite worth of the human soul.
—**Carol Schlorff**, author of *How to Kill a Giant*

With shades of *Pilgrim's Progress* and *The Screwtape Letters*, this novel takes the reader alongside Billy Yates's journey from disbelief to faith in Christ. In the presence of angels and demons, we are treated to glimpses of his past life and the challenges of the present which he must reconcile to make a decision to follow Christ. Speculative fiction readers will particularly enjoy this book, but I recommend it for general audiences as well.
—**Linda Wood Rondeau**, author of *Lessons Along the Way* and *Ghosts of Trumball Mansion*

True Status is a fictional account of God's nonfictional ability to bring skeptics to faith. This page-turning book is a must-read for modern readers as it chronicles the reality of a journey many people in our secular society frequently experience. It's not farfetched to read a really good book, but rarely are readers afforded the opportunity to read a life-transforming book. *True Status* is such a life-transforming book that possesses the ability to inspire the reader to possibilities of tremendous proportions. I'm grateful my eyes have been privy to peruse through the pages of such a powerful book that is packed with eye-opening information.

—**Bryan C. Jones**, Senior Minister of Newburg Church of Christ in Louisville, Kentucky, author of *Finding My Good Thing*, *The Art of Soul Winning*, and *The Converted to Christ Personal Bible Study Series*.

There are big questions in life that bind all people together. We each seek answers for these questions in our own ways. Is there a spiritual realm? Do I have a spirit, and if so, how is it connected to my body? What happens to my spirit when my body dies? Is there such a thing as spiritual warfare? If so, how do I keep from getting hurt in it? What does a good life look like? Is there an "afterlife" that shapes how I live in this life? In *True Status*, the author, Chuck Richardson, crafts an intriguing story that takes the reader into the consideration of these big questions we all have. As the events of the life of Billy Yates unfold, readers may find themselves asking how such events are unfolding in their own lives. This is a book that is worth reading, sharing and discussing. Enjoy the journey this book can take you on.

—**Kerusso**, author of *When God Speaks...Will You Hear?* and *Leviticus Alive! Your God May Be Too Small*

True Status is a modern account of coming to follow Jesus. The story revolves around Tennyson William Yates as he has an encounter with a supernatural messenger after surgery. At first, Yates struggles with the vision and the reflections it causes. Yates spends time reviewing his life and wrestling with the memories the vision brings up. Eventually, Yates decides that the vision is calling him to learn more about the faith he was raised in, and he starts to engage that faith and discern not only if God is real but whether God is a God worth following.

There are certain things that stand out in *True Status*. First, the story really excels in drawing from the prophetic and apocalyptic literature of the Bible. The visions and encounters with other worldly creatures are clearly a homage to the individual visions of the prophets in the Hebrew Bible. Later in the book, when Yates starts engaging Christianity more directly, there is a real strength in the conversations that come from the Bible classes that Yates attends. These conversations are especially rich with the discussions that occur outside the Bible class, with many ideas and questions coming up. In these conversations you get a glimpse of the nuance and complexity that comes from following Jesus and studying the Bible.

—**Stephen Lamb**, Associate Pastor of Youth Ministry, Living Water Community Church, Chicago, Illinois

True Status

CHUCK RICHARDSON

ELK LAKE PUBLISHING INC.

PUBLISHING THE POSITIVE
Plymouth, Massachusetts

A Christian Company
ElkLakePublishingInc.com

COPYRIGHT NOTICE

PUBLISHED BY: Elk Lake Publishing, Inc., 35 Dogwood Drive, Plymouth, MA 02360, 2023

Library Cataloging Data
Names: Richardson, Robert C. (Robert C. Richardson)
True Status / Robert C. Richardson
322 p. 23cm × 15cm (9in × 6 in.)
ISBN-13: 9798891340008 (paperback) | 9798891340015 (trade hardcover) | 9798891340022 (trade paperback) | 9798891340039 (e-book)
Key Words: Lost Soul Book; Christian Fantasy; Demons and Angels Books; Black Authors Christian Books; Black Christian Fiction Books; Christian Mystery and Suspense; Christian Mystery Kindle Books
Library of Congress Control Number: 2023xxxxxx Fiction

TABLE OF CONTENTS

DEDICATION

This book is dedicated to the Lord Jesus Christ, and to his work to seek and to save that which is lost. The words of Jesus should fill us with hope, fear, and wonder that the salvation freely offered to all will be embraced by so few. Let us, you and I, enter through the narrow gate.

> Truly, truly, I say to you, he who hears My word, and believes Him who sent Me, has eternal life, and does not come into judgment, but has passed out of death into life.—John 5:24

> Enter through the narrow gate; for the gate is wide and the way is broad that leads to destruction, and there are many who enter through it. For the gate is small and the way is narrow that leads to life, and there are few who find it.—Matthew 7:13–14

ACKNOWLEDGMENTS

Thank you to my wife, Ruby, and our two daughters, Brittany and Jillian, for your continual loving support. Ruby, you have been beside me every day and have patiently read everything I write and rewrite and revise, and I know you wondered when I would finally get it all done. I love you very much. Jillian, your own creative efforts inspired me to begin writing this book. Brittany, your review of my earliest chapters let me know I had a lot to learn about punctuating dialogue.

Next, I must thank one of my coworkers, Cassandra Frost, for her thoughtful feedback about *True Status*. Cassandra, your insightful comments helped me put the finishing touches on the manuscript and improve the story in numerous ways. Also, Cassandra, thank you for telling me about the 2022 Kentucky Christian Writers' Conference. It was at the conference that I met Deb Haggerty of Elk Lake Publishing, who, three months later, became my publisher. I also want to thank another coworker of mine, Jill Elswick, who read an early version of *True Status*. Jill, your feedback helped me realize I had a long way to go before the book was ready for publication. Your comments helped guide me as I did a complete rewrite of the book.

Thank you to all the brothers and sisters in the church, my friends and teachers, who have helped me along the way and prayed for me since I was baptized as a twenty-four-year-old young man. Thank you to the faithful followers of Jesus at Newburg Church of Christ, Watterson Trail Church of Christ, Park Forest Church of Christ, and Schenectady Church of Christ, where I was born again in 1982. Thank you to Joe Aniskiewicz, a very old friend. Your example of faith in Jesus led to my own faith in him.

Finally, I want to thank the team at Elk Lake Publishing, Deb Haggerty, Cristel Phelps, and my editor, Mary W. Johnson, for believing in *True Status* and for being in the business of bringing the message of Christ to the world. Mary, thank you for your guidance and helping to make *True Status* the best book possible.

F<small>ROM DEATH INTO</small> L<small>IFE IS A</small> P<small>ERILOUS</small> P<small>ASSAGE</small>.

CHAPTER 1

WEEK 1—MONDAY

On the third Monday in April, the battle burst from unseen realms into my consciousness and altered the course of my life. It was also the day of my surgery.

The pre-op room was chilly, but without a word from me, my nurse brought me two warm blankets, sky blue and silky as a cloud. At first, I'd thought she might be an angel, but she turned out to be as human as me, and I soon learned angels are not sweet lovely things unless they're in disguise.

My name is Billy Yates. I had a personal dilemma I hoped surgery could resolve, but my nurse gave me the first hint my problems were bigger than just a dilemma. At forty-two years old, I was four weeks from a fork in the road, an intersection which would force me to choose which way my life would go.

When she breezed in, she said, "Hello, my friend. I'll be taking care of you."

She leaned her tall frame close as she spread the blankets over me, gave me a pat on the chest, and said, "Is that better? Comfy now?"

I nodded. The warmth from the blankets flowed into my body and helped relieve the knots in my stomach, which were there because of my impending operation. After adjusting a nearby cart, she went over my medical history, how I was feeling, and when I had last eaten. She focused on getting me ready for surgery, and to my dismay, her eyes did not meet mine. Her oval face and dark brown skin had the gloss of burnished bronze, and light flickered in her brown eyes like lightning flashes across a clear sky. She had a small scar under her left eye and another on the side of her face, but they'd healed long ago and the scars could not detract from her beauty. She enchanted me, and the electricity of desire surged in me.

Did she feel it too?

No rings on her fingers, but she also had some scars on her hands. What kind of brawls do angels get into?

She pulled on medical gloves, settled herself on a stool with wheels, and commenced preparing the surgical site on my right underarm.

Her name tag read *A. Otl*. I couldn't recall if she'd said her name. I asked her, "Does the A stand for Angel?"

"Pretty good guess. It's Angeline."

All right, I'm a genius.

My attention then shifted to saying her last name.

"Angeline Oh ..."

I could not figure out how to finish it. After a few moments of study, I said, "I've got it now. It's not a name at all. They're your initials. Angel of the Lord." Pride beamed within me at my own cleverness.

She smiled and, finally, turned her gaze on me, and I drank in the sight of her lovely eyes.

"My name is Angeline Otl. It rhymes with bottle, not Angel of the Lord. That's way above my pay grade. You're really silly."

Angeline made an on-target assessment of my demeanor, but it was likely the medicine they gave me. My mood was relaxed, sleepy, and goofy. A few weeks later, I learned some other things I'd said to her as the anesthesia took effect. Angeline moved over to work on the site under my left arm.

This surgery was my last hope. My overactive sympathetic nerves caused me to produce too much sweat, ruining a lot of nice shirts—and dinners with lovely women. And concentrating for a class or waiting calmly to be interviewed for a job while sweat poured down my sides? Forget about it.

I'd tried many less drastic remedies. Nothing solved my problem. But I did my research and learned about the surgery, so there was hope. I'd told all of my students there is always a solution if you put in the work to figure things out. I taught math at a community college and worked with kids fresh out of high school, adults who hadn't been in school for years, and all ages in between. As long as they put in the work, I would do everything in my power to help them succeed.

My approach to life was the same. Each of my problems had a fix, and I just had to put in the work to uncover the solution. I was glad I'd done the research and found out about the procedure that could solve my problem—endoscopic thoracic sympathectomy. The doctor said he would make a few incisions under each arm and then use some special instruments to disrupt the nerves in my underarms and stop the sweating in that area. The surgery required general anesthesia, so I would be unconscious for about an hour, but I'd be able to go home the same day.

Angeline had removed the hair from my left underarm. She looked startled, stopped working, and peered at the spot. She leaned closer and said in a low voice, "Why does it say that?"

"What?"

She sat up and looked directly at me. "Why does your tattoo say that?"

I laughed. I had no idea what she was talking about. "I don't have any tattoos."

"Whatever you say," she said. "It looks like a tattoo to me, and it has a message for you." Then she said in a whisper, "Lord, it may be his true status, but don't let it be his final status."

I smiled. "Did you just say a prayer for me?"

"Yes. I pray for all my patients."

As I drifted off to sleep, she leaned over and said, "My friend, do not give in to fear and despair anymore."

I laughed to myself. "I know them well. They're old friends. They'll be so disappointed."

"They are demons."

She looked worried. She saw me, and I think she liked me. A chuckle again left my lips.

"Angeline, are we friends?"

"Yes, Mr. Yates, we're friends."

"That's good, because this procedure worries me. You can call me Billy."

"Okay, Billy." Angeline looked puzzled when she said my name. She squeezed my hand. "We're going to take good care of you."

That was the last thing I remember her saying before the surgery.

When I woke, my mother was gazing down on me.

"Hi, Mom."

Adorned with earrings and a matching necklace framed by black hair with a few streaks of gray, my mother presented a striking image of beauty. She answered gently, "Hi, baby. How are you feeling?"

"A little tired and sore, but otherwise I feel good."

"The doctor said everything went fine, and you just need to take it easy for a few days."

TRUE STATUS

Her complexion and eyes were dark brown, just like mine, and her face was symmetrical, perfectly balanced. At seventy-three years old, her skin was still smooth, almost flawless. Any scars she had could not be seen from the outside. Mom and Dad—June and Lancaster Yates—had six children—Dolyana, Sabrina, Henry, Rueben, Daphne, and me, the youngest. People always said I looked just like my mother, but as I grew up my mustache, goatee, and closely cut hair ruined the resemblance.

Ezriah Reynolds, my best friend, stood next to Mom beside my bed. Ezriah, an attorney and my elder by nine years, also taught at the community college where I worked.

Before meeting Ezriah, I often saw him in the student center playing chess with students. One day he, a clean-shaven, broad-shouldered Black man, sat alone in front of a chess board in the student center. I paused briefly to eye the chessboard, and he looked at me and said, "Pawn to queen four."

He saw my blank look and added, "That's an opening move. Have you ever played chess? It's a great game."

"No, I haven't."

We introduced ourselves, and Ezriah proceeded to teach me the game of chess. He loved people, and continually found ways to reach out to all kinds of folk to make them feel at home, a talent I admired and wished was mine.

Ezriah helped me from the hospital bed to a nearby recliner, and I daydreamed in the tan vinyl pull-out sleeper chair while waiting to be discharged. My thoughts drifted to Mom's little brother, my Uncle Jimmy. He was two years older than I, and we were inseparable until he left Chicago for college in Louisville.

Jimmy had died in this same hospital twenty-five years earlier at the age of nineteen. I couldn't fathom why

God allowed such things to happen, and the thought of it always brought tumult to my mind and tempted me to shake my fists and curse God to his face. So with clenched teeth and a trembling body, I did something I hadn't done in years.

I prayed silently. "God, I believe you exist, and that makes what I've seen all the more maddening. My parents have always said to praise you. I love them, but I cannot praise you because I don't trust you. Why do you crush the innocent and never rescue them? You let my uncle die and left my mother to dissolve in tears and did not help her. Show me if I am wrong. Show me if you even care."

Sorrow for my insolent prayer immediately gripped me. My parents had taught me better than that, but strangely, I felt better. I really needed to rest. At least for the next few days, I was going to eat, sleep, and read, and try not to think too much.

As I sat there, Ezriah and Mom talked about getting me home. My thoughts returned to Angeline, and I hoped she would reappear in my hospital room so I could gaze into her eyes again and hear her calm, low voice. Angeline had such romantic loveliness, but more than that, she was refreshingly good, graceful, and attractive. My aim was to see her again.

But instead of Angeline, a giant in white clothing as bright as lightning bent down and squeezed himself under the door frame, pushing a wheelchair. When he straightened up, his hair brushed the ceiling. He looked like a warrior bent on vengeance and destruction. I shivered, and the hair all over my body stood at attention. I wanted to scream, to look away, to run and hide as his eyes pierced my soul, but instead I froze and sat silent. The giant wheeled the chair right past Mom and Ezriah and over to me. He motioned for me to get in the chair.

I didn't move. Human beings were not that big. He was not, could not be human, and I had no intention of going with him. With the doorway blocked, I considered vaulting from my chair and crashing through the window to escape. Instead, I remained motionless.

He reached down, touched my shoulder, and said, "I am Alexander. Do not be afraid." He again gestured for me to get in the wheelchair.

I wobbled as I rose. Alexander reached out and steadied me, and as though I were a child, he lifted me and placed me gently in the wheelchair. Ezriah and Mom continued to talk as though they did not even see Alexander. Then Mom turned and said they would pick me up at the front doors of the hospital, and they left me alone with the giant.

The thing I'd feared from the moment I learned the place of my surgical procedure reappeared in my mind, and I slumped in the wheelchair. Had Death come for me? Would this angel bear me to my final resting place? He was nothing like my sweet Angeline. Grief would strike my mother hard again, as it had when Jimmy passed away. Her grieving was unbearable to me. It was unfair. How could God be so unfaithful as to bring this repeated suffering upon my mother?

She would never even think such a thing. No matter what, she would always be a devoted child of God. But to me, God was not reliable or faithful. He had allowed my uncle to die, he allowed my father to be crushed in a work accident, and he had never answered my prayers for a wife and children, even though I had done much good in my life. God allowed untold millions to suffer all kinds of mistreatment and injustice. Now perhaps I would meet him. I had plenty of complaints and had forgotten all fear of God.

"Why do you think such miserable thoughts about our Father?" Alexander said, as he wheeled me down the corridor. "He determined precisely when and where you were to be born and gave you family, friends, and every resource to care for you. All the gifts and blessings he provided, so you would reach out and find him. He has always been near you, but you refused."

"You've been eavesdropping on my thoughts?" I sat up and slapped my knees. "That is really rude."

"Did you not know all your thoughts and deeds are an open book? You should examine your own life, rather than cast aspersions upon the God you barely know. Then make peace with your God."

I was silent, never having considered unseen observers and commentators had witnessed my life and judged it. I swiveled my head from side to side, wanting to discover the spiritual spies that might be surrounding me. There were only a few of the hospital staff, and we passed them in a blur while Alexander whisked me along.

"Do you remember Millie St. Vincent from high school?" he said.

"I've never heard that name before. Who is she?"

"You should ask yourself. Do you remember Eddie, Rose, Sharon, and Miros?"

"Of course. They meant everything to me at one time." I sighed and slumped back in the chair. "But that was a long time ago."

"Where are they now?"

I didn't answer, because I didn't know. I said, "Aren't you going to ask me about Mrs. Heaviland?"

"Why? Are you responsible for what happened to your beloved teacher?"

"Yes ... no." I wasn't sure. "I wasn't, but maybe ... I always felt I was."

"If so, you were a very powerful little boy. You have much to sort out in the past, but don't dwell on it too long."

"If I'm dead, why should I look back at my life? Isn't it too late for that? I *am* dead, aren't I?"

"Yes, you are. But who knows? Perhaps you will live again." Alexander chortled as if he had told a joke.

"You mean like reincarnation? I don't believe in that."

"Do you believe in anything?"

"Yes, I believe in doing good. I've helped a lot of people. My life is about helping, and I've always done that."

"My time with you is coming to an end for now. You are headed for all you fear. When you see the parable, heed the warning."

"What?" I paused, and my thoughts returned to Angeline. "What about Angeline? Will I see her again?"

"So you fancy the woman Angeline?" The grin in his voice was obvious.

"If I survive today, I'm going to marry her." I twisted in an attempt to look Alexander in the eyes.

"You are overconfident. But I did not come to bring you romantic advice. I will tell you a mystery. May you solve it and be blessed. One day ago, Angeline took her life and plunged it into death, yet now she truly lives. How can that be?"

That sounded like a riddle. I'd never been good at riddles, so I didn't even try to answer.

As we approached the final long hallway to the front of the hospital, the translucent doors revealed flickers of red and yellow flames. I cringed, finally realizing where Alexander was taking me. I slammed my shoes to the floor, and pressing myself back into the wheelchair, I strained with all my might to stop. My leg muscles cramped as I resisted my destiny, but I slid on. I tried to get up, but kept falling back. I wasn't strong enough to stop rolling to my punishment.

"Stop, stop. This isn't right," I yelled. "This is not fair. I don't deserve hell. I've done much more good than bad."

I couldn't stop the wheelchair. I pulled my feet up and prepared to leap over the side of the chair when the rolling stopped with a jerk, tumbling me to the floor. As I got up, Mom and Ezriah walked through the doors.

"You lied to me." Shaking my fist, I prepared to take a swing at Alexander. "I'm not dead!" As I got up and turned to face him, the giant was gone. In his place stood an unfamiliar tiny white-haired old woman, barely five feet tall.

"I never lie, Billy," she said. Her eyes were familiar, and then I knew. Alexander was there, looking out at me from those old but piercing eyes. "Have a nice day."

She whipped the wheelchair around and proceeded back down the hallway.

Mom and Ezriah helped me to my mother's rental car, and she drove me back to my apartment with Ezriah following in his car.

I sank into the front passenger seat and stared out at the evening sky painted with the sunset's lovely orange, red, and yellow reflections—heaven's fire—but there was no pleasure in the sight.

The ease and rest I craved would not be mine. They would burn on a funeral pyre of fear.

CHAPTER 2

WEEK 1—MONDAY

Bethesda Apartments provided three hundred fifty tidy dwellings, including my own garden apartment. The building consisted of a two-story U-shaped red brick structure with five gleaming white porches, each with an entryway into that section of the complex. Each porch had four white columns supporting a small roof emblazoned with the Bethesda Apartments' golden logo. A park-like courtyard in the back included a pool which many residents, including me, enjoyed during the warmer months.

Ezriah and Mom talked in the kitchen while I sat on my couch and stared at a framed drawing on the wall of Uncle Jimmy and me. A spider plant on a nearby shelf dangled one of its baby spiderettes above the picture as if reaching out to caress the frame. We had been shooting baskets at my parents' house, and a friend took a picture of us and later gave the photograph to Jimmy. In just fifteen minutes, he sketched the picture of us from the photo.

Ezriah entered the living room and said, "I'm taking off now. The girls have a play tonight. I'll check on you tomorrow." Ezriah had a wife, twin daughters, and an older son.

"Okay. Thanks for everything. Tell the girls I wish I could see them perform, but their uncle needs to rest." A seven-foot bamboo palm stood like a sentinel near my apartment door, and Ezriah brushed by the plant, opened the door, and then turned back for a moment.

"Don't forget the class starts next Tuesday night at seven." Then he was gone.

Ezriah attended classes at a seminary, and he had extracted a halfhearted commitment from me to join a class called 'Jesus in the Old Testament.' I'd had enough of Bible study from my childhood and teen years. Ezriah meant well—he was always trying creative ways to save me—but my intent was to come up with a reason why I couldn't make the class. Ezriah reminded me of Miros Rybakov, an old friend who'd studied for the ministry twenty years earlier. And thinking of Miros reminded me of Alexander, the peculiar big being—imaginary or real—who wheeled me to the door of the hospital. He'd mentioned Miros, among others from my past.

The savory aroma of Mom's cooking filled my apartment. Roast beef, mashed potatoes and gravy, green beans—she was a master at making the best meals in no time. While we were eating, Dad called, and Mom sequestered herself in my office and filled him in on everything concerning my surgery so they could do their usual parental plotting.

Dad was retired due to injury. Five years earlier, his spine had been crushed in a work accident when an overloaded pallet rack collapsed on him, and he traveled only rarely these days. When Mom returned, I still sat at the kitchen table and pretended to read the news on my tablet. Meanwhile, I racked my brain, still thinking about Alexander, without gaining traction as to what direction to take.

I looked up from my tablet. "How's Dad?"

TRUE STATUS

"You better call him. He wants to know when you're going to visit."

"I might do that and extend my time off from work an extra week." A worthy excuse to avoid next week's class with Ezriah.

My father was built strong and lean without an ounce of fat, and his limbs were like pieces of black wire woven together to form long legs and arms. People said I looked like my mother, but my build was like my father, tall and wiry. Dad used to keep factory machines humming as an electrical and mechanical maintenance man. No one was more skilled with machinery than he.

Dad suffered catastrophic, faith-busting injuries from his accident with the overloaded pallet rack. Fast action by first responders got him to a trauma center and into surgery that saved him from bleeding to death internally. Following the emergency surgery, Dad had two more surgeries, each lasting about twelve hours, to treat his neck and back injuries. We weren't sure if he would be permanently paralyzed, or if he would even survive. After three months, Dad was able to walk with a walker, and after a year he was able to walk normally, but he couldn't sit, stand, or walk for long without leg pain.

Mom strolled to my living room picture window and took in the lovely view of car tires, fenders, and the parking lot asphalt. Most people thought my garden apartment was half underground, but in my view it was more than half above ground. During the day, sunlight poured in and filled my place with warmth and light.

She sighed. "You really like this place, don't you?"

"Yes. It's my sanctuary."

"I can see that." She thought it more of a dungeon.

Mom walked over to one of the bookshelves that graced the three walls of my living room. The shelves were not only replete with books, but with pictures of family and friends, awards, souvenirs from family vacations, metal and wooden masks, and plants. All manner of greenery and flowers thrived under my care. They filled my apartment, making it a garden paradise. My affection for plants was only exceeded by my love of books, resulting in an impressive literary collection amassed over decades.

"You loved books before you could even read, always the smartest kid in school. Our little professor. We're so proud of you. We always knew you were going to be a teacher." Mom ran her hands along one of three small desktop bookshelves that had no hardware or glue holding them together—only slots and pegs. "These are really beautiful. Are you still doing woodworking?"

In the back of Bethesda Apartments stood a separate structure that consisted of a series of single-car garages. I rented one of the garages and used it as a woodworking shop. I stained rather than painted my pieces, because stain was semi-transparent, allowing the beauty of the wood grain to be seen. I experimented with different colors of stain like antique jade, hunter green, mustard, white, charcoal gray, and antique red, as well as traditional wood colors of walnut and oak. My oversized living room housed twenty of my bookcases, and the room was a beautiful and colorful tribute to life and learning—a space full of the knowledge of many things. The rest of my bookshelves were in my bedroom, kitchen, and home office.

Altogether my home had three-hundred-forty feet of shelf space filled with about 6600 books, and I had read almost all of them. It was a good thing I had an e-reader, because if not, there wouldn't have been room for me to live there. My books represented much of my learning since middle school, and I treasured them. I read and studied a great deal, and my love of reading had served me well. Strangely though, I didn't remember the contents of most of my books. If I couldn't remember them, what was the point of having read them?

As Mom stood there, a quote from Ralph Waldo Emerson came to me. "I cannot remember the books I've read any more than the meals I have eaten; even so, they have made me."

I agreed with Emerson, but I would've gone further and said books not only made me, but they also saved me. Books had been not only my comfort and refuge, but also my creators and my saviors, so they were due my honor.

In answer to Mom's question, I said, "I haven't had time for woodworking, not in quite a while. I've been putting in extra hours at work. Some of my students need a lot of help."

I taught different math classes, from remedial math to calculus. Many of my students were adults in their late twenties and thirties, just a little younger than me and, in some ways, not so different. In many cases, they'd admit they didn't pay attention when they were in grade school. They'd given zero thought to their future. As adults, they deeply regretted their childhood foolishness when they couldn't get the jobs they wanted or make the money they needed to take care of themselves and their families. They didn't realize until too late how important it was to pay attention to their teachers and parents, so they ended up paying for the education that could have been theirs for free. They'd been immature, but when they got to me, most of them were serious. It was my pleasure to help them prepare for a new and better life.

A few months before my surgery, one of my former students, Jeremy Jordan, surprised me when he stopped by my office. He'd graduated with his associate degree and had moved on to engineering school.

Jeremy said, "Mr. Yates, can you help me? I'm struggling with differential equations. I can't understand a word my professor says."

We met after work every day for weeks, and he aced the class. I had to brush up on differential equations, but the knowledge came back to me quickly enough. A request like Jeremy's was something I'd never turn down, because it was my purpose and reason for being put on earth. And my students' needs were not always academic. Sometimes, they were financial or emotional, so my support might be money for rent or food. Sometimes, it was a word of advice or encouragement, or even a place to stay for a few nights. My joy and honor was to help—to see them reach their goals. My math blog attracted learners from all over, so my service to students extended around the country and the world.

"How long have you been at the college?" Mom said, as she examined my books. She loved reading too. She was the one who'd infected me with the reading bug. "I worry sometimes. You hear so much these days about colleges having financial problems."

"I came to Louisville when I was twenty-four, so it's been eighteen years." I paused a moment, ordering my next words in my mind. "Mom, did you see the humongous guy that wheeled me out of the hospital?"

She laughed.

"Very funny. She was the tiniest woman I've ever seen. But it looked like you were upset. Did she say something to you?" Mom returned to the kitchen and placed a hand on my forehead. "You don't have a fever, but you don't look well."

"Did you realize my surgery was at the same hospital where Uncle Jimmy died?"

Mom gripped the back of one of the kitchen chairs. "I knew it, but I tried not to think about it. Jimmy's surgery was supposed to be just as low-risk as yours."

"I was nervous about my surgery. How did you deal with the fact that God ignored all our prayers and let Jimmy die?"

Jimmy was on a run on his college campus when he made a misstep, fell, and broke his leg. The repair required surgery, so my parents and I drove to Louisville to visit him while he was in the hospital. It was then, before the surgery, that Jimmy drew the picture of the two of us from his friend's photo. The day after the surgery to repair his leg, a blood clot hit Jimmy's heart, causing a fatal heart attack. At nineteen years old, he was gone.

Jimmy's death devastated us all, especially my mother. Seeing Mom suffer so much broke my heart all over again. Why God let Jimmy die was beyond my understanding. It made no sense. Without Jimmy, there would have been no me, as in Professor Yates, math instructor. In middle school, math became a struggle for me, but Uncle Jimmy tutored me several times each week until what had been my weakness became a strength.

"I know my God did not—" Mom's voice rose. "—he did not ignore my prayers." Mom clasped her hands, took a deep breath, and spoke deliberately. "He heard me. He just didn't answer the way I wanted him to. I just had to accept he is God, and I am not. He is a good God. Romans 8:28 says all things work together for good for those that love God and—"

"But we didn't get good. We got bad. We got the worst possible outcome."

Mom put one hand on my shoulder. "He was my baby brother. Not everything is good, but God works everything together for good for his people. We've all got to die at some point. That's not God failing us."

I knew she would answer like she did, but to me her answer was not acceptable. Mom and Dad always gave answers like that, but in my mind, God had let us down. Why would God let one of his faithful servants go through so much suffering? God was supposed to be faithful, to love those that loved him. To me, God was unreliable.

"Another thing," I said. "The verse in Romans leaves out those who do good, because it is right. Not all of us love God, but we still do good. Is God so self-centered he only appreciates those who love him? Why can't he appreciate the good people who do good just because it's right?"

"Because our good works are not that good. They're always flawed, and often, they're mixed with our self-interest and pride. But God can redeem them and use them for his glory and our good, if we love him. If God based his grace and favor on our good deeds, we'd all be in trouble." Mom put her arms around me and hugged me tightly and added, "Billy, I hope you'll go to that class with Ezriah. You need to think about spiritual things."

"I think about spiritual things all the time, just not about Jesus. My calling as a teacher is spiritual. My work is important to the well-being of my students and their families."

"Billy, we've been over this a million times. No matter how much good work you do, good work is not going to save your soul. Jesus is the only one who can do that."

"I'll think about going to the class. Do you remember my second grade teacher, Mrs. Heaviland?"

"Isn't that the one who nicknamed you Billy Goat Billy? You thought you were a superhero that year." Mom laughed at the memory.

"Actually, I gave myself the name but because of her class. In my mind, I was a superhero for a while. I've always been sorry I couldn't go back and visit her and show her what I've done with my life."

"You had nightmares about her for a while. What made you think of Mrs. Heaviland?"

"Someone at the hospital today mentioned her. Do you believe God sends people visions?"

Mom took a chair at the table and sat. "I know God revealed things to his prophets and apostles in Bible times, but I don't think he's still doing it today. Why do you ask?"

"I think a vision of an angel appeared to me at the hospital. He was terrifying, and he spoke to me. I thought angels were supposed to be sweet little things."

"Oh my goodness, baby, what are you talking about?" The pitch of her voice rose. "When did this happen?" She was sitting directly across from me, studying me, ready to weigh my every word and figure out the mystery I'd become.

"That little bitty woman you saw at the hospital had been a huge man, but he wasn't human."

"What did he say? What did he want?"

"When I first saw Alexander—that was his name, Alexander—he wasn't human, so I started thinking I'd died." The daylight outside was rapidly becoming dark, so I got up and moved around the apartment, closing the blinds and draperies in the kitchen and living room. "I'd already been worried from thinking about Uncle Jimmy's death, and I just got angry thinking about how much you would suffer from my passing away. I wanted to give God a piece of my mind, and as I stewed and brooded, Alexander interrupted and reprimanded me for thinking ill of the Lord." I came back and sat opposite her at the table.

"He'd invaded my thoughts and read my mind. He said God had always been near me, and that God had given me all kinds of blessings, and I hadn't appreciated any of them. He said I needed to examine my own life instead of criticizing God. He named some of my old friends." I squeezed the tightness at the back of my neck. "Alexander lied to me, because he said I was dead. I asked him what was the point of examining my life, if I was already dead? He said maybe I could live again. What does that mean?"

"So, he wanted you to examine your life. Was there anything else?"

"He said something about seeing a parable and heeding the warning. He was trying to scare me, and he did a good job. Now it's making me angry and afraid. Do you think I imagined it?"

"Do you think it was real? That's what matters. Was it something you just imagined, or was Alexander God's messenger to you?"

"I don't think I imagined it. He spoke in defense of God, not something natural for me, even in my imagination. I really just want to forget about Alexander, and reliving the past is the last thing on my agenda. What good would that do, right? But what if he comes back?"

"Well, it doesn't sound like he told you to do anything really crazy or dangerous. If you believe it was real, then maybe you should examine your past. What could it hurt?"

"There are some things better left forgotten. Plus, if he lied to me, how could he be God's messenger? I am not dead."

"You're thinking about physical death, but there's such a thing as spiritual death also."

"You mean like when a family disowns someone and they become dead to them? So Alexander was saying

I'm dead to God? That doesn't make sense. God should recognize the good I've done."

Mom shook her head.

"You know what? We covered this ground a few minutes ago. I'm going to bed. I have an early flight tomorrow, but I'm going to give this some serious prayer. You should try praying about it also, especially if you think this was a message from God."

I had no intention of praying, but my encounter with Alexander reignited my memories of second grade, especially of Mrs. Heaviland and Eddie Frogman. Mrs. Heaviland, my second grade teacher, inspired my own teaching career. I loved her, but she often haunted my thoughts, and each remembrance brought a burden of guilt that made no sense.

Eddie, on the other hand, was my best friend back then.

CHAPTER 3

Second Grade

The goats climbed up the mountain's sheer rock face, and the video images of the mighty goats with their pointy horns, black and sharp, captivated me. They were so brave. They weren't afraid of falling, because their hard heads protected them if they fell. Even more amazing were the Moroccan goats who could climb trees. They stood at the tops of argan trees, munching on the fruit which looked like shriveled golden apples.

I fell in love with goats, and upon learning boy goats were called billy goats, I took on a new persona and transformed into Billy Goat Billy, a hero who climbed mountains, trees, and anything else. He also helped kids solve every kind of problem.

That day as I went out of the room for recess, I stopped at my teacher's desk and leaned toward her and said in my most serious voice, "From now on, call me Billy Goat Billy."

Mrs. Heaviland looked at me and smiled. "You really like the goats, don't you, Billy?"

"Yes," I said, punching my hands up into the air. "I am a goat. My name is Billy Goat Billy. I have heart."

Mrs. Heaviland laughed and said, "Yes, I can see that you do." Then she stood up and said, "Come with me, Billy."

We walked out of the room and down the hall. I didn't know where we were going, but it was going to be good. I loved Mrs. Heaviland, and she loved me too, because I was her favorite student—at least that was the case in my mind. As she walked and I bounded along to keep up, I looked up at Mrs. Heaviland. I had already decided I was going to be just like her and teach boys and girls everything. We reached our destination, the school library, and Mrs. Heaviland spoke to the librarian, who then left for a few minutes and returned with a big book.

Mrs. Heaviland turned to me. "Billy, you can keep this book for one week."

The book was all about goats. While the other kids played games on the playground, I plopped myself into a soft rocking chair in the library and began soaking in the book's images and the story of goats. I envisioned the good deeds superhero Billy Goat Billy would do.

Later that day at home, I went outside and looked for my two best friends—Eddie, who was White, and Sammy Parker, who was Black like me. They did not attend my school. They both went to a private Christian school. Sammy had moved to Frankfort as a kindergartener from Rome, New York, and we three had been friends ever since.

Neither Eddie nor Sammy could come out to play, so I returned home, went to my backyard, and stood in Tall Tower and looked out across the yard. To my mother, Tall Tower was a swing and slide. My father called it a sky fort skyscraper, but from the time I saw it and understood what it was, it became Tall Tower.

My father had built Tall Tower for my fifth birthday. About six weeks before my birthday, the hardware store delivered the wood for Tall Tower, and a huge pile of pressure-treated lumber filled our garage. Every day after he came home from work, whether he was tired or not, my father would pour himself into building it, and over the next forty days Tall Tower rose to life. I watched as Dad cut the wood and assembled the entire structure, with wood screws holding it all together. I helped out some, but mostly I watched Dad build it. At first it looked like the skeleton of a small house standing in our back yard, but slowly it took shape, and it came to life for me with the spirit of my father.

At its pinnacle, the tower portion was twelve feet in height with a ground level and a platform halfway up. The platform level was a nice hiding place, because it was completely enclosed with boards except for three openings. One of the openings was accessible by a rope ladder, and the other by a wooden ladder. The platform level had a third opening where an attached enclosed yellow turbo tube provided spiral sliding transport to the ground. A multicolored tarp covering a top board formed the peaked ceiling of Tall Tower.

Attached to the tower at a height of seven feet was a twelve-foot-long support beam held up at the other end by an A-frame structure. Two swings dangled from the support beam secured with bolts and nuts that protruded through the beam.

My father's protective power lived in and surrounded Tall Tower, so in my mind nothing bad could happen to me while I stayed in or on the Tower. But that day, the day I got the goat book, something evil invaded the sanctity of my safe place.

Standing in Tall Tower, the sun baked my skin in the hot, dry air. No wind gave relief, and an eerie silence filled our neighborhood, normally a noisy place with the sounds of children playing.

Just before I headed back inside to cool off, a voice said, "If you're really Billy Goat Billy, then climb up here."

"Who is it?" I looked around and saw no one. "Where are you?"

I sometimes heard the sound of my parents' voices when they were not around, but this was a new and strange voice.

"I am the god of this world."

God of this world?

"Climb up?" I said. "Climb up where?"

The voice said, "You know."

I looked up and saw the upper beam of the swing station. The two swings hanging from the beam swayed slightly. I walked out from the main section of Tall Tower to the A-frame that held the other end of the upper beam, raised my left foot and placed it against one of the A-frame supports. I stood for a moment, my right foot on the ground and my left foot on the A-frame, trying to figure how I could climb up.

Years later, I calculated the A-frame support formed a steep sixty-five-degree angle with the ground. I grabbed the underside of the A-frame support with my left hand and pulled myself up, stepping up with my right foot and grasping the underside with my right hand. There I was with both feet on top of the support and both hands wrapped around to the underside. Pain racked my hands as I struggled against gravity. I took small step after small step and with each step repositioned my hands until I reach the top.

At the top, I crouched and rested in the hot stillness. The top support was three inches wide, and I stood up and began to traverse the top beam. With my first step, the wind began to blow, but I took several small steps and stopped as the wind whipped the tarp on Tall Tower. The tarp undulated back and forth, one side pushing in and the other side blowing out. The trees in front of our house swayed wildly, and the strength of the wind horrified me.

Wind blew against my face, and incredibly, tiny crystalline balls of ice fell and bounced off my narrow pathway.

The voice came again, laughing. "You won't make it. You're going to fall."

"I am *not*."

My defiant spirit clashed with my trembling body, and I froze on the top beam. I was seven feet off the ground and six feet away from the safety of one of the twelve-foot posts. My imagination stretched the distance, making me feel much higher up and farther away. As I stood there, the bolts threatened—I had forgotten about them. The top parts of the bolts protruded up, about an inch above the top beam. I don't know why I didn't trip over the first set of bolts. The bolts supporting the second swing were ahead of me, seeming to reach up, ready to trip me.

The voice laughed an evil laugh, and the beam glistened with icy water droplets. I stood motionless, but only for a few seconds. I took several short steps and avoided the bolts. I grabbed one of the twelve-foot posts and held onto it, terrified at my accomplishment, but also exultant. I'd done it, walked across the top beam of Tall Tower.

I stood on the top beam and held on to the post for several seconds and then bent and stepped down under the tarp, which still whipped back and forth in the wind, and onto the platform. I sank to my knees and threw my hands up.

"I really *am* Billy Goat Billy. I'm amazing."

As I knelt there, a kid's voice said, "He's up here."

It was Eddie and Sammy. Eddie was trying to climb up the turbo slide the wrong way. Sammy crawled onto the platform from the rope ladder.

"Billy, what are you doing?"

"Did you see what I did?" We both knelt and sat back on our heels.

"What did you do?"

"I walked all the way across this beam."

Sammy looked at the beam and then back at me. "Why would you do that? You could kill yourself."

"To prove who I am." I pounded on the platform.

"Why? We know who you are. Don't you know who you are?"

Eddie called out, "Guys, let's go to the river before it gets dark."

"I had to prove it to the voice. He told me to do it. Can you believe it hailed?"

Sammy said, "What voice? You're hearing things. And we didn't have hail."

"He said he was God. He laughed at me. He wanted me to fall. I had to show him."

"God would never tell you to do something and then hope you can't do it. My dad says God always helps us do his will, and he's with us no matter what."

"Come on guys, let's go," Eddie said again.

Eddie was still trying to climb up the slide the wrong way, pulling himself up.

I said, "Yeah, let's go."

The voice softly said, "Yes, get going, Billy Goat Billy. This is only the beginning of your work for me. If you walk in my ways, you will remove anyone who falls short in your eyes. Let your impulsivity reign."

The message went over my head, but to escape the menacing voice I jumped up, pushed Sammy aside, and dove into the slide head first. Sammy dove in right behind me. We screamed with glee and crashed into Eddie, pushing him backward out of the turbo slide. We shot out like triplets—Eddie belly-down and feet first, then me, and Sammy last of all. We sprang up and ran for the river.

Trees lined both sides of our street and stretched up and over the street and met in the middle to form a high arch over the road with bits of fading sunlight showing through. We raced down the middle of the street, as if running down the main aisle of some ancient cathedral up to the altar. Eddie led the way with long loping strides. Sammy and I jostled against each other as we tried to keep up with Eddie for the three blocks to the Tiberias River. Gradually, Sammy pulled away from me and caught up to Eddie.

Like running in church and playing in the middle of the road, going down to the river without a sibling or parent was forbidden, but that didn't enter my mind. I thought about Eddie and his interesting knack for things involving nature, especially animals—frogs, turtles, and other creatures. Rivers, lakes, and ponds were Eddie's favorite places.

The street ended, and we left the asphalt and the tree canopy behind and emerged into a field of grass that sloped down toward the river. Heat enveloped us as we emerged from the shade. As we ran, grasshoppers, crickets, and other bugs fled before us, trying to avoid being trampled. Eddie and Sammy were running stride for stride, and they elbowed each other until Sammy lost his balance and took a hard tumble.

"What did you do that for?" Sammy yelled. He tried to get up, but fell down twice more before he righted himself. He looked so funny. Eddie and I laughed, but I could see Sammy was mad.

Eddie finally stopped laughing and said, "Sorry. You're okay. Let's go."

He started running again, and we followed him down to the river bank. He crossed the bridge over the river every day on his way to school, and the previous day he'd spoken about a huge tree that had fallen half into the river. He said he wanted to explore it.

The river's scent grew stronger as we approached. The smells of algae, wet grass, and wildflowers filled the air, along with the audible greeting of swirling, rushing water splashing over the rocks. We raced down the river trail to a place I'd never been before. When we got to the spot where the tree had fallen, we could see part of the trunk was under water, but a lot of it was above the surface. The monstrous tree stretched diagonally in relationship to the river bank, and many of its tangled branches reached back over the land. Eddie climbed onto the trunk of the tree and walked quite a long way out into the river, then got down on the tree on his stomach and reached for something in the water.

Meanwhile, I climbed up on a large rock that loomed over the area near the water and stood on it. Sammy, still sulking, wandered down the trail away from the tree, angrily throwing stones into the river. From my perch, some strange-looking fruit hanging from the fallen tree's branches beckoned me. Some of the branches hung above the rock where I stood, and I grabbed one of them and held on to it as the water distracted my attention from the fruit.

The ever-flowing water captured my imagination.

Where'd it come from? Where is it going? How come it never runs out?

My thought was to climb onto the tree branches like the goats I'd seen in the video and the book. As I stood there muddling, Eddie called my name. I turned my head and saw a snake right in front of my face, hanging from a branch. The snake, about two feet long with dark brownish green skin and a distinct scale pattern, wiggled a yellowish tail. Its belly was a series of white rings that ran the length of its body and met the darker colored skin at its nose. The snake's head was shaped like a triangle. Its eyeballs had black slits in them.

TRUE STATUS

The wind blew hard against my face as the snake floated up and down in front of me, and I felt the same way as earlier that day when the voice invaded Tall Tower. The voice wanted me to die then. Now he wanted to possess and destroy anything he could reach. I didn't hear the voice, but I felt it nearby.

Maybe, it was inside the snake.

I fell backward onto the rock as the snake coiled itself up, flicked out its tongue, and opened its jaws to reveal a white mouth and huge fangs. It moved toward me, gliding slowly. Then abruptly Eddie stood over me. He grabbed the snake around the neck.

"He can't hurt you now." Eddie shook the snake and laughed. "It's a small one, but it could have killed you." Eddie's face lit up with excitement. "I haven't seen this kind around here before."

"Kill it," I said. "Bash its brains out and kill it. Smash it."

"Why? It's just a dumb animal. We probably scared it out of the tree."

I quickly got to my feet. "I hate it. It wants to control me. Bash its brains out. Make it die. I can hear him laughing."

"You're nuts." Eddie laughed again and shook his head. "How can it control you? It can't hurt you now. I'll just throw it in the river." Eddie threw it over his shoulder, and it landed in the water with a splash.

Eddie probably didn't hear the snake hit the water because he slipped and fell as he threw the snake. He flailed his arms to regain his balance, surprise and fear on his face, but he'd gone over too far. He fell backward, and his head slammed onto the stone with a thick thud. The light in his eyes went out, and he slid down unconscious in a heap at the base of the rock. Blood gushed from Eddie's head, soaking into his shirt and the ground.

Over and over, I shook Eddie and told him to wake up. When he didn't, I looked for Sammy but didn't see him. I started screaming his name, and finally Sammy came running. He stayed with Eddie while I dashed, full of adrenaline and fear, to find help. I was scared we would get in trouble, but happy to get away from the river, because the snake would be coming back to get me. It would be back.

An ambulance came and took Eddie to the hospital.

Certainly, he'd get better, and we'd be able to play together again soon. It would be several days before I learned how bad Eddie was hurt.

That evening, the prospect of going to school the next day excited me. I would be Billy Goat Billy and in my element as a huge benefactor to my teacher and classmates. Being Mrs. Heaviland's helpful helper would be my job, and she would, of course, be very pleased with me.

I did not dream my idea of being helpful would be miles from hers.

CHAPTER 4

Second Grade

White porcelain matched Mrs. Heaviland's skin tone, and sharp angles defined her facial features. Her nose and chin seemed chiseled from some translucent mineral. When she introduced herself to the class at the beginning of the school year, she told us her name was Mrs. Chrysolite Heaviland. She laughed and said she was from a place where everyone was heavy. A tall and big woman she was, like a mountain extracted from its foundation and transported to our classroom. When I first saw her name, I thought it said Heavenlyland which was a much better indication of where she was from. She'd served in the military, and that discipline showed in her seriousness in teaching and in the strength of her guidance. Though she was not soft or jovial, we knew she dearly loved us.

Mrs. Heaviland passed out worksheets for our in-class assignment—math word problems. Some kids groaned and others rolled their eyes, but I loved those problems. As Mrs. Heaviland walked around the classroom, our principal rushed in, said something to her, and then left. Her face changed. Something was wrong. She began walking to the door of the room, and as she reached the door, she turned toward us.

"Boys and girls," she said, "I have to go to the office for a few minutes. I'll be right back. I want you to stay in your seats and keep working on your worksheets."

With the assignment finished, my eyes scanned the room to look at the faces of my classmates. Word problems were fun and interesting, but I sighed at the confusion in many eyes. Some had trouble reading and others had trouble with math, so word problems were the worst for them. Joel Johnson, a kid I'd known since kindergarten, saw I was done with the assignment and waved me over. I got up to see what he wanted.

Joel said, "Is this answer five?"

"Read it again and circle the numbers and important words. You have to know what kind of problem it is—you know, times, adding, taking away, or dividing."

After re-reading the problem, Joel said, "Oh, okay, I get it. The answer is six."

I also helped a new kid who sat next to Joel. Then I turned away and started walking around the classroom, imitating the way I had seen Mrs. Heaviland make her rounds.

As I left Joel, the new kid said, "Is he trying to show us up?"

"No," Joel said, "he can't help helping. He's always been like that. A brainiac-math-wizard kid. But he's cool."

Billy Goat Billy was a brainiac-math-wizard cool kid. I liked Joel's answer. Then Suzy Harris and Frannie Simpson waved me over. I explained a problem to Suzy and then clapped my hands and bounced over to Frannie. Explaining things to my friends was my wheelhouse, a satisfying place to be lost in, and they seemed to understand better after my help. I was helping Frannie when Mrs. Heaviland returned. My back was to the door, and I didn't hear her come into the room.

"Billy Yates," she screamed. "I told you to stay in your seat. Now sit down."

Her voice sounded completely different and hit me hard, like a punch. My legs got weak and I almost doubled over. Confusion filled my mind, and I had trouble thinking or even remembering where my desk was. I *never* got into trouble at school.

When I turned around and saw her, fear flowed through me and settled heavily in my shoes. I didn't move. I didn't say anything. Her face was bright red, and sweat flowed down her temples and cheeks. Terror anchored me to that spot like a little black nail a big red hammer was about to pound. I envisioned a scene from an unfunny cartoon where someone was drilled into the ground.

"He was helping us, Mrs. Heaviland," Frannie said softly.

"I don't care what he was doing. Billy, you have been disobedient, and you know what? In this world bad, bad things happen to disobedient little boys. Now *sit down*." Violence filled her voice, like she wanted to break something.

I almost sat down on the floor right there. I leaned against Frannie's desk for a second.

Frannie gave me a little push and said, "Go, Billy."

Disoriented, I stumbled back to my seat, sat, and put my head down on the desk. I was a bad boy. What had I done? What would happen to me? It was right after lunch, so we had another three hours of school left. I don't remember anything else Mrs. Heaviland taught for the rest of that day. I tried to listen, but I couldn't understand anything. My brain had shut off.

When the bell rang, and it was time for us to go home, we all began to gather our things and head out the door. Mrs. Heaviland stopped me and told me to wait by her

43

desk as she said goodbye to all the other boys and girls. I was trapped. Her eyes pierced my broken heart and surely saw how bad I was, but I couldn't tell if she was sad or mad. I no longer knew her.

"Billy, I am so sorry I yelled at you. Please forgive me. I shouldn't have done that."

"Why did you yell at me?" I started crying. "I was being your helper."

"I know you were. I just got some really bad news from one of my sons. Sometimes, when I talk to him, I get so frustrated and angry ... and I took it out on you." She began to cry also. "Will you forgive me? I'm very sorry." She wiped her face with a tissue. Years later, my mother revealed she'd heard several of Mrs. Heaviland's younger children had substance abuse problems, with one daughter who died in a car wreck and a son who was a persistent felon.

"Yes, I'll forgive you."

"Now, Billy, from now on you must obey what I tell you. You must learn to respect authority and follow the rules, because what I said about bad things happening to boys that don't follow the rules is true. And sometimes things are very unfair in this world."

"I will. I'll listen."

Mrs. Heaviland had dark blue eyes. She didn't look like my mother, but at that moment she reminded me of my mother. I felt safe with Mrs. Heaviland, and we were friends again, but how was it that adults, who were usually so good, could sometimes be so dangerous?

"You know what? You remind me very much of one of my sons. He's done very well. I expect you will do some great things one day also and help many people, but sometimes I worry about you. The world is often not kind to Black boys. Have I ever shown you this picture of my family?"

Mrs. Heaviland showed me a picture of herself, her husband and seven children, four boys and three girls. I was surprised to see her three oldest children, a girl and two boys, were Black.

I counted the children. "Wow. Your family is bigger than mine."

"I always wanted a big family, but when my husband and I first married we were unable to have children, so we adopted our first three. Then after ten years of marriage and many, many prayers and tears, God blessed me, and I started having children."

"Why did you have tears? Was God too busy to help you?"

Mrs. Heaviland shook her head and leaned forward in her chair. "How can I explain it to you, Billy? You are so young. I cried many tears, because I wanted to give birth to babies, but six times my babies died before I could give birth to them, and their loss made me and my husband very, very sad."

"Why did your babies die?"

"I don't know why." Mrs. Heaviland's bloodshot eyes glistened with moisture like red window panes full of water, until slowly, drops fell like pieces of crystal, shattering as they hit the floor. "I can only tell you those years of grief made me trust and rely on the Lord more, because I knew he understood how I felt, and he helped me through each loss. Now, I know I can face what life brings and still have hope. Billy, I want you to always remember Jesus understands when you hurt really bad, and he cares. Will you remember?"

"I'll remember." I'd been taught about Jesus every Sunday and Wednesday of my life up until that time but still didn't understand the things Mrs. Heaviland was saying about Jesus. Looking back over the years, I failed to remember the charge she gave me that day. Even at that tender age, the seed of skepticism was present. Did God really know? Did he really care?

My repaired relationship with Mrs. Heaviland also restored within my mind my heroic status as Billy Goat Billy, so my heart was happy that day after school. I had no idea my session with Mrs. Heaviland would be the last time I'd see her alive, for that very night she had a stroke and spent several weeks in intensive care before she passed away. My classmates all knew I was the last of her students to see her alive, and many of them asked me what happened. I felt I should have known, but I didn't know what happened. For some mysterious reason, in my young mind, responsibility for Mrs. Heaviland's death fell on me.

On the way home from school, I always walked by Sidoni Fields, an expansive park with baseball fields, basketball and tennis courts, and acres of grassy spaces. Usually people thronged the park enjoying the community pool, picnic areas, jungle gyms, or many other amenities, but that day an eerie quiet hung over the park. The Tiberias River flowed nearby, and Eddie was on my mind. His house was on my way home, and my plan was to stop by, hoping he could come out and play.

Shrieks of glee pierced the quiet. Two small kids bounced on the oversized stomach of my classmate, Gary Hugh-Manson, who was splayed out on the ground. Every time one boy crashed down on his belly, Gary made an awful high-pitched squeak as the air rushed out of him and a horrible wheeze as he inhaled.

"Get off him," I screamed, rushing down a small hill and slamming my book bag to the ground.

The first boy said, "He's ours."

"Yeah, he's ours. Get your own bouncy," said the second little imp.

A third delinquent yelled, "I'm next. Leave us alone. We're not hurting anybody."

Tears mingled with dirt streamed down Gary's face. Grass clung to his hair. I grabbed the two little monsters and shoved them into the third kid, and all four of us went tumbling in the grass. Gary struggled to his feet and slowly lumbered away. I slammed my fists into their faces over and over. My insides burned to inflict pain. Maybe they would suffer and die.

"If you ever do anything to Gary again, I am going to kill you." I spit out the words and saliva flew everywhere.

I staggered away as though drunk. That was, in my mind, Billy Goat Billy's debut as a righteous avenger.

***

On the way home, I stopped by Eddie's house to see how he was doing, expecting to play. The front door hung open, and I rang the doorbell, pressed my face against the screen door, and peered into the dark foyer. It was quiet inside the house, and no one seemed to be home until there was a repeating thump, each thump followed by shuffling steps. An ancient woman with a cane emerged from the darkness and wheezed into my face through the screen door. I jumped back, thinking she might hit me with the cane. It was Eddie's great-grandmother.

"Is Eddie home?"

"Eddie's in the hospital." She struggled to catch her breath. "I'm the only one here. Everybody's with Eddie," she said, tilting her head and eyeing me. "What happened to you? You've been fighting, haven't you? Good boys don't fight. You know that, don't you?"

"I haven't been fighting. Just playing with my friends."
A small lie wouldn't hurt.

"You're one of the boys that were down there at the river when Eddie got hurt, aren't you?"

"We were playing. He fell and hit his head."

The way that elderly woman stared at me punctured my spirit, so I turned and ran for home. It was as though she'd seen in me something much worse than my ragged, grass-stained, blood-flecked exterior. When I arrived home, my mother had already learned I'd been fighting, and she grounded me for the rest of the week.

Later, Mom told me Eddie had a severe brain injury, and he would need months, maybe years, of therapy to get better. Within the next year, Eddie's family moved so he could be closer to doctors that specialized in the treatment he needed.

I never learned if Eddie recovered or not. Over the years, I sometimes wondered what had caused Eddie's fall. Once, during one of my visits to him, he asked me what happened, because he had no memory of how he got hurt, and Sammy hadn't seen what happened. All I knew to tell Eddie was he'd saved me from the snake, and then he slipped and hit his head when he threw the snake into the water.

The lie came naturally and without thought or memory, a signpost to the darker road ahead.

CHAPTER 5

WEEK 1—TUESDAY

Peaceful sleep eluded me Monday night because of a deep duality of heart. Part of me craved a return to a normal adult life, but my conscience interrupted my rest. It insisted I continue in the pursuit of my memories and the meaning of the words of Alexander—a messenger sent to me, perhaps, by God himself. I'd already recalled Eddie's accident—something I'd forgotten for years—and the remembrance was unbearable. Remembering further was dreaded work. More forgotten memories might bring additional pain.

★★★

At seven-thirty Tuesday morning, I rose from an air mattress in my home office to the tantalizing fragrance of my favorite meal. I found Mom in the kitchen enjoying a breakfast of toast, scrambled eggs, and bacon.

"Morning."

"Good morning. How are you doing, baby? Did you have a good night?"

"It was okay. I thought a lot about Mrs. Heaviland, and some of the things that happened when I was a kid."

Mom said, "Last night I spent a lot of time praying, talking with the God of heaven and earth about you."

"You know what? Last night, I remembered the weirdest experience of talking to God too, but it wasn't a prayer. It was more like a challenge. He called himself the god of this world."

My mother's jaw went slack, and the eggs almost dropped out of her mouth. She swallowed hard. I feared she'd had a stroke right there in front of me.

"Mom? Are you okay?"

She coughed and cleared her throat before she spoke.

"Billy, the god of this world is *not* the true God. The god of this world is the devil. I can't believe you don't remember that."

I shook my head and raised my hands. "I guess I forgot." I felt like kicking myself for mentioning the term *god of this world*.

"What challenge did he give you?"

I told Mom about climbing on Tall Tower. I'd never previously told my parents about walking across the top beam.

Mom shook her head and looked down at the floor, then turned toward me. "I can't believe you'd be so foolish. You could've been badly hurt if you'd fallen."

"I know, I know. Sometimes my own recklessness is unbelievable even to me. And I was terrified of the voice and of walking across that beam. But you know what? After I did it and proved I really was Billy Goat Billy, the feeling was great, like I'd accomplished something. Ridiculous, yes, but I was so proud of myself. But scared too. For days afterward."

"Pride can be a bad thing. The devil is tricky, and you can be sure he wants nothing good for you. The devil only comes to kill, rob, and destroy. You must have been crazy to accept a challenge—"

"Mom, I was just a little kid."

I crossed my arms and stood rigidly across the table

from my mother. "What I think is really crazy is that your God, the God of the entire universe, would make the devil the ruler of this world. That makes no sense. It's as if the devil's working for God, and if the devil is so bad, why would God do that? Makes absolutely no sense."

"Why are you such a skeptic?" Mom got up from the table and put her dishes in the sink. "You're the one having all these spiritual experiences. You better start asking God to help you figure out what's happening to you, and what you should be learning from it."

She turned from the sink to face me. "And it's not God giving the devil power. We and the devil all have free will to make our own decisions. *We're* the ones that give the devil power over us by going along with his schemes and lies. God is the one who always works for the good of humanity. God even uses bad things to bring about good."

Mom would never give up defending God, and the voice had truly wanted me to fall. Sammy had probably been right when he said God wouldn't ask us to do something and then want us to fail. But what did God want, and why he would give the devil so much power?

"Mom, did you know Mrs. Heaviland had six miscarriages?"

"No, I didn't. How did you know that?"

"She told me one day after school."

Mom's expression went from frowning to puzzlement. "That's sad, but it's a strange thing to tell a second grader."

"She showed me a picture of her family, and she said after many prayers and tears God blessed her to be able to have children. She told me about the miscarriages when I asked her why she had the tears. She wanted me to remember Jesus knows about our pain and he cares."

"She was right, Billy. I just wish you'd believe it." Mom hugged me and tapped my chest. "There is a Scripture passage that says God sustains us when we are at our weakest, and it's then God's power works the best."

Her words reminded me how much my parents loved me, and how pleased and relieved they would be if I were a believer in Jesus. But I couldn't say I believed. I didn't want to lie.

"I truly wish I could be like you and Dad, but I can't make myself believe if I don't. My heart is not feeling it, but … there are a lot of things I want to understand."

Mom had a flight to catch, so our back-and-forth had to end. I grabbed Mom's suitcase and walked her up the stairs from my apartment.

"Don't forget. Your father wants you to visit."

"I will. Soon." I watched her pull away in her rental car and wished I could've been driving her to the airport.

Between the exit from the building and my apartment was a small laundry room several tenants shared, and while returning to my little hole in the ground, I heard gleeful howls coming from the laundry room. Looking through the window pane of the laundry room door, I saw a young man doubled over with laughter, apparently at something an older man sitting in a motorized wheelchair had said. I'd seen the man in the wheelchair before—he had recently moved into Bethesda—but I hadn't met him, so I went in to introduce myself.

The older man maneuvered the wheel chair deftly with his left hand, the only hand I saw him use, along with his left arm and his head. He looked to be about twenty years older than I, with a head of long white hair and a full beard. The man studied me while he grasped my right hand with his left hand, as if he sought to read my mind. His gaze made me uncomfortable. My new neighbors were E.J. Landes and his son Edmund from somewhere in Wisconsin. Mr. Landes seemed familiar, but I was not sure we'd ever met before. After a few minutes of small talk, I returned to my abode.

A maintenance notification hung on my door.

THIS WEDNESDAY, FROM 10 PM–5 AM, THE WATER IN YOUR UNIT WILL BE TEMPORARILY TURNED OFF TO PERFORM MAINTENANCE. DURING THIS SCHEDULED TIME, YOU WILL BE UNABLE TO ACCESS ANY WATER SERVICES. YOU ARE ENCOURAGED TO PLAN ACCORDINGLY.

WE APOLOGIZE FOR THE INCONVENIENCE AND THANK YOU FOR UNDERSTANDING.

I made a mental note and then threw the notice away once I was inside.

It was easy to question my mother about God and her faith, but confronting myself about my own behavior proved much harder. The guilt I'd felt for Mrs. Heaviland's death was clearly misplaced, since I had no knowledge or control over her passing. The memory of beating the kids who abused Gary Hugh-Manson troubled me because of the murderous exhilaration of my heart while it happened. But my worst recollection was what I'd done to Eddie.

He didn't slip. I pushed him. The snake filled me with fear, because to me the god of this world had sent it to take me away, and when Eddie let the snake go, I was furious. He heard me say "bash its brains out," but he laughed and ignored me. So I bashed Eddie's brains out in a fit of fear and rage.

Did Eddie ever recover and have a normal life? Why did I have such a fearful and violent spirit within me? Why would I assume guilt for Mrs. Heaviland's death while conveniently forgetting the things I was actually guilty of?

No answers came to me—only dread and remorse. I sought to escape and ran to the entryway, but at the door,

Eddie's frightened, confused expression appeared.

You're my friend, Billy. Why are you killing me?

I couldn't touch the doorknob, and so retreated, trapped. At the kitchen sink, I turned on the water and wanted to wash, but there was no hope for cleansing. Instead, I bent over the sink, where my tears mingled and vanished in the drain with the faucet's flow.

★★★

I regretted accepting Alexander's challenge to examine my past. Still, the good I'd done would mitigate my crimes. I was sure of it, convinced that my intentions had always been good. The bad only came out when I was gripped by fear, or by anger caused by others. I'd loved Rose, Sharon, and Miros in their time, but I had no desire to relive those memories.

Questions needed answers, but did my past hold those answers? My fear and guilt would have to be set aside, and I'd have to focus on what I wanted to know.

After several minutes' reflection, these questions came to me.

1. Why was Alexander sent to me?
2. Why did Alexander say I was dead? Was he lying?
3. What does it mean to be dead and live again? How is that possible?
4. How does suffering result in greater faith in God, as Mom and Mrs. Heaviland seemed to believe?
5. Why did God give the devil power over the world?
6. Why did God tolerate so much heartache, injustice, and suffering?

I had no idea how I'd get those answers, and maybe a more important question was left off my list. Believe it or not, I took my mother's advice and spoke to God.

"God, what is it you want me to know and to do?"

CHAPTER 6

WEEK 1—TUESDAY NIGHT

I woke up the next evening and went for a swim. In the sea, I got tangled in a ragged rope that briefly pulled me away from the land, but I escaped from its dragging clutches and felt relief at reaching shore.

The night was hot, so I walked near the water's edge. The sea splashed me as I went along, cooling and soothing my legs, and the wet sand shifted like moving silk beneath my feet. Waves broke and rushed over the shore and then retreated. Serenity reigned.

In the distance, the waves met the sky, and the rays from the setting sun shone through the layers of perfectly placed clouds. Who planned and constructed that seascape? I anticipated something dramatic or miraculous happening, but no. It was the close of another ordinary day, like days had closed since the beginning of time.

***

The light faded quickly and the darkness grew thick, making seeing hard. My thoughts turned to good times I'd just had with family and friends. What had possessed me to go for a swim alone? I quickened my walk, intent on getting back home as soon as possible.

I broke into an anxious jog, and then I saw them ahead of me. Thousands of workers—fishermen—pulling nets from the water, nets holding innumerable fish. The workers sorted through the fish, throwing some onto a hot grill, while throwing others into baskets to be carried away. The fish sizzled and crackled on the grill, but the smell was rotten-egg awful. I inched closer, and saw not a grill but an oven being used to bake the fish. Thick, dark smoke poured from the oven, staining the air like ink. The sounds of screaming, moaning, and cursing were worse than the smell. Why were the workers screaming and moaning? Every impulse in my body cried for me to turn and run, but someone was in terrible trouble. I wanted to help.

I looked again, closer. The workers were not cooking fish, but burning dead bodies. The workers worked silently, and they were not crying. Who was making that awful sound? Why were they incinerating dead bodies? What had happened to the fish?

I knelt and began to crawl, appreciating the cover of darkness. Sweat blurred my vision and smoke stung my eyes. I strained to see what was happening, until finally I saw the human bodies writhing in the oven in unspeakable agony. Burning, but not burned up. Why did they stay in the fire? I could see them moving around. How long would they burn? Why didn't they jump out of the flames? Pulling them to safety was my hope, but the oven was too hot to get close, and the stench of burning sulfur was overwhelming. My lungs seized and tried to shut down. My stomach churned. I vomited.

One of the workers came toward me, moving without hesitation through the impenetrable darkness. I jumped to my feet and ran, but the worker, faster and stronger, overtook me. He clamped an iron hand on my shoulder and spun me around. He seemed an inhuman—perhaps superhuman—soldier, holding me effortlessly as I beat on his arms, fighting to get away. I screamed at the sky and at him.

"Who are you? What do you want?"

He lifted me off the ground and said only, "We are the gatherers."

We are the gatherers.

He possessed an aura of holiness overlaid with anger, a deep anger directed toward me. In my emotional whirlpool of dread and fear, the specter of death seized its chance and bubbled up from within me. Boils formed and burst through the skin of my arms, revealing all manner of gross creatures that crawled and squirmed out from the inside. My screams of pain and horror floated out over the water, washing back to me with the waves.

My rotting, insect-ridden flesh reeked of the grave. The gatherer eyed me with disgust and hurled me into the air. My vision flashed to a point outside my body, where I could see myself as he threw me. At the bottom of my field of vision, a masculine hand wrote what looked like a title.

A Parable for Billy Yates.

★★★

I awoke in my bedroom, nauseous, trembling, burning with heat and drenched in sweat. I went into the bathroom and lay down for several minutes on the cool, blessedly real tile floor.

Eventually a terrible hunger took center stage. I got up off the floor, ate a cheese sandwich at the kitchen counter, and went back to bed, but not to sleep. Sheer weariness overtook me only after Alexander's prophetic message had replayed in my thoughts for hours. I understood now what he'd meant.

When you see the parable, heed the warning.

CHAPTER 7

It was just a dream. A stupid, stinking dream.

No. It was a parable foretold by God's messenger. Representing a reality?

Where is the light? There should be daylight by now.

My little hole in the ground was sinking. Soon the windows and door would be blocked by earth, and the gatherer would strike the match. I threw back the covers and flew to my bedroom window. Darkness. I sprinted to my apartment door and flung it open and ran down the hall, bare feet slapping the cold tile, and peered through the entryway door. A streetlight illuminated the parking lot. I returned to my apartment breathless and trembling.

Not trapped. It's still early in the morning.

If Alexander had sought to terrorize me into becoming a Christian, he'd made a good start. But would the fear of hell make me a faithful Christian? Jesus told parables, but I doubted Jesus told hellfire-and-brimstone parables. Jesus always preached about God's love and kindness.

I planned to get Ezriah's take on the parables Jesus preached to draw followers.

Did the gatherer who grabbed me inject me with the feeling of death, or did he simply reveal what was already inside me?

I dragged myself out of bed, feeling dirty and disgusting, and headed to the shower in the hope of feeling clean again. After viewing myself as decrepit and decaying though still alive, I hesitated to even peek at myself in the mirror. I stripped off my pajamas, took several long deep breaths, and approached the bathroom door, wary of the waiting mirror. Would my hell-bound soul be reflected in the looking glass, or would my face be so deformed by sin that I wouldn't recognize it? When I crept through the door and saw my anxious reflection, I sighed with relief. I didn't look too bad.

The warm soap and water of the shower washed away my feeling of wretchedness from the previous night. I dried off, stepped out of the shower, stood in front of the mirror, and raised my left arm out of habit to put on my deodorant. Then I froze, remembering the post-op instructions not to use deodorant until the incision healed.

That was when I saw it.

At first, I didn't see it clearly. My imagination took over. A black and red roach appeared to be clawing its way through my skin. I tried to brush it away before I realized it wasn't alone. Thousands of them crawling, squirming all over me, not just roaches, but ants and centipedes.

"Where are they *coming* from?" I yelled.

I looked around the bathroom but didn't see anything. Then they came from my ears, nose, and mouth, out of my back and my legs. Their dirty bodies were on me. I frantically tried to brush them off my body, but they kept coming.

"Stop. I'm not dead. Don't bury me."

They stopped. There were no bugs.

I found myself lying on the bathroom floor staring at the ceiling. My head throbbed. My face had apparently hit the toilet on the way down, and my lip and right knee bled. Sweat poured from my head, back, and legs as I struggled to my feet, wobbling as if my legs would not support me. My arm felt heavy, but I forced myself to raise it up and leaned close to the mirror and saw a red circle with dark black letters coming out of the circle. I vaguely remembered seeing the red circle as a child, but not the letters. I squinted at the mirror and tried to read what it said, but couldn't because the letters were backward. I swung open one of the three doors of the medicine cabinet, looked in the second mirror, and clearly saw one word.

Rejected.

I touched it and tried to peel it away, but someone had emblazoned it on my skin. I couldn't feel it, but with my underarm hair cut away it was plainly visible.

I'd been labeled a reject.

My thoughts raced.

Who'd done this?

Someone had told me there was a tattoo under my arm. Questions flooded my mind.

Who was it?

I had never gotten a tattoo.

Who had done it?

Then I remembered Angeline.

Did Angeline, my angelic nurse, do this?

No, it startled her when she saw it. She'd prayed for me.

She'd said, "Why does your tattoo say that?"

That surgery was the first time I'd ever had general anesthesia.

How could someone have done this to me without my knowledge?

It seemed like I'd seen the red circle before, but not the letters. Could it be a birthmark I'd forgotten about?

My next move was to call Mom. She was at work, so I didn't want to keep her on the phone long.

The call rang only once before she answered. "What's wrong, baby?"

"Nothing's wrong, Mom," I responded, tempering my anxiety and steadying my voice. "Why do you ask?"

"Because you usually don't call me this time of day, and I was worried about how you were doing after the surgery."

"I'm doing fine, and the recovery is going well." I paused for a moment and then asked, "Mom, do you recall a birthmark under my left arm?"

Now, it was her turn to pause before she answered.

"It wasn't there when you were born. You were eight- or nine-years-old when I first noticed it. A red circle. I took you to the doctor, and he examined it. He said red birthmarks can be caused by blood vessels close to the skin. I told him it wasn't there when you were born. He said usually they're a patch, not just a red circle like yours. The doctor couldn't explain it. He told me to keep an eye on it and to let him know if there were any changes in it. I checked every few months for years, it never changed, and I eventually forgot all about it. Is it giving you trouble now?"

"No. I'd forgotten all about it too, until I had the hair cut away for the surgery." Telling my mother her son had been labeled a reject was not an option, so I said, "It was just a red ring with no marking inside it, right?"

"Right, just a red ring with no markings. Have you seen any changes? Is it bothering you?"

"No, it just surprised me, because I forgot it was there."

We talked for a few more minutes and then said goodbye.

I sank into my living room couch and wondered when the reject label had shown up, and what it meant.

It reminded me of the little round labels you sometimes find in a pack of T-shirts. Each shirt has a sticker with something like 'QC Checked'—evidence the shirts have passed all quality control checks and are fit to be worn.

What did they do with the rejected shirts?

"Has God rejected me?"

I surprised myself when I said that out loud. Those words echoed in my mind, and they stung. Even though I didn't trust God, my body grew tense with anger at the thought he would reject me. In my nightmare parable, I had felt death in myself and thought the gatherer had caused that feeling. Alexander had said I was already dead while in the hospital, even though I still lived. My explanation was Alexander had lied, but he must have meant I was dead because God had rejected me. To be rejected by God is to be dead, even if you're alive on earth.

Mom had said, "There is such a thing as spiritual death."

Was I spiritually dead? How could I be spiritually alive again? Alexander said it was a possibility, but what were the prospects for me? How could I trust a God I did not trust, or believe in a God I did not believe in?

Ezriah and I had scheduled that night to meet for a bite to eat and then to go to the park and shoot some baskets. I decided to talk to Ezriah about it. I took another shower and scrubbed my tattoo and picked at it until it bled, but those feeble efforts had no effect. I felt like taking a knife to it and carving the invader out of my flesh.

CHAPTER 8

Day 3—Wednesday

Ezriah and I met at a fast-food chicken place. We settled into a booth with our meals, and Ezriah blessed the food with a prayer of thanksgiving.

I asked, "Does the Bible talk about God rejecting people?"

Ezriah raised an intrigued eyebrow. "Yes. There's a passage in the Old Testament that says God rejected Saul. Saul was the first king of Israel."

"Why did God reject Saul? And how did God let him know he was rejected?"

"God sent Samuel to tell Saul God had rejected him as king, because Saul had rejected the word of the Lord. Basically, Saul had previously rejected God, so God rejected Saul. Saul begged for forgiveness, but it was too late."

"If Saul begged for forgiveness, why didn't God forgive him? Doesn't God always forgive you if you ask for forgiveness?"

Ezriah pondered for a few moments.

"Interesting question. I'd say when a person repents of their sins and obeys God, he forgives their sin. Remember, God knows a person's heart and whether or not they've sincerely repented."

Ezriah sat back in the booth and chomped some more on his huge chicken sandwich before continuing. "In Saul's case, it seems to me that even though he admitted he'd sinned, he was still more concerned about himself than honoring God. But even if he'd truly repented, it was clear God had decided Saul was no longer worthy to be the king. God has a right to make choices, you know. We should read that in the Bible and see exactly what it says."

"So when God rejects someone today, that's the same as being spiritually dead, right?"

"Yes, and the reality is that everyone who ever lived, except Jesus, has rejected God. So God has in turn rejected every one of us. That's our true status, and we're all in the same boat. At one point, we all stand condemned before God. It's just that Christians have come back to God and received forgiveness." He eyed me closely. "Why are you asking all these questions? What's going on?"

How could a good God condemn everyone?

I took a deep breath. "You're not going to believe this, but you know those little labels that come on T-shirts that say 'QC Checked'? Well, I have one of those, only mine says 'Rejected.'"

Ezriah looked at me as though the gravity of my existential crisis eluded him. "That sounds pretty strange, but just take them back to the store and get your money back."

"What?"

"You got some bad T-shirts, right? Just take them back to the store. Do you have your receipt?"

"Ezriah ... the rejected label is on *me*."

Ezriah didn't say anything for quite a while—then he looked at me and said, "Peel it off."

We both started laughing.

I said, "What do you suppose they do with rejected T-shirts?"

"They probably cut them up and sell them as rags. Wait—what are you *talking* about?" Ezriah laughed harder, and he shook his head and waved his hands in a dismissive gesture. "Let's rewind this conversation. You came with a label? A *reject* label?"

★★★

We left the restaurant and drove to the park. Ezriah impassively listened to my weird tale, starting with what Angeline had said when she saw the tattoo, and then Alexander and the nightmare parable. When we found an open basketball court, I took my shirt off and showed him the tattoo.

"So you had a nurse named Angeline who discovered that tat in your armpit, you were rebuked by an angel at the hospital, and you had your own personal parable about hellfire delivered to you in a dream. Man, that really is the pits." He doubled over and roared with laughter.

"You know what?" I said. "This is not funny. So far it's been the worst week of my life, and I don't deserve this." I took a shot at the hoop, and the ball flew over the rim and beyond the backboard, missing them both.

"What was that?" Ezriah bounced the ball a few times and passed it back to me. "Try again. You have no idea how this tattoo got there?"

"Zero idea." Another attempted shot got the same airball result.

Ezriah took a shot and the ball arced up and over the rim and dove in, rattling the metal mesh of the net. "That's how you're supposed to do it …. Maybe you got drunk one night, got the tattoo, blacked out, and forgot about it."

"In all the years we've known each other, have you ever known me to drink like that? I haven't been drunk since high school." I went in for a layup, and the ball ricocheted off the bottom of the backboard and almost hit me in the face.

"You've played this game before, right? It's called basketball." Ezriah dribbled toward the basket, spun around me, and put in another basket with a jump shot. "Maybe you were drugged? Maybe Angeline did it."

"First of all, I'm just getting warmed up out here on the court. Second, Angeline was shocked when she saw it, so she's innocent. What about Alexander and the nightmare parable? Are they all sending me messages from God?"

"Maybe the stress of the surgery and the mysterious tattoo set your imagination to working overtime." Ezriah added with a smile. "Plus, maybe you're worried about the class you promised to attend with me and the fact you're going to have to actually read the Bible. You might have biblephobia, which might be causing a psychotic break."

"Come on, man, this is serious." I slammed the ball into the asphalt several times before tossing the ball to him. "You need to pray for me."

Ezriah outweighed my one-hundred-eighty pound frame by about forty pounds, so he began backing me down toward the post like a bull. When he got to his spot, he turned to take his shot. I stood three inches taller with long arms, so I jumped and swatted the ball away. I raced past Ezriah and retrieved the ball at half court, then turned and drove quickly on him, and though he tried to block me, I went high over him and jammed the ball in the basket with a mighty dunk.

"Ha-ha. You been posterized." My chest ached, so it was minimal exertion for me after that, but it felt good to dunk on Ezriah.

"You got me, my friend. You know I'll pray for you. I've prayed for years God would reach you somehow. Why have you never believed?"

"I don't understand the Bible. I can't believe in something that doesn't make sense to me. I believe God exists, but I think he's not trustworthy. God should protect his people, but he doesn't. I've told you about my uncle and my dad, how God didn't save them from what happened. And just look at the evil condition of the world. Why does God allow it?" I shrugged. "I used to ask him to help me. I prayed he'd give me a wife and children, but I've never gotten an answer. I still feel the same way about God, but now I'm scared."

"Do you think my kids understand and accept every decision Deanna and I make for them?" Ezriah said. "No. They're just children, and they don't understand a lot of things. They just deal with it because we're their parents. They trust us because we love them. It's the same way in our relationship with God. We trust him to do the best thing for us, even if we don't understand everything. God shares the pain of humanity, but he doesn't enjoy our suffering." He pointed an accusing forefinger at me. "You blame God for all the bad things in life. To whom do you credit the good things?"

I didn't respond to that question, but the answer was, I credited myself. I'd worked hard for everything I'd accomplished.

"God freely loves us," Ezriah continued, "and he wants us to willingly love him in return. He always takes the first step, but he doesn't force anyone to serve him. You're free to choose."

He absently dribbled the ball for few moments, then said, "There's a book of the Bible I think you should read. I once heard a preacher compare the Christian faith to a car. He said if you want to learn how a car operates, you take a close look at what's going on under the hood. The preacher said that, for Christians, the best way to look under the hood is to read the book of Romans. He said it's the clearest and most complete explanation of the Christian faith in the Bible. Why don't you read the book of Romans over the weekend, and we'll talk about it next week. Will you do that?"

I made a counter-proposal. "I've already agreed to take the 'Jesus in the Old Testament' class with you. That starts next week, and it'll probably involve quite a bit of Bible reading. So how about I take the class, and then afterward, I'll read the book of Romans?"

Neither taking the class nor reading the Bible was my preference, but my best friend was giving his heartfelt advice, and desperation drove me. "I'll dig out my Bibles tonight. Who knows, all this prodding might push me to do some advance reading."

"Fair enough, my friend. Just keep an open mind. I can see God's hot on your trail, and that's a good thing, even if it is scary. He wants to bless you, man. No one comes to Jesus except those the Father draws."

Right before we parted, I remembered my question about my nightmare parable. "Did Jesus tell any fire-and-brimstone parables? Kind of like my nightmare?"

"I think he did. Jesus spoke a lot about the reality of hell. Let me find it." Ezriah typed in a search engine on his phone, and in a split second, he found it. "Check out Matthew 13 and see for yourself."

***

I returned home to my little hole in the ground. The mention of Angeline's name reminded me that my intended quest of two days ago—to see that beautiful woman again—had been interrupted by Alexander. I would find my Bibles, and my plan for the next day was to reach out to Angeline. If God really did want to bless me as Ezriah said, then bringing Angeline into my life right away seemed like a great way to do it.

I took off my T-shirt, stood in front of the bathroom mirror, raised my left arm, and spoke to my rejection label.

"I'm going to read the Book, but you will not bully me. Even if God kills me, I will not accept what I think is a lie."

I remained stationary with my eyes glued on the tattoo for several minutes, and just when I was about to turn and go, a wrinkle passed through the mirror and the face of the man in the mirror changed. He was a younger and taller version of me. With his right hand raised, he spoke.

"Will you condemn God to justify yourself? You weren't even honest enough to credit God for all the good things in your life." He shook his head, and the mirrored reflection shimmered. "There are things you will never understand. God does share our suffering. You've ignored God so long you don't even know where your Bibles are. Do you really think it will be so easy to find God? Are you seeking him now only to soothe your fears? Humble yourself, and open your heart."

I remained motionless and silent. A spirit who looked just like me had hijacked my reflection and rebuked me. Still, my heart sensed the compassion of this fourth miraculous messenger.

As I stepped back from the mirror, my reflection became mine again. I turned and stumbled out of the bathroom to find my Bibles.

CHAPTER 9

Day 3—Wednesday night

Upon my confirmation at age twelve, I received my first real Bible, one covered in red leather. My second Bible, a tan hardback book, was the assigned text for two 'Bible as Literature' college classes. My third Bible had a fancy black leather cover with gold letters on the spine, with pages edged in gold. My dear old friend, Miros Rybakov, gave me that Bible as a gift.

The red, the tan, and the black—three books treasured for sentimental reasons, but not for their message—were all missing.

My collection, almost seven thousand books organized by genre, included technical and academic books, English literature, science fiction, African-American authors, poetry, religious books, and more. The bamboo palm standing at my entry door guarded the religious and spiritual books. I expected to find the objects of my search there.

Before beginning the search in earnest, I hesitated before the bookshelves, paralyzed.

The angel, the parable, the tattoo, the man in the mirror ... imagined? ... all real?

Hide ... but where? Home's not safe. What's next? No more, please.

My beloved plants dig their leaves into their pots and fling dirt on me and scream, "Get right with God." What about the good I've done? Doesn't that count for anything?

Will anyone speak up for me?

I will defend myself. I will fight.

What if I read the Bible and actually believed it?

I don't want to change. I will atone, but I don't want to change my life.

Can a Christian believe in science, mathematics, literature, and the Bible at the same time?

Crazy thoughts, yes, but everything was crazy then.

More questions popped in my mind like bubbles, and I debated with myself.

Wasn't the Bible a centuries-old collection of writings by ignorant and superstitious people? Does something become less valuable just because it's old? Aren't there many writings hundreds or even thousands of years old we still honor? The Declaration of Independence and the United States Constitution are over two hundred twenty years old. The works of Shakespeare are about four hundred years old. Homer wrote the Odyssey and the Iliad almost twenty-eight hundred years ago. Are we really different from—or smarter—than our ancestors?

There was no justification for dismissing the Bible, but I honestly didn't want to read it either. Other books on the shelves tempted me to pick them up and reread them. They wanted to be loved again, and they enticed me, calling out to me like long-lost friends. Given the weirdness of the recent past, I questioned whether my library consisted simply of inanimate objects, or if it had been transformed to possess some spiritual power and a will of its own.

I refocused and returned to my task. My Koran just sat there, and I felt no attraction to it. When I tried to read the Koran, it never resonated with me, and I couldn't understand it. The next book was *Man's Search for Meaning,* then a commentary on Genesis, and several Bible dictionaries and handbooks. There were books by Josephus and Max Lucado, and a novel called *Left Behind.* Though an unbeliever, I probably had read more about Christ than many Christians.

I could not find any of my Bibles.

I plopped on the floor crossed-legged and sat fuming, until I noticed the first three books from *The Vampire Chronicles* by Anne Rice were definitely out of place among the religious books. I pulled out the second of the series, *The Vampire Lestat*, one I'd read many years earlier. I admired Lestat for his resilience. He was almost completely destroyed, but after a long time he regained his strength. Again temptation created in me a desire to reread those books.

Why I'd placed *The Vampire Chronicles* in the spiritual section of my collection was a puzzle to me. Did I at one time believe vampires had spiritual or theological implications? A scene from one of the books depicted a vampire god hearing the prayers of thousands of his vampire children, and all the pleas and needs drove the vampire god nuts.

How could any god handle and respond to the prayers of billions of people?

It seemed impossible to me. I put the book back on the shelf.

Loud knocking shook my apartment door, jarring me out of my contemplative musings.

"Billy, you in there?" Surely the entire apartment complex heard my neighbor, Joseph Pullman.

My middle-aged joints had locked in place, but slowly I unfolded myself, rose from the floor, and opened the door to wave him in.

"Hi, Joseph. What's going on?"

Joseph was in his late fifties, several inches taller than me, with a slender build. As a young adult, he'd had brain surgery to remove numerous benign tumors. The surgery had left Joseph with weakness on one side of his body, so he limped, and avoided walking long distances.

Joseph's wild curly silver hair grew into an afro when he didn't cut it for a while. Lumps and bumps covered his round face and forehead, as if more tumors were trying to break through his pale white skin. Joseph's normal tone of voice boomed like a megaphone.

"Mom and me just got back from Nashville. We was visitin' my uncle. How you doin'? Your operation go okay?"

"Yes," I said, "it went really well. I've just been resting the last few days."

"I brought you somethin'." Joseph held out a plastic bag with one arm while he steadied himself with his cane. A whole apple pie waited in the bag.

"Oh, Joseph, thank you so much." From when I first moved in, Joseph, motivated by his Christian faith, had consistently done kind, neighborly deeds such as this.

"We remembered you liked apple pie."

Joseph followed me into the kitchen. I got plates for both of us, warmed two big pieces of pie in the microwave, added some vanilla ice cream, and we both scarfed down a delicious dessert. Joseph informed me his uncle had surgery to remove a cancerous tumor, and they'd visited him in the hospital. Joseph's father had died from cancer a few years earlier, and he feared his beloved uncle might be next. Sometimes, he dwelled on the dread idea his mother would die and leave him alone. He knew he shouldn't worry, he said, but he couldn't help it, because his mother was his best friend.

TRUE STATUS

Joseph had tried to share the gospel with his older sister, and she was not happy about it. She told Joseph not to mention Jesus to her again. Something similar happened with one of Joseph's brothers. Joseph's voice cracked, and the more he talked about his family sorrows, the quieter and more solemn he became.

How many families had Jesus fractured? And why?

After rinsing our plates and putting them in the dishwasher, I said, "I've got to get back to work."

"What kind of work was you doin'?"

"Looking for my Bibles. I don't know where they are."

"I read my Bible every day," Joseph said as he got up. "I'll let you borrow it. I'll get it right now."

"No, that's okay. I really want to find my own Bibles."

"Okay, then. I can help you look. Any idea where they're at?"

"I thought they'd be over here, but I haven't found them yet."

"How many you lookin' for? You going to have a small group Bible study or somethin'?" He started laughing at the thought of me conducting a group Bible study.

"Three Bibles," I said. "Why don't you start at the other end of the living room? I'll go back over here, and we'll meet in the middle."

Joseph had often invited me to his church, especially when they were having a special event. I had visited a few times. Surely, he wanted to ask why I was interested in the Bible all of a sudden.

I had several books on astrology, and at one time in my life astrology may have been my religion, as it revealed much about me and how to conduct my life. Like the prophets of old, the wisest astrologers made amazing predictions using science, art, and the positions of planets and stars rather than the word of God.

Where would I have put my Bibles?

The Bible contained poetry, and the King James Version was considered a great work of English literature. Next stop, poetry and English literature books.

Joseph said, "I don't believe how many books you got. Have you read them all?"

"Not all. I've read most of them."

"I never was much of a reader. You know, I used to be in the LD classes." Joseph paused for a few seconds and added, "You know what LD stands for, don't you? My brother said it meant 'Little Dummies.'" Joseph roared with gurgling laughter for a moment, and then stopped. I wanted to laugh too, but I held it in.

"But that wasn't funny." His voice became low and distant. "My brother was mean. Not a nice guy."

"I'm sorry, Joseph."

"You don't have to be sorry. You didn't do nothin'."

I tried to focus on my poetry and literature books. Here was *The Complete Poetry of John Milton*. I remembered reading Milton's poem, "Samson Agonistes," and comparing it to the biblical story of Samson, a task which rewarded me with new insights about God and man. I returned the book to the shelf and continued looking. I took pleasure in perusing my books, and they continued pleading their case they'd make much better reading than the Bible.

They might have been correct. They grew more insistent and angry. The books stomped on the shelves as they slid up and dropped themselves down in a discordant wave of protest.

Which book should I read first? Which of you deserves to be read first?

No answer from the books. They didn't care who I read first, as long as it wasn't the Bible. At that moment,

TRUE STATUS

I remembered I wanted to read the thirteenth chapter of Matthew to see if it matched my nightmare parable. The books' noisy protest continued.

Annoyance grew in me. "Be quiet. That's enough," I yelled, and they obeyed.

But Joseph flinched as if I'd struck him. "Why are you shoutin'? I did not say one word. Not one word."

"I'm sorry, Joseph. I thought I heard someone. Did you hear the noise?"

"No, I didn't hear nothin'. It's been all quiet."

I spotted a book from my high school English class, *Three Centuries of English Literature*. It contained the works of many different poets. It included a poem called "A Poison Tree" by William Blake, a poem about the sad results of anger and unforgiveness. It was simple and short. I had never forgotten its opening stanza.

"Listen to this, Joseph."

> *I was angry with my friend:*
> *I told my wrath, my wrath did end.*
> *I was angry with my foe:*
> *I told it not, my wrath did grow.*

Joseph said, "That's true. Jesus said somethin' like that in Matthew 5 and 18 and other places too. Never stay angry. No, no, no, get it out and get it over and done."

The poem ended with a murder. I put the book back on the shelf, even though it contained many other poems I would have loved to reread. There were no Bibles among the poetry and English literature.

Maybe they were with my science fiction books. Inappropriate, but such might have once reflected my attitude. I located some of my favorite science fiction books—*Rendezvous with Rama, Dune,* and *The Illustrated Man.* I found *Invisible Man* by Ralph Ellison. Not science fiction, but his main character lived in a basement apartment like mine, full of light. Considered one of the best books of the twentieth century, it told the story of a Black man whose race rendered him invisible and won the National Book Award for Fiction in 1953. I don't think I fully understood the book when I read it in high school. It would've been nice to read *Invisible Man* again. There were my biographies of Abraham Lincoln, Martin Luther King Jr., Malcolm X, and Anwar Sadat, but no Bibles.

"Now look at that," Joseph said. "That up there looks scary, like a demon."

Joseph stood in front of three bookcases that held my academic books. Each bookcase was eight feet tall, with intricate crown molding at the top. Two of them were finished with an antique vintage walnut stain. I'd finished the one in the middle with a burnished black stain on the exterior and a red stain on the interior.

At the top of the middle bookshelf stood a metal mask, part of a warrior's helmet, and for the first time I realized the mask atop the bookshelf gave the impression of a sinister foe staring down on us.

"I don't like that face up there," Joseph said. "And that in there"—he pointed to the red stain inside the bookcase—"looks like blood."

Those three shelves and their books were what I was most proud of, from both a woodworking as well as academic perspective. I grabbed the mask and showed it to Joseph.

"This is just a very old metal mask. It's nice workmanship. Part of a warrior's armor." I held it out for Joseph to hold.

He backed away. "Unh-uh. Not touching it."

"Joseph, are you getting any sort of feeling from the mask?"

"Don't know. Somethin's not right."

That worried me, because Joseph seemed in tune with spiritual things. He'd known right away the Bethesda Apartments handyman and resident, Mr. Accusio Ubel, was nasty. Though the books, the shelves, and now the mask seemed imbued with a contrary supernatural presence, I suppressed my anxiety and put the mask back on the bookshelf and turned my attention to what was on the shelves. What else could I have done? Fled my apartment, screaming the place was haunted?

I paced.

It was not the place. It was me. They would follow. When I yelled for silence, they complied. I had the power to resist.

I had work to do.

The books on these shelves were thick and heavy, full of complexity. If one of those bookcases had fallen over I could have been hurt. Earlier I had fastened each one to the wall with metal brackets and screws so they were secure.

The books included textbooks for the hardest college courses I'd taken. The titles included a physics textbook, *Mechanics and Special Relativity*, a philosophy book, Kant's *Critique of Pure Reason*, and a computer science textbook entitled *Pseudorandomness and Cryptographic Applications*. Somehow, I managed to do well in all those classes. These once intimidating books became monuments to overcoming challenges in my life—like monsters I'd slain, they could no longer hurt me. Long before I got to college, I would often struggle academically, eventually succeeding each time with the help of my parents. Those struggles made me strong and determined. I learned early I could overcome adversity.

I liked the idea the shelves were screwed to the wall.

The middle bookcase with the red interior and the warrior's mask at the top had a large knot in the back panel. The red stain accented the wood grain around the knot, and it appeared to be a heart full of blood with veins and arteries swirling around it, as if it was a living thing. Joseph had spooked me a little.

Maybe there was something in my academic career I hadn't slain. Maybe I had overlooked something—maybe an opponent I hadn't considered. Maybe it was the Bible—I had never really tried to understand the Bible. Was the Bible more challenging than the things I'd already studied? Did Jesus teach anything that was really new? Didn't other great teachers come up with the same kind of ideas?

How would the Bible resolve my present torment?

I would never know if we didn't find my Bibles. The search resumed.

I stopped and looked again at the bloody heart in the back panel. It bothered me. Why had I never noticed it before? I reached into the enemy bookcase, slowly stretching my hand out toward the bloody spot, and ran my fingers across it. No blood, only wood. I gave a sigh of relief. As I touched the wood my hand brushed against something else, and I pulled it out. It was a paper I had written about *Crime and Punishment* by Fyodor Dostoyevsky when I was in eleventh grade.

"Hey, Joseph," I said. "I just found something I wrote about *Crime and Punishment*, one of the supreme masterpieces of world literature. Listen to what I wrote in my summary. 'Crime and Punishment is the story of Raskolnikov, a young man, who murders a corrupt old woman and steals her money, based on the belief that he is a great man who will use the money for a higher purpose. He believes he is above the law. His human weakness is revealed in his subsequent guilt and psychological suffering for his crime. It's a study of the dramatic battle fought between good and evil.' Wow! Doesn't that sound intense?"

Joseph said, "Why would a great man use his powers to murder someone weaker? That's no challenge. My great man, Jesus, held back his powers to save us all."

I didn't understand what Joseph meant. How could Raskolnikov have felt murder was justified in the first place?

I resumed my search through my literature books and found *Their Eyes Were Watching God* and *The Pilgrim's Progress*, but no Bibles. I scanned every shelf looking for the Bibles. There was a book entitled *The Woodworker's Bible*, but I didn't think that was the word I was seeking. I started at the bottom of each bookshelf and worked my way to the top. No longer lingering over the books or thinking about their contents, I raced through the shelves.

The search continued for more than ninety minutes through every foot of shelf space in my apartment. Then I repeated the process a second time. After two and a half hours, exasperation won and my search ended. Joseph had gone home an hour earlier.

He'd said, "I almost forgot. I have to get Mr. Fluff and Patches from Miss Dianne." Miss Dianne was a neighbor who always kept Joseph's adored cat and dog when he and his mother were out of town.

The couch received my sulking frame. I finally wanted to read the Bible, and God wouldn't let me.

Would God really make it hard to find him just because I'd ignored him for so long?

Tremendous thirst seized me, so I went to get some water, but nothing came out of the tap. Then, I remembered the memo taped to my door about the water being turned off Wednesday night. I looked in the refrigerator, and there was nothing to drink. After getting the notice, anyone with any sense would have filled a pitcher of water just in case, but not me. I slammed the refrigerator door.

I was dying of thirst. I had gone to and fro through my apartment and had come up empty. I began again to go through the bookshelves. I must have missed them. My Bibles had to be there. All my searching stirred up dust from the books and I began to wheeze. I tramped into the bathroom and took two puffs from my inhaler.

I pulled off my shirt and addressed my reject label in the mirror.

"This is all your fault. Why did you and Alexander show up and ruin my life?" I was losing my mind, but at least this time my reflection gave no retort.

Downloading a Bible to my Kindle crossed my mind, but I really wanted to hold a physical book. I should have accepted Joseph's offer. I would go to a bookstore and buy a Bible. I trudged out of my apartment and raced up the stairs and out a side entrance to the parking lot.

I'd forgotten how late it was. I stood outside the building and the night air engulfed me. My phone said it was eleven thirty. No bookstore would be open. I'd have to wait until morning. A crescent moon grinned, mocking me with its crooked smile, and laughter floated down on the night breeze.

The small universe of my apartment contained so much knowledge, yet when I considered the stars, I felt small in comparison to the sky's vast expanse. I gazed upward and wondered if God could be concerned about someone like me. My guess was he probably took no thought of me at all. The demons of fear and despair Angeline had warned me about crept closer, clawing their way into my heart.

Again there was laughter—an evil sniggering—the same as before, many years earlier when I was small, standing in Tall Tower. I turned and saw a figure partially hidden in shadows. It was Mr. Ubel, standing on the balcony of the apartment above mine, which was strange because his apartment was on the other side of the complex. He held a lit cigarette in one hand and a half glass of brown liquid in the other.

I guessed he was doing maintenance work up there, even though the hour was quite late and he appeared to be drinking. The cigarette smoke spewed out of his mouth and nostrils and curled up around his head. He'd once told me he thought I was making coffins when I was building bookshelves. I probably should have told him I was making a coffin for him.

He laughed an old man's laugh and took a sip of his drink.

"The way you busted through the door, I thought your ass was on fire, and then you stopped. Did you forget where you were going? Do you even *know* where the hell you're going?" The drunken old man cackled wickedly again.

He was not worthy of any reply. I shuddered to think Mr. Ubel had access to my apartment. My skin crawled—like insects swarming—at the mere sound of Ubel's voice, the same as when I first saw my tattoo.

"Lord, help me," escaped from my lips. Strangely, small prayers were becoming a new habit.

I retreated back down into my little cave. He called to me as I went.

"It's hell, ain't it? Ain't it hell?"

After changing and getting ready for bed, as I was about to lie down, I saw them.

My nightstand had a single drawer with a small shelf underneath, and my three Bibles peeked out over the edge of a wicker basket on the nightstand shelf. They were barely visible. No wonder I couldn't find them.

Laughing, I drew the Bibles out of the basket. I surprised myself with how pleased and thankful I felt at that moment. A small wooden desk in the living room was the place for my treasures, and my examination of Scripture would begin in earnest at that desk. I opened my red Bible and flipped over a few pages to the "Presented to" page. Someone with lovely handwriting had printed my name—Tennyson William Yates.

Is my nightmare parable really in the Bible?

I have to find it.

I have to read it for myself. Tonight.

CHAPTER 10

Week 1—Thursday

Just past midnight on Thursday morning, I reflected on the search for my Bibles, as well as on the opposing forces whose objective had been to make my Bibles almost impossible to find. One force aligned itself with the good man in the mirror, the vision who'd warned me my own terrible attitude would make the Bible search difficult.

The other force was pure malevolence, a force which didn't want me to find the Bibles ever again. The strange alliance between good and evil—and the strength of the two forces, perhaps equal and opposite as in physics—perplexed me, and led me to ponder whose purpose was served by such an arrangement.

I flipped through the pages of the red Bible in hopes of stumbling across the book of Matthew. Ezriah had said Matthew was the book where Jesus told a parable matching my nightmare. I had no idea where the book of Matthew was, but a check of the table of contents revealed it to be the first book in the New Testament.

I went straight to the thirteenth chapter. As I scanned the pages, my palms grew sweaty and my stomach roiled. I kept losing my place as my eyes skimmed past the verses, requiring me to return to the beginning. The chapter consisted of a long series of parables. One phrase in my Bible summed up the chapter as "parables about the mysteries of the kingdom of heaven."

Finally, near the end of the chapter, there was a section of just four verses entitled "Dragnet," similar to my nightmare. Verses forty-seven through fifty hit me hard.

> Again, the kingdom of heaven is like a dragnet cast into the sea, and gathering fish of every kind; and when it was filled, they drew it up on the beach; and they sat down and gathered the good fish into containers, but the bad they threw away. So it will be at the end of the age; the angels will come forth and take out the wicked from among the righteous, and will throw them into the furnace of fire; in that place there will be weeping and gnashing of teeth.

I shivered, and my mouth became dry as I read the passage and relived my swim in the ocean at the beginning of my nightmare. The rough rope of the dragnet from which I'd barely escaped brushed against my legs again. The sickening odor of burning sulfur filled my nostrils, and my ears heard the shrieks of pain coming from the furnaces, and my face felt the fire's intense heat. I remembered the fear of being thrown into a burning furnace by a pitiless angel, a being whose supernatural strength overwhelmed my own power. The warning was loud and clear—believe in Jesus or else—but I was trapped, frustrated because I didn't know how. Shaken, I returned to the beginning of the chapter and read carefully, to better understand the meaning of the parables, and to see if they held any hope for me.

Large crowds of people gathered around Jesus, according to Matthew 13, and they listened to his teaching, which he did through stories called parables. The chapter related seven parables Jesus told. He gave the crowds only the parables and nothing more—no explanations or interpretation of the parables' meanings.

At first, I was disturbed and angry that Jesus, the supposed savior of the entire world, would explain the parables to only a few of his followers, leaving the vast majority of people in the dark. Then, I had a change of heart after considering my own students. I loved all of them, but some students received far more of my time and attention simply because they sought me out more than most. They had a greater desire to learn than the rest. No doubt Jesus realized any in the crowd who truly desired to understand his teaching would remain with him and ask questions as his disciples did.

The parables showed me how the devil worked. In one story, a sower of seed, who represented Jesus and his disciples, spread the seed, the word of God. The devil stole the word from the hard path—the hard hearts of some of the people. Hearing the word did those people no good. Other factors in this parable—the worries of life, afflictions, and the pursuit of wealth—made God's word equally ineffective. The soil determined the effectiveness of the word of God. Good soil yielded good results.

Two other parables showed how the devil tried to disrupt God's work by placing followers of the devil in the midst of the followers of God. In both parables, God allowed his people and the devil's people to coexist until the time of judgment, when God sent his angels to separate the two groups.

Why would God allow the devil's children and God's children to intermingle?

None of the parables answered that question, but I concluded God had no fear of the work of the devil. Perhaps God's purpose was to allow people time to sort out and choose which side they wanted to be on. In the end, the angels of God sorted the people and sent them to the places the people themselves had chosen.

The words of Mrs. Heaviland meant more now. "I can only tell you those years of grief made me trust and rely on the Lord more, because I knew he understood how I felt, and he helped me through each loss. Now I can face what life brings and still have hope."

It seemed the devil's attack on Mrs. Heaviland only served to strengthen her faith. Maybe that was why God allowed the devil to be the god of this world. It served God's purposes.

Now, I had some understanding of why God gave the devil so much power. I understood why Alexander said I was dead, and to live again would require me to have faith and trust in Jesus. Based on Matthew 13, there were only two options.

Belong to Jesus, or belong to the devil.

My spirit was downcast. I'd hoped for some middle ground, or at least a means of penance that I might atone for the wrong I'd done to Eddie. Where did faith in Jesus come from? Would it ever come to me?

It was still very early Thursday morning, and I planned to get at least a few hours of sleep. Later in the morning, I would reach out to Angeline. After that, I would return to examine my past as Alexander had challenged me to do, even as I feared such self-scrutiny.

What would I do if my recollections proved me even more wretched than I'd thought?

CHAPTER 11

WEEK 1—THURSDAY

I arose around ten o'clock Thursday morning. Rays of sunlight insisted on pushing through the blinds in my kitchen and the draperies of my living room windows, so I opened them and the light poured in. My little cave had not been so bright in a long time, and the thought of Angeline also brightened my spirits. My proclamation to Angeline that the letters on her name tag, *A. Otl*, stood for Angel Of The Lord had been incorrect. After meeting the fearsome Alexander, I was sure she was not an angel, especially if he was the general representative of that species. The thought that Angeline was a mere mortal like me made me smile.

I hoped I'd get to see her and talk with her again. She'd been the first to see my "Rejected" tattoo, and I wanted to tell her about all the strange occurrences of the last few days. I feared she'd think I was deluded, but I still wanted to tell her about everything, plus maybe she would share with me the secret of her scars. Someone had treated her cruelly. Some rotten guy had tried to destroy her lovely face. He'd failed, and she somehow became more radiant than before.

How could she be contacted? The first step might be to call the office of the surgeon who had done the surgery. I dialed the phone number.

"Hello, my name is Tennyson Yates. May I speak with Angeline Otl?"

The receptionist said, "Mr. Yates, there is no Angeline Otl working here. Are you a patient of Dr. York? Maybe I can help you. My name is Susan."

"Yes, I had surgery on Monday. But I—"

She interrupted me and said, "Let me pull up your file."

She put me on hold, and returned after a few minutes. "Mr. Yates, we needed to do a follow-up phone visit with you anyway. I'm so glad you called."

Susan asked me a series of questions about how I'd been doing since the surgery. Then she said, "Mr. Yates, thank you for calling. We have all the information we need, and you seem to be recovering very well. We'll check in again with you in a couple of weeks."

"Susan, do you have any idea how I might contact Angeline Otl? She helped with my surgery."

"She probably works for the hospital where the surgery was performed. Try calling over there."

Perhaps trying to reach Angeline by phone might not be such a good idea. It might be hard to say what I wanted to ask during a phone conversation. I decided to send Angeline a thank-you card and include a brief message, along with my phone number. That way she could decide whether or not she wanted to call me back.

I bought a thank-you card designed for healthcare workers. On the front it said, "Thank you for taking such good care of me." It had a stethoscope formed into the shape of a heart. The inside was blank. I wrote:

TRUE STATUS

Dear Angeline,

You got me ready for surgery a few days ago. Thank you for praying for me and for being a friend. I'm the one you asked about my tattoo. Do you remember? I'm the one that had the strange message in my left underarm.

Your question, "Why does it say that?" started me on a mystical and terrifying spiritual journey these last few days, and I have a feeling it is not yet over. I would love to tell you about it in person. If you would like to hear my story, please call me at the phone number shown below. I would like to hear your story as well.

Your friend,
Tennyson "Billy" Yates

I dropped the card in a mailbox and hoped for the best. I'd initially thought she was unattached when she had no rings on her fingers. Later, I realized she probably took off her rings whenever assisting with surgery. In any case, I'd done something to reach out. There was satisfaction in making the effort. The rest was up to Angeline.

After mailing the card, I sat at the little desk in my living room and began flipping through my red Bible. A sheet of paper fell out—a schedule of confirmation classes from thirty years earlier, with dates, topics, and the first name of the teachers for each session. I studied the sheet and found, to my surprise, the classes lasted an entire school year, but I couldn't remember any of the teachers, topics, or my fellow classmates.

Some of the topics seemed important—Sin, Redemption, Holy Spirit, Way of Discipleship, Way of Salvation, and Living a Holy Life. Definitely significant things to know about, but what kind of explanations had been provided? And did the explanations really make sense? Hard to believe I'd actually been taught about all those things. I'd apparently never learned them.

As usual, I asked myself a long series of questions about my lost memories.

How was that possible? Did I learn the material and then just forget it all? I'd always been such a good student. Had I been robbed of those memories? Was that part of the devil's work?

Or did I, even at the age of twelve or thirteen, possess a heart so hard the word of God could not penetrate? Did the devil take advantage of my hard heart and steal the words away, as the birds consumed the seeds in the parable of the sower?

The title 'Renounce, Reject, Repent' sent my mind back to the previous day when I saw my "Rejected" tattoo in the mirror that first terrible time. For the hundredth time, I asked myself how it got there? What did it mean?

I went into the bathroom and took as hot a shower as I could stand and scrubbed the tattoo with soap, even though I knew it would not come off. After drying off, I examined the tattoo again in the mirror and waited in vain for the man who had appeared to me in the mirror before.

Ezriah said God had rejected everyone, but not everyone got an actual label confirming the fact.

Why me? Why was I the lucky one? Why was I rejected? Was it because of what I did to Eddie? That surely was a sin, but it was also an accident. I didn't intend to hurt him so bad.

How could I believe in a God who'd already rejected me?

After getting dressed, I sat at my desk and focused again on the first topic on the list that had caught my eye.

Sin.

What was sin?

I swiveled around in my chair and looked at my thousands of books. Those authors had their own ideas about what was right and wrong, and I didn't always agree with them.

"What do you guys think?" I said out loud to my books and bookshelves. "What is sin? Surely someone among you has an answer."

There was no reply.

Some things were unarguably sinful, like murder, rape, human trafficking. Those were some of the big ones. Lying and stealing could also be considered sins, but I wasn't certain. *Couldn't lying and stealing sometimes be justified?* It could be to protect someone, or to feed your family. I didn't think God would condemn someone who stole food to feed his family, or lied to protect someone. And churches seemed to always be passing judgment on sexual behavior, like living with someone without being married or for being gay or for just having sex.

Church people seem to be really hung up on sex. Christians are always judging the people they don't like, and a lot of them are doing a lot of the same things they frown upon.

Why does Christianity always seem to attract hypocrites?

If Ezriah were here, I'm sure he would have said something like, "Billy, you know anything good is going to attract hypocrites. It's not just the church. Everyone wants to be part of something good, even phonies."

I thought again of what I'd done to Eddie—a bad sin, so I was no better than the hypocrites. I told myself it was an accident, and I hadn't intended to hurt Eddie, but the reality was in that moment I'd wanted to kill him. My plan was to find some means of penance so I could atone for the sin against Eddie, but I didn't know what my penance should be. I needed to think about that.

I also knew that to complete Alexander's directions, I needed to spend some time thinking about my past, especially as it related to Rose O'Leary, Sharon Fields, and Miros Rybakov. There was one other person, but I couldn't remember who Alexander had mentioned, and I had no intention of spending any time dwelling on who it might be. Recalling Mrs. Heaviland and Eddie brought me some relief, but mostly my recollection brought grief and sorrow over what I'd done out of fear.

I wanted to get the whole project of reviewing my life over and done.

CHAPTER 12

BILLY AT COLLEGE—NINETEEN YEARS OLD

I attended college in Bowling Green, Kentucky, and as a sophomore I purchased my second Bible, the tan one, as the textbook for my first 'Bible as Literature' course. I hoped the class would kindle my spark of faith in God. Sadly, love for God eluded me, but I did fall for a classmate—Rose O'Leary.

I had been introduced to Rose as a freshman, but she didn't capture my imagination until sophomore year, when after our second Bible Lit class session she saw me sitting alone in the student center. She and a girlfriend of hers named Sarah approached me.

In her jeans and multicolored V-neck tee, Rose folded her five-foot-ten-inch frame into the chair, a serious look on her face. She spoke to me in deep, low tones, in contrast to her normally high-pitched singsong voice.

"I read our assignment in Genesis 1 in the evening and in the morning and ... I saw that it was good. Then I read Genesis 2 in the evening and in the morning and ... I saw that it was very good." As she proceeded with her declaration, her green eyes sparkled with glee, and I laughed at her silliness.

"Did you like that? I knew I was going to like you, charming Billy Boy." Rose threw her head back and laughed. "Now I'll challenge you with the riddle I wrote last night. Listen to this and tell me who I am, and what my name is."

She paused and looked around at her audience of two for dramatic effect before she began.

"I am not the creator, but life I brought forth. Flora and fauna are my children, I their first source. I first appeared on creation week's dividing line, when my shimmering cover fled and I could no longer hide." Rose stopped and demanded, "Who am I and what is my name? Easy, if you did your homework."

I said, "So you're a poet and an orator. I read the assignment, but I can't answer that riddle." Sarah wasn't in the class. She was even more dumbfounded than I was.

"I am dry land, and my name is Earth," Rose declared with a grin as she shook her head and waved her hands in the air. Rose had waist-length red hair braided in a single chain and wrapped like a halo around her head. It was funny to watch the way her head bobbed and her hands flowed as she expressed herself.

Sarah asked, "How did the dry land create the animals? I thought God did that."

"I'm so glad you asked that question." The scatter of freckles on Rose's oval face danced on her cheeks. "It's really interesting to see how Genesis explains what happened. God initiated the processes of plant and animal life by first commanding the sea to teem with swarms of living creatures, and then he did the same with the land by telling it to bring forth living creatures. It's really similar to how scientists believe life developed on earth."

One minute Rose would tell a ridiculous joke, and the next, she'd make a comment of surprising insight and wisdom. Her combination of humor, braininess, and good looks made her something special. Rose and I shared time together daily in the student center or the library, and we became great friends. I dreamed of an intimate relationship with Rose, but I didn't get the sense she felt the same way until we both happened to be at the same off-campus party.

My roommate and I walked a few blocks to the house party under the bright light of a happy moon. The home pulsated with music and the warm welcome of a hundred young people, most unknown to me. Rose was there, also unknown to me, until a few minutes after our arrival when I saw her red mane pop up above the crowd. When she finally pushed through the revelers, and I saw her clearly, she took my breath away. Her hair was down and hanging loosely around her shoulders and back, and she wore a simple black dress.

She immediately took my hand and pulled me to the dance floor. We spent the entire evening together, talking and dancing. I held Rose so close I felt her heart beat, and she seemed to melt, soft and vulnerable, in my arms. I dared to hope she might have a romantic interest in me after all. The next week, I invited her to a party at my dormitory, and she accepted. I envisioned a future with Rose as my loving partner.

The following week, I greeted Rose at my dorm's front door, and we walked through a lifeless maze of hallways to the party.

Where was everybody?

She was dressed in white jeans and a multicolored T-shirt with her braided hair wrapped around her head like a laurel crown. I touched the back of her hand with the intention of clasping it in mine, but Rose moved her hand subtly away.

The party was subdued, a much quieter affair than the house party had been. Rose appeared intent on scanning the room to see who was there, and she seemed uncomfortable being in that setting with me. The awkwardness between us was palpable, and we both struggled for things to say. I'd intended to tell Rose how I felt about her, but as the evening dragged on, I realized my love for Rose might be unrequited.

At the end of the evening, the sky sprinkled us with sad tears.

"I'll walk you to your car." I pushed through the dorm doorway and held it open for her.

She shook her head. "That's okay. It's raining. I don't want you to get wet. I'll be fine. I'll see you Monday in class." And she sprinted away.

We continued to talk almost every day, but it was agonizing for me to be around her. One day in the student center, Rose—a photography major—lugged in a heavy box, probably photography equipment too heavy for her to carry. When it was time to go, I grabbed the box and carried it to her car.

As we walked along, Rose looked at me and laughed. "You know, my other friends say you just want to be my slave."

I couldn't believe she would say something like that to me. I'd grown up going to predominantly White schools and lived in mostly White neighborhoods. I was used to being around White kids and felt comfortable. However, wherever I went, I always scanned the room and counted the Black faces, often finding none. Yet I didn't feel different or out of place. I felt I was among friends.

As I got older, I came to understand many of the White people felt *I* was the one out of place, and wondered what I was doing in *their* presence. They would have been much happier for me to not exist. Rose's comment made me wonder if she felt the same way.

When Rose saw the look on my face she said, "I'm sorry I said that. It was a really stupid thing to repeat." She shook her head. "I can't *believe* I said that."

After I loaded the box into her trunk I asked, "What do you think about me?"

"I think you're a nice guy."

"That's it? Nothing more?"

What did I want her to say? *I love you* would have been ideal. *You're the man of my dreams* would have been wonderful. *You're my best friend* would have been fine, but *You're a nice guy* felt like an insult. I supposed she thought I was nothing special. Maybe barely good enough to be her slave.

"What do you want from me? You've been so mopey lately." She pinched her lips together and then continued. "I can't help that I don't always react the way you want me to, or say what you want to hear. You never tell me what's really on your mind. You've always been a closed book. If there's something you want to say to me, you should just say it."

I didn't realize I'd been so obviously down in the mouth, but I didn't say anything. I should have told her how I felt, but I'd already given up.

As she got in her car, she cursed under her breath and said, "Billy, you make everything so hard."

The last time I was with Rose, we rode together in an elevator after leaving a class. We were both headed for the first floor, but the elevator stopped on the second floor, and I decided to get off. I barely said goodbye, and didn't turn back as the elevator door closed. I kept walking, because I had to get away from her. Someone said something to me, but I didn't pay attention or understand what the person said, since my sadness consumed me. As I walked along, tears rolled down my face.

But I felt free.

The semester's end approached, and after a few days of avoiding Rose, I took a bus to my parents' home and spent a month at home for Christmas break.

And just like that, I put Rose O'Leary into my past for good.

CHAPTER 13

BILLY AT COLLEGE—TWENTY YEARS OLD

When I returned to school after the Christmas break, I took a second course on 'The Bible as Literature.' Rose was not in the class.

One afternoon, I sat studying at a table in the library and heard someone say, "Hi. Is it okay for me to sit here?"

The woman was Sharon Fields. Sharon worked for the English department. I'd seen her many times, but we'd never been introduced. Sharon, a little over five feet tall, had large inquisitive eyes, black marbles in a pool of milk. Her face was a triangle with high, wide cheekbones and a square chin. A lean, athletic beauty with muscular arms, shoulders, and legs, she had dark brown skin and black, braided hair with strands of gold woven in.

"Of course you can," I said. "Have a seat."

"You're Tennyson Yates, correct? I'm Sharon Fields." She held out her hand, and I shook it.

"Yes, but you can call me Billy. Most people call me Billy, or Bill."

"Billy? How do you get Billy out of Tennyson?"

I smiled at her. "Well, my middle name is William, and my parents have always called me Bill or Billy. Usually it's been Billy."

"You know what? It's really great to see you smile again."

"What do you mean?"

"All last semester, you and your girlfriend were either here or in the student center almost every day, and you both always looked so happy. This semester, when I see you, you're usually alone, and you look miserable. Did you guys break up?"

It surprised me that anyone would think Rose and I were dating.

"She wasn't my girlfriend, so we didn't break up. We were just friends. We spent a lot of time in here talking about school work."

"Oh. I guess I misunderstood about you and Rose. Speaking of school work, you know what? Part of my job is helping professors grade papers and tests. I've read several of your papers. You're an excellent writer and a top-notch scholar. I've been very impressed with your work."

My chest puffed out a little bit. "Thank you. Writing is enjoyable, and I'm planning to teach on the high school or college level."

"I'm working on my doctorate." A relaxed smile crossed Sharon's face as our eyes met. "I intend to do some research, but like you, I'm also planning on teaching."

"We have a few things in common."

"Hey, have you ever been to the Temple After-Hours?"

"No. What is it?"

Sharon explained the Temple Museum—recently renamed for Mr. and Mrs. Malachi Temple—threw a party several times a year, called the Temple After-Hours, especially designed to attract new and younger members.

She said, "Would you like to go to the Temple After-Hours with me tomorrow night? They have several bands and an open bar. It's really a good time."

"Sure, sounds good."

Sharon clapped her hands and rose from her seat. "Great. Meet me near the student center main entrance tomorrow at six-thirty, and we can walk over to the museum together."

The next evening, when I arrived at the student center, Sharon was already there talking to several of her colleagues. When she saw me, she came over quickly and took my hand, and we strolled to the museum with a small group of other people. I had just turned twenty and was the youngest person in the group, but I felt right at home. Sharon, kind and attentive, seemed to like me a lot. I was excited for what the night might hold.

We spent the evening looking at exhibits and discussing them, and we listened to the music and danced. Sharon had to get my drinks for me—I later learned she was thirty-one—but we both drank. Sharon drank quite a bit more than I did, and the more she drank, the more she said what was on her mind.

While we lounged at a small table listening to the music, Sharon leaned toward me.

"I think you and Rose O'Leary were more than just friends. I saw you and Rose right before Christmas break. You both looked so sad, as if you'd been crying."

Sharon's comment caught me off guard. What had Sharon seen or heard?

"Where did you see us?"

"On the second floor of the English building. I was surprised to see you guys, because the second floor is for English department staff offices. We don't usually see students on the second floor. I actually spoke to you. You stopped for a split second, but you looked right through me. I don't think you even heard me. You were in your own little world."

"I got off the elevator on the second floor alone."

"Well, Rose was right behind you. She looked confused, and just about as sad as you did. After I spoke to you, I looked up, and Rose was gone. What was going on with you two?"

I was amazed Rose had followed me off the elevator, but I didn't dwell on what it might have meant. I didn't know what to say to Sharon, so I lied.

"Like I told you yesterday, Rose and I are just friends. We sometimes critique each other's work. I was a little harsh about one of Rose's papers. Rose got upset, and we had an argument. That was all."

Sharon leaned back in her chair, shook her head, and chuckled. "That's your story and you're sticking to it, right?" After a moment, she sat up and pointed at me. "Or maybe you're a heartless lady-killer."

I smiled and raised my hands widely. "But I didn't do anything. I'm an innocent man."

"Okay. Doesn't matter." Sharon stood unsteadily. "It's getting late. We need to be leaving."

"Sharon, we've both had too much to drink. Neither of us should drive."

She laughed again. "I didn't drive. I walked. I just need you to walk me home. It's at the corner of Amoreof and Self Streets."

We retrieved our coats and left the museum about midnight. As we stepped into the night air, Sharon shivered and wrapped her arm around my arm, snuggling against me. We walked to her house, four blocks from the campus.

Snow covered the ground on that February night, but the plowed sidewalks made the walking easy. Trees lined the street, with snow and ice hanging from their branches, and the stars appeared low and close by in the clear night sky. Peacefulness and quiet reigned as the snow crunched under our feet.

Sharon leaned on my arm and said, "You know, at times like these I feel really close to God. I believe he has a special call on my life. I really want my life to make a difference for people so God will be pleased."

"What god are you referring to?" I asked, trying to be provocative.

Sharon looked at me like I was crazy. She leaned away from me and said, "The Father of our Lord Jesus Christ is the God I serve. Do you believe in Jesus?"

"My parents are believers. I'd like to believe, but you could label me a skeptic."

We arrived at Sharon's home, a large two-story brick house where Sharon lived in a two-bedroom apartment on the first floor. The second story had three bedrooms which she rented out to students. The renters had their own kitchen and shared two full bathrooms and a living room.

Sharon unlocked her door, and I hoped she would invite me in. Instead, she took my hand and pulled me down and gave me a long kiss, the sweetest I'd ever received. Then she disappeared through the doorway. Enchanted and spellbound, I drifted back to my dorm room dreaming of the next time I would see Sharon.

CHAPTER 14

Billy at College—Twenty Years Old

Our relationship blossomed like a rose in springtime, and by summer I was Sharon's live-in companion and her soul mate for life. I'd landed a summer job at a company called Daniels Machining, Inc., DMI for short, so when one of Sharon's tenants departed, it made sense for me to rent a room from her. Sharon and I continued to spend almost all our free time together in her apartment, but when it got late, I always went back to my room. Three weeks into the summer, things changed.

One evening after watching a movie with Sharon, I stood to go, but she shook her head.

"This is ridiculous. You should just stay here with me. We're together all the time anyway. I don't want you to leave."

That was fine by me. In a few short months, I'd gone from lonely college sophomore to living with Sharon. She was like honey to me—my sweet, most beautiful, trusted friend.

Sharon wanted me to meet her family at a summer reunion in her hometown of Admah, Kentucky. Sharon and Lillia, Sharon's cousin who was more like a sister, talked almost daily, and they led the reunion planning committee.

One day, I arrived home from work in time to catch the tail end of one of their marathon phone conversations. Sharon perched on a black high back bar stool, sipping wine, with one elbow on the marble-topped kitchen island. I kissed her and then peeked in the pans on the stove to find the source of a savory aroma—pork roast, carrots, and potatoes next to simmering collard greens. Satisfied, I headed to the alcove to read.

I found myself eavesdropping when I heard Sharon laugh into the phone.

"Billy's all of the above and more. Yes, delicious. And he has more sense than my ex-husband."

Lillia shouted and laughed on the speakerphone. "Well, that's not saying a lot."

"You know what I mean, girl," Sharon said, chuckling again. "Billy's young, but he's also mature, smart, and strong."

Lillia hooted laughter again, but I couldn't hear anything of what she said.

Sharon said, "Well, that was my idea, and I don't care about that old saying. I deserve some pleasure in my life."

Again, I couldn't make out what Lillia said.

Sharon said, "I don't care what she *or* the church ladies say. They can't judge us. I've worked harder for the Lord than any of them. I deserve this." Sharon sniffed. "Anyway, hasn't Mrs. Johnson been married three or four times herself?"

I heard Lillia's shout. "I got to run. Kev just arrived. Love you. 'Bye."

"Love you to the moon and back. 'Bye."

When Sharon got off the phone, I came into the kitchen.

"You know, you should be more concerned about what other people think. You're getting to be a well-known figure in Christian circles. You've got two thousand people following the blog for your counseling ministry. You're speaking at women's conferences, and—"

"What are you talking about?" Sharon put her glass down. Her fingernails clicked as she tapped them on the countertop.

"I mean you just told Lillia you don't care what the ladies at church think. You need to protect your image. You and I shouldn't stay in the same hotel room when we go to the reunion. Either we should get separate rooms, or I could stay with one of your relatives."

"The last thing I worry about is protecting my image. God is my protection and shield. I'm not concerned with what other people say. And anyway the hotel is already sold out, and I don't want you to stay with anyone in my family. My family is crazy, my father is crazy, my cousins are crazy, my aunts and uncles are crazy, and sometimes they make me—"

"So, why don't we just stay home then?"

Sharon had had a chaotic family life, starting as a young teenager with her parents' divorce and continuing through her first marriage. She'd had two abortions because her husband didn't want children. She'd vowed she'd never do that again.

"I love my family. It's just that with them you never know what's going to happen. But I do want them to meet you and see what a good man I've found." She rose from the stool, threw her arms around my neck, and swung herself around me. "Billy, you make my life so sweet. I love you and I need you ... Are you happy here? Do you feel at home with me?"

"Yes. I love you too. As long as we're together, I'll be at home."

Sharon pressed herself against my chest and sighed. "That's all I need to know. You shouldn't worry about anything anymore. No one can judge us."

I didn't say anything else, but my stewing over it didn't stop. Sharon's mention of "church ladies" reminded me of my mother, a church lady, who was not judgmental. However, Mom would not approve of our relationship. I had no faith, but I wanted to keep my life hidden.

Sharon didn't care what anyone else thought. She trusted in Jesus and engaged in premarital sex while teaching against such immorality. Sharon's duplicity confused me, but I loved her and would do anything for her. Being with Sharon felt really right.

The Fields family reunion weekend was the next weekend. We would drive to Admah on Friday afternoon.

CHAPTER 15

BILLY AT COLLEGE—TWENTY YEARS OLD

On Friday afternoon, we both got off work early so we could leave for Admah—a three-hour drive—by four o'clock. Sharon's dad, David Fields, was a well-connected regional banker in Admah, and her mom, Michal Fields, owned De Saul's, a local women's clothing store established by the De Sauls, Michal's parents. And Sharon had a sister, Marta, younger by thirteen months.

Sharon had only briefly mentioned Marta, so I asked about her.

"So it was just you and Marta growing up. How did you girls get along?"

"Yes, just Marta and me. We got along great. We were best friends as children, and only one grade apart in school. We also have a half-brother named Arnon, but he's much older than us."

She seemed uncomfortable talking about Arnon, David's son from a previous marriage and sixteen years older than she. Arnon had left home at eighteen and joined the military, rarely coming back to Admah. At the age of fourteen, Sharon met Arnon for the first time. She didn't expect him to attend the reunion.

As we got closer to Admah, the land's elevation steadily rose. Eventually, we crested a mountaintop and saw the whole region.

"Look, look," Sharon said. She drummed her feet against the floorboards like an excited young girl. "See how beautiful this part of the country is? It's in a valley. You can see how gorgeous it is for miles around." Her voice held a dreamy tone. "I didn't expect this to bring back so many memories."

I took in a vast field of yellow and purple flowers, a forest, and a network of streams and glistening lakes. We began our descent into the valley of Admah, a region that abounded with wealth from fresh fruit and vegetables, as well as a steady crush of tourists who enjoyed water recreation, camping, hiking and fishing.

"It *is* gorgeous," I said. "We'll make some great future memories here."

The idea of future memories must have triggered my mind's ghastly response, whether imagination, premonition, or ancient history I did not know. The luscious valley disappeared in a flash of blinding light, and a fierce wind blew superheated air bearing the scent of scorched flesh. The formerly tall green forest exploded into haphazard giant charred toothpicks spread on the ground, with scores of dead animals and human bodies strewn about. Those still dying writhed in pain or stumbled through rubble with eyes that could no longer see. Steam rose from where water had flowed.

I turned to Sharon. My love, no longer lovely, was a haggard old woman whose face fragmented slowly into dust as if blown apart by the wind. She reached a wizened hand to me and before I could pull away from that awful claw, she clutched my arm. I screamed, and the vision stopped.

TRUE STATUS

The car swerved left, then right, and then bumped over the rumble strip toward the guard rail as an eighteen-wheeler flew by, blasting its horn.

"Watch out! Billy, what are you *doing*?"

I straightened the car and pulled to a stop behind the truck at the end of the ramp.

"Sorry." I gasped for air. "I must have dozed off for a second." A green and white sign pointed west to the city of Canaan and east toward Admah and Lot's Landing.

"Are you okay?" Sharon said with concern. "You look like you've seen a ghost."

"I'm okay." I forced the crazy vison out of my head and didn't consider what it might mean. With clammy hands and great apprehension, I turned the steering wheel, and we headed east.

At six-thirty, we arrived at the Garden Resort, home base for the Fields family reunion. The Garden, a resort and conference center, consisted of condos in a series of gray and white three-story clapboard buildings. The buildings connected in a large rectangle around a huge open-air courtyard.

From our third-floor condo, we could see the courtyard's manicured lawn, flowering trees, and sculpted bushes. Families of the Fields clan claimed gazebos, pavilions, and shelters scattered around a big white tent, its sides rolled up like a canopy. Seven hundred people were expected. Lillia and Sharon planned a full weekend of activities, including time for awards and talent performances under the big tent.

Miss Hannah, an old friend of Sharon's from the nearby town of Canaan, called Sharon, who happily promised to stop by. Sharon called her dad, and we soon found David in the courtyard standing alone. Before we reached him, another man appeared from the opposite direction. Sharon stopped in her tracks and took a step back.

"Arnon," she breathed. "He's here."

David hugged Sharon, shook my hand, and stood back to size me up. Arnon also greeted us warmly.

"So you're Billy," David said. "It's great to finally meet you. You know you have a lot to live up to, the way Sharon's bragged on you."

I laughed and said, "It's great to meet you as well, sir."

"Sharon tells me you're a great math scholar," he said, "and you're planning on being a college professor. That right?"

"Yes, sir. I'm hoping to teach at the high school or college level. I've always loved helping people learn new concepts, especially when they don't think they can succeed. The challenge of learning how people are thinking and figuring out how to help them learn has always appealed to me."

"You might want to consider the banking field. We can always use smart young people like yourself, and there's a lot more money to be made in my business."

David was in great shape for a man in his late sixties, and tall, maybe an inch or two taller than I. Probably about six three or four, with a much bigger frame than mine. He looked like a football player. Arnon's looks were like David's—both had light-brown skin and curly black hair with streaks of gray—but Arnon was built much smaller. He stood a few inches less than six feet in height with a slimmer build than David's, more like my body type.

My first impression was that Arnon was David's older brother rather than his son. Deep lines ran on each side of Arnon's mouth, and he had sunken little black beads for eyes in a face like worn-out leather.

Sharon had also called Marta, and as we were talking, Marta and Michal approached. Sharon introduced me to them, and we hugged and talked. Like David, Michal was very attractive, and youthful enough in appearance to easily pass for Marta and Sharon's older sister rather than their mother. The three of them were of similar height and build, about five feet tall with lean, athletic bodies. Sharon worked out several times each week, and I learned Marta and Michal were devoted to weight lifting, aerobics, and yoga.

Then David said, "Hey, Billy, would you take a picture of me and my children?" He handed me his phone. "There's no telling when I'll have them all together again."

For the next several minutes, we laughed, talked, posed, and took pictures with each other's phones, and I took several photos of Sharon and her family. At some point, another relative came up, and she took pictures of all of us.

Finally Sharon said, "I'm starving. Let's get something to eat. It all smells so good."

***

Everyone in our group had eaten except Sharon and me. We told everyone goodnight, assuring them we'd see them on Saturday. After the crowd dispersed, it didn't take us long to pull together a good meal. For me, a beef brisket sandwich, baked beans, and coleslaw. Sharon chose pulled pork, baked beans, salad, and a beer.

After we ate, we discovered a little towel hut in the courtyard, and we got two large hotel towels and headed down to the lake. We found a deserted spot on the beach with one of those big wooden lounge chairs, and we spread our towels on it. The lake had bar service, and a waiter offered us some wine. I declined, but Sharon took a glass. We kicked off our shoes and strolled along the shore, watching the water, the clouds, and the setting sun. Down the beach, a long horizon of trees were silhouetted against the setting sun's light, which was softened and partially blocked by clouds.

I imagined the wind parting the clouds like a curtain and revealing a mystery, but the clouds' secrets remained hidden. Eventually, a dim starless sky and a shrouded crescent moon hung low over us, and we returned to the wooden lounge chair and stretched out there. The waiter brought Sharon another glass of wine and took back the empty one.

"You know," Sharon said as she leaned against my chest, "you really have to watch out for my daddy."

"What do you mean? He seems like a pretty good guy. A very successful person with a lot of responsibility."

"Successful in business and ministry, but faithless to his first and second wives. Does that make him a successful man? He uses people. Especially women."

"Were the problems in his marriages all his fault?"

"No, but he's a troubled person. His father died when he was a baby. I love him, but I don't think Daddy really loves anyone except maybe Arnon. No matter what I do, he never appreciates or even recognizes my successes."

"Arnon is his favorite? He didn't look too special to me."

"Arnon used to be a really good-looking guy, and very athletic when he was younger. In Daddy's eyes, Arnon could do no wrong."

"Maybe there's still hope for your dad. Maybe he'll surprise you one day. You should tell him you feel overlooked. I can't believe he's not super-proud of all you've accomplished."

"I don't know. It's probably not worth the trouble." Sharon shook her head. "I hate the thought of a big confrontation. Anyway, I could tell he was trying to size you up today."

"That's okay. Maybe he has some ideas or connections that would be helpful to both of us."

"All right, I warned you." Sharon laughed. "You know, there's a proverb in the Bible that provides a warning when dealing with people like my daddy. It's the first eight verses of Proverbs 23. I have the verses memorized. It goes like this."

Sharon sat up in the lounge chair and took the dramatic pose of a performer. She punctuated the biblical recital with her own commentary.

> When you sit to dine with a ruler,

"And Billy, my daddy *is* a ruler. He thinks he's a prince, or maybe a king."

> ... note well what is before you, and put a knife to your throat if you are given to gluttony.

"You have to be very careful. The ruler is always evaluating you to see how he can best use you. Don't be led by your appetite. If you make a mistake or act too eager, you could be through, as if cutting your own throat with a knife." Sharon grimaced and made a slow slashing motion across her throat. "Even his children have to be on guard— even *we* are of no value if we don't serve his purpose."

> Do not crave his delicacies, for that food is deceptive.
> Do not wear yourself out to get rich; do not trust your own cleverness.

"The ruler doesn't wine and dine you for nothing. A ruler is tricky. Don't be too eager to achieve the wealth and pleasures the ruler offers. They will come at a heavy price. You may get all you desire and lose your soul."

> Cast but a glance at riches, and they are gone, for they will surely sprout wings and fly off to the sky like an eagle.

"Remember, material success can evaporate quickly. You should never put your hope in wealth. It can be gone in a snap."

> Do not eat the food of a begrudging host, do not crave his delicacies; for he is the kind of person who is always thinking about the cost. "Eat and drink," he says to you, but his heart is not with you.

"The ruler didn't become wealthy without being careful with his money. Even when he seems to be generous, he's always counting the cost and looking for a return on his investment. His friendship comes with strings attached. There may be a heavy price to be paid to get your desires."

> You will vomit up the little you have eaten and will have wasted your compliments.

"The tasty meat will turn out to be poisonous, and it will make you sick. You could end up with nothing but a bellyache or a heartache. So beware, Billy Yates, and be on your guard."

Sharon fell back into the lounge chair, laughing, and placed a hand over her heart.

"Did you like my dramatic presentation of Proverbs 23? Plus I included my commentary at no extra charge. You should be grateful for my wise counsel and theatrical interpretation."

"It was terrifying, and I think you've had a little bit too much to drink. I wish I had a Bible to verify you quoted it correctly."

"Very good, Billy, you're thinking like the Bereans. There's hope for you yet."

I didn't know what she meant about the Bereans, so I said, "Miss Preacher, let's go. It's getting late, and I have no idea what you're talking about." I laughed. "You're too much."

***

The next morning we washed up, got dressed, and had breakfast at about nine in the courtyard. Sharon said she had a family meeting at ten thirty, and she'd meet me for lunch at noon. We planned to meet at the same picnic table where we had breakfast, right at the edge of the big tent. Sharon kissed me and disappeared into the crowd.

I hiked down to the beach, found a lounge chair, and relaxed by the lake, scanning the photos taken the day before. I'd not noticed Sharon and I had much darker complexions than the rest of her family. In fact, the images on my phone were the first pictures I'd ever seen of Sharon's family. She had all sorts of framed art in her home, and she displayed a picture of her and me taken six months earlier at the Temple After Hours, but there was not a single picture of her siblings or her parents.

Did her darker skin make life hard for Sharon within her own family?

I hoped she hadn't internalized and carried the wicked weight of lies from the damaged psyches of people who'd been taught to hate themselves. I turned back to the pictures on my phone and looked at pictures of my family taken during Christmas eight months earlier. My parents had been married almost thirty years at that time, and they were still going strong, in love and committed to each other.

How did they do it?

Sharon and I had talked about getting married when I graduated, and I looked forward with excitement to joining the fine family of Fields.

My phone alarm alerted me it was almost noon, so I headed back to the picnic table for our rendezvous.

CHAPTER 16

Sharon was not there when I returned to the picnic table. I scanned the hundreds of people relishing the warm sunny day in the courtyard and on the surrounding balconies. She didn't reply to my text, so I hiked back up to our third floor condo and found it empty. I hustled down to the front desk and asked where their meeting rooms were. The meeting rooms were also unoccupied.

With no idea of the location of the family meeting or even the room numbers of their accommodations, I tramped back outside and stalked around the courtyard. Hunger and anger grew in me.

At one o'clock, two of Sharon's cousins, Castor and Pauly Chemosh, twin brothers, passed my way.

"Have either of you seen Sharon?"

"She ditched you, dude," Castor said. He chuckled, shook his head, and kept walking.

"You're Billy, right?" Pauly said, smirking.

"Yes, I'm Billy Yates." Heat flushed through my body. I was in no mood for more foolishness.

"Billy," he said, "David and Arnon are wicked as hell. And Sharon is just like her daddy."

"Who the—"

"Don't get offended," he said, as he pushed by me and laughed. "I'm just trying to help you out. Run for your life."

"You go to hell. You *and* your brother can go to hell." My curses continued as he laughed.

Famished and furious, I found food and brought it back to the table. As I ate, the poison words of the Chemosh twins and Sharon's warning from the previous night replayed in my mind. Maybe the supposed bad faith of David, the ruler, was really a red flag about Sharon. The wine had loosened her tongue and she'd revealed her true self, full of treachery and bad intentions.

I stared up at the condos and imagined Sharon in one of them with another man. The thought made my blood hot with searing anger. In my mind, they peered down at me through one of those windows and laughed. Hatred for both of them filled me.

If I found them, I would kill them.

A door in my heart cracked open, and outside that door was an acquaintance who had for some time longed to enter into a deeper relationship with me, not out of a desire for love or friendship but to take over my soul. It had been crouching at the door of my heart like a ravenous animal, and as my anger grew, I slowly opened the door to invite it in.

Near the table where I sat, metal stakes secured the big tent to the ground. They stood every five or six feet near the picnic tables at the edge of the tent. A stake protruded from the ground to my left, just within reach.

I touched the stake with my left hand and allowed its sun-baked, flat-topped knob head to burn my hand. I didn't care. The pain felt good. The stake, I imagined, was about eighteen inches long and would make a fine weapon as either a club or a dagger. I grabbed my weapon and pulled with all my might, but it didn't budge. I began to wrench the stake from side to side to loosen the ground around it, and finally it began to come out. I shivered with pleasure, thrilled at my progress. Soon the weapon would be mine.

I stopped pulling for a moment, and as quickly as it had commenced, my madness stopped.

I slowly unwrapped my fingers from around the stake and raised my bruised and aching hand.

"I'm not a murderer. And I don't want to spend the rest of my life in prison."

My fantasy of killing someone I actually loved was the stupidest plan I had ever concocted.

How could I have thought of doing something so idiotic? Where did such a thought come from?

All I had to do was make it through the weekend. Then, I could move back on campus and try to forget Sharon and her crazy family. I put the murderous spirit out and slowly closed the door of my heart, but anger still coursed through my veins. My aching left arm and my injured palm aggrieved me even more. Even so, I didn't need to kill her. I could hurt her in another way, and that thought gave me comfort.

After I finished eating at about two, I decided to patrol the grounds and make my rounds through the courtyard, through each floor of the condo's hallways, and through the condo buildings on all four sides. At three o'clock, I came out of the stairwell at the far end of the hallway onto the third floor to see Sharon and Lillia tumbling out of one of the condos about halfway down the hall. I couldn't tell which door they came out of.

I moved closer to them, but they didn't see or hear me.

Lillia said, "So what are you going to do about your little boy?"

"He'll be all right," Sharon said.

"You know you're just using that boy," Lillia said. "You're just like me. I know you."

Sharon said, "No, I love him. I'm never going to let him get away."

"You can't have your cake and eat it too."

"Yeah, I can," Sharon said, and laughed.

Lillia turned and went down a hallway to the left and Sharon went to the right, to the elevators. We were alone. Sharon pressed the button for the elevator and stepped back a couple of steps to wait.

A small table with a flower vase sat between the two elevators, and above the table hung a mirror. If Sharon had looked in the mirror, she'd have seen me standing right behind her, but she looked away from the mirror as if avoiding seeing how she looked—or perhaps to avoid having to gaze into her own guilty eyes.

I bent down and growled softly, my breath on her neck. "Where have you been?"

Sharon nearly jumped out of her skin.

"Lord Jesus! Don't do that! You scared me half to death!" Her face changed, growing solemn and then alarmed. "Billy, don't look at me like that. You look like the devil. What's wrong with you? You're scaring me." Sharon held one hand to her chest as she backed away from me.

I ignored her question and hissed, "Where have you been? You're three hours late for *lunch*."

Her appearance shocked me—her body shrunken and shriveled up, her eyes bloodshot in a ghostly pale face.

"I lost track of the time," she said. "But I don't answer to you, Billy Yates."

Sharon ran to the stairwell door and went down the stairs, and I wanted to strangle her. As the door to the stairwell closed, the elevator door slid open and a few people got off, and I got on the elevator and went down with a grin on my face. It had felt good to frighten her.

Activities ran for the rest of the afternoon and evening under the big tent. Lillia, Sharon, and several other family members were responsible for making sure everything went as planned. Games, speeches, performances, and later dinner and dancing filled the rest of the afternoon and evening. I brooded in the audience for a couple of hours and watched.

Sharon didn't come near where I had ensconced myself, so we didn't speak about the scene at the elevator. She sang with a group that performed two or three songs, and she glanced my way a couple of times, looking apprehensive. It could have been a nice evening, but everything was ruined, so even though the festivities would go on for many more hours, at seven-thirty I went back to the condo and watched television and got ready for bed.

The plan had been for us to head home after a late breakfast Sunday morning, but I doubted Sharon would come back to the condo that night. She might stay with Lillia or someone else, since I was certain we were through. Tired and broken-hearted, I just wanted to make it through the night, get back home to my room, and put it all behind me. Sharon might even take off and leave me stranded at the resort, but I could always rent a car and make my own way home. Might turn out to be the best thing.

I left the light on in the bathroom and turned in at about ten thirty.

CHAPTER 17

Sharon crept into the condo a little past midnight, retrieved her nightclothes from the dresser, and withdrew to the bathroom. A few minutes later, she came out and climbed into the bed. I pretended to sleep, because I had no desire to talk to her. All I wanted to do was get back to my room.

After a few minutes, she sighed.

"I am so sorry for what happened today. I'll never do anything like that again, I promise you. Will you please forgive me?"

She wept soft, quiet tears that almost brought me to tears as well, but I kept quiet. I'd resolved to be done with her.

Sunday morning, I got up at six thirty, took a shower, and went out to locate a Garden restaurant open for breakfast. One was open, overlooking the lake. Another lovely day had begun, with bright sunshine and a light wind making small ripples on the water. Two birds flew low, darting in and out of the water, getting their breakfast as well, I supposed. I envied the birds, since they were likely partners for life.

I enjoyed a deluxe basic breakfast of two fried eggs over well with the yolks broken, bacon, fried potatoes, and wheat toast with butter and grape jelly. While eating at an outdoor table, I alternated between reading the news on my phone and gazing out at the shimmering silver-blue lake.

After twenty minutes, Sharon came and sat at my table. She looked lovely, like her normal self, nothing like the wraith she'd been the afternoon before. I found myself being drawn back to her. There was no helping the way I felt when I was around her. She was everything to me.

"How did you know where I'd be?"

"You love a hot breakfast when you can get it, and this is the only restaurant open for breakfast in the Garden. I think breakfast is your favorite meal."

"It probably is. I love breakfast."

"How can you stand those hard eggs? They're like rubber." She laughed.

I chuckled. "Those runny eggs you like are awful. Yuck."

Sharon ordered breakfast, and we sat and talked as if nothing had happened.

Finally she said, "You haven't answered my question."

"What do you mean? What question?"

"From last night. You ought to know I can tell the difference between when you're asleep and when you're just pretending to be asleep."

"Oh." I looked out at the lake for a moment before I spoke. "I just can't answer you right now. I need some time to think."

"That's okay. I can wait, but I meant what I said. I *will* be better." Sharon dropped her head and looked at her hands.

We didn't discuss what happened any further. We returned to the condo, packed up our things, checked out, and headed home. I drove, and except for the music from the radio, we rode in silence. Sharon slept most of the trip, and when we arrived at her house, she headed for the entrance to her apartment while I headed to the second floor to my rented room.

When Sharon saw my direction, she grabbed my hand lightly. "No, Billy your home is down here with me. We can work through this."

I pulled away from her. "I need to be alone for a while."

I got to my room and closed the door and lay down on the bed. Early in the summer, it had been so exciting when Sharon wanted me to stay with her, but now it was a relief to be alone. The dormitory opened for the fall semester on the coming Thursday, and I would move out of Sharon's house and return to campus.

It was early Sunday afternoon. I stayed in my room the rest of the day reading except for going out once to walk to a local fast food place. I'd been spoiled that summer, because Sharon, a very good cook, made a home-cooked meal almost every night. Soon my fare would be cafeteria food.

I had three more days of full-time work at DMI. After that, I would continue working there part time during the school year. On Monday morning, when I left before seven to catch the bus for work, Sharon's car was not in the driveway. She didn't have to be at her office until eight-thirty, so I wondered where she was.

When I returned home after work, Sharon was still not there. My worry accelerated when she didn't show up Monday night or Tuesday morning. She didn't answer my call on Monday night. Tuesday, during my lunch and breaks, I called friends who might know where she was.

Finally, I called her office at school, and they told me she had scheduled a few days off. I was relieved to learn she'd planned to be off, so she probably didn't have an accident—just time off she didn't care to tell me about.

She might have gone back to Admah. Certainly, she'd met someone else down there.

Thick clouds and drizzling rain made Thursday morning dark as nighttime. I planned to move back to the dorm that afternoon, and I fretted about the rain soaking my things. At nine a.m., while I dried off after a shower, Sharon knocked on my bedroom door and called my name. Silently, I waited until her footsteps receded as she went back downstairs. Then I went to my room and got dressed. Sharon's voice brought me both relief in knowing she was okay, and anxiety because I'd hoped to avoid seeing her when I moved out.

A few minutes later, she returned and knocked again, and I opened the door.

"I wanted to let you know I was back. Can we talk for a few minutes?"

"Come in. It's messy right now, but I'll have it cleaned up by this afternoon. I'm glad to see you're all right. I was worried. I haven't seen you since Sunday."

Suitcases, boxes, and other things that needed to be packed formed a messy collage strewn everywhere, including across the bed and the only chair, so we ended up sitting on the floor. I sat under the only window in the room and leaned back against the wall as rain streamed down the window. Sharon sat opposite me, and she rested her arm on a footlocker that sat at the end of the bed. She leaned back against the bed. We probably looked like two very young kids getting ready to play a game—children who had not yet learned to keep secrets out of shame and fear.

"I went to see Hannah Samuel," Sharon said. "She lives in the next town over from Admah. Remember? We were supposed to go see her during the family reunion, but I forgot. I called her Sunday when we got back here."

"Yeah, your friend Miss Hannah. She called you on Friday night, right?"

"Yes. I needed someone to talk to, so I called her and she invited me to come stay with her a few days. She helped me a lot." Sharon's tears began flowing, and she pulled her legs up and wrapped her arms around her knees. "Miss Hannah helped me see where I'd gone wrong, because she's known me so long, since before I was born. While I was growing up, Miss Hannah loved me and treated me like more than just a big bundle of bad behavior—which I definitely was. But she loved me anyway."

Sharon stopped, wiped her eyes, and then continued.

"She had a beautiful meal ready for me when I got back down there Sunday evening. She and her husband had already eaten, but Miss Hannah sat with me, and we talked while I ate. She wanted to know about school, my ministry, and my life and plans. I told her the truth. I tried to be honest with her about everything, including you." She paused and looked at me for a few seconds as if searching for some expression of affection from me, but I remained stone-faced.

"I know you've lost trust in me," Sharon said, "but I really do love you."

"How did Miss Hannah help you? What did she say?"

I got up and found a box of tissues and gave it to Sharon. I don't know why I didn't do that sooner. Sharon had never been so emotional in my presence before.

"She made me see my sinful, stupid pride, and I'm so ashamed of myself," Sharon sobbed. "Miss Hannah said, 'Honey, you've worked hard, and you've sacrificed in service to God, and you've had more than your share of suffering. But you sound like you think God should make exceptions for you, as if God is in your debt. The Lord Jesus Christ suffered and died a horrible death to save us from the punishment our sins deserve. Honey, you've preached and taught the word of God, but you're not living it out. You've got to submit yourself to the Lordship of Jesus Christ and obey him. You're beautiful, smart, and talented, but you didn't make yourself. God gave you so many gifts so you would honor him in every part of your life.'"

"What did she mean by 'submit yourself to the Lordship of Jesus Christ'?"

Sharon said, "It's in the seventh chapter of Matthew, at the end of the Sermon on the Mount." She looked away from me, and her eyes grew distant as she recalled the verse and quoted it.

"Not everyone who says to Me, 'Lord, Lord,' will enter the kingdom of heaven, but he who does the will of My Father who is in heaven will enter. Many will say to Me on that day, 'Lord, Lord, did we not prophesy in Your name, and in Your name cast out demons, and in Your name perform many miracles?' And then I will declare to them, 'I never knew you; depart from me, you who practice lawlessness.'"

Her eyes returned to mine.

"I've preached and taught the gospel, but I was doing evil. Now I want to live according to the Father's will. I don't want to be in rebellion against Jesus anymore. He's done too much for me for that. He showed us his love when he laid down his life for all of us ... so it means a lot of things. Billy, I don't know if you even want me anymore, but one thing it means is if you and I are going to continue our relationship, we can't live together. The intimate sexual part of our relationship will have to be put on hold."

I shook my head and scoffed at her. "How could I possibly want to continue our relationship? Sharon, you were three hours late for lunch, and you never gave me an explanation. From that day, I felt you were cheating on me with another man. Who were you with?"

"I know I betrayed you." She hesitated and added, "I was with Arnon."

My mouth slackened. I didn't know what to say. "Arnon is your brother. What do you mean, you were with Arnon?"

"He never seemed like my brother. I was almost fourteen when I first remember meeting Arnon. He had the most beautiful dark eyes. His shoulders and arms were so defined and sinewy, like strong rope—he was not a big guy, but he was a well-made man. We were enthralled with Arnon.

"He took our childhood. First, it was Marta. I was so envious of the attention he gave her, and then he turned to me. When Mom found out, she had him arrested. Arnon went to prison for seven years. He corrupted us. He ruined himself, and destroyed our innocence."

"He took advantage of you when you were a child. You're an adult now. Why did you let this happen, now you're grown up?"

"I know I'm a grown woman now. I don't know why I did it, but I felt like a young girl again. I guess I felt sorry for him. I always felt guilty he went to prison. But Saturday, right afterward, I was so disgusted with myself.

"Arnon made me sick. I told him I would never see him again, and he looked so lost. I remember looking down from the room, and I saw you waiting for me in the courtyard. I betrayed you, but I wanted to come to you."

"So why didn't you?" I asked, raising my voice and waving my arms. My façade broke, and my own tears began to fall. "We could have avoided all this."

"I felt dirty and disgusting. I couldn't go to you, my innocent man. I just knew you would know. I cried instead.

I left Arnon and found Lillia, and we had a little party with booze and pills, and I felt better for a little while. It makes no sense, but that's what happened.

"I'm sorry for all the ways I've failed," she said, "and I'd like a chance to regain your trust. Either way, I'm going to live a new life. My eyes have been opened."

My dream of Sharon had crumbled over the previous week. But now someone new and unexpected confronted me, a broken and humbled Sharon I didn't understand. Part of me wanted her back. In my heart, I didn't believe in the kind of change she claimed, so I was not up to the task of giving second chances. My trust in her had departed. I'd heard her say with my own ears she'd have her cake and eat it too. I was determined it would not be at my expense again.

My friend from work, Miros Rybakov, showed up about four thirty. We moved my things out of Sharon's house and back into the dormitory.

Sharon and I were no more than distant friends for the final two years of my undergraduate career.

CHAPTER 18

BILLY AFTER COLLEGE—TWENTY-THREE YEARS OLD

After five years of college, I graduated with both a bachelor's and master's degree in mathematics, but I didn't pursue my teaching career right away. I continued to work at DMI for another two years before moving on.

I was a Production Engineer for DMI, a producer of stainless steel cryogenic pumps for liquefied gases for the power industry. Our group worked with product design engineers and the shop to make sure the products met design requirements.

Around this time, my sweating really became a problem. I began bringing extra undershirts and shirts to work, and changed clothes several times every day. I hoped the condition was temporary, but the sweating only got worse over time.

The DMI plant was a huge facility. Miros Rybakov was the production scheduler, responsible for making sure the right products got shipped on time, and he spent a lot of time riding around the plant on an electric scooter. We got along well, and Miros became one of my all-time best friends. I had dinner with Miros and his wife, Athena, most Sundays.

Miros, thirty years old, stood about six feet four inches, with thick arms and legs and a broad torso. His devotion to his faith made him act in ways that seemed peculiar to me, but Miros hadn't always been that way. He regularly tried to persuade me to become a Christian.

One Sunday after dinner, Miros and I went outside and played with their dog, Oliver. Their backyard smelled like the sweet aroma of a puppy lying down in fresh-cut grass. After Oliver had worn us out, we sat in the patio chairs, and he began telling me what he'd been like before and after Jesus changed him. Miros called it "my transformation."

He said, "Billy, God has a funny way of showing us how screwed up we are. If we pay attention and respond, it will really pay off for us."

I rolled my eyes and got ready for the God pitch. "What are you talking about?

"When I first met you, I thought you were full of hate and anger. You would have never been hired if the decision had been up to me."

"That's not true. I don't hate anyone. I love everyone." I jumped up. I wanted to kick Miros right out of his chair. "Who told you that bull?"

Miros jumped up too, laughing and taking a boxing stance.

"Mm-hm. I love how you show your love." Miros took a fake swing at me. "This'll give me a chance to whip your butt. I only outweigh you by seventy pounds. Two hundred and fifty pounds of pure muscle, baby." He pounded his chest and bounced and shadow-boxed around the patio.

"I'm way too quick for you. You'd never land a punch on me." I started throwing air punches. Oliver got into the act, barking, jumping, and running in circles around us, until Athena opened the back door.

"What in the world are you two doing?"

She came out and handed each of us a glass of lemonade. Athena was also tall, about six feet, with a slender build and long limbs and fingers. Strands of her long honey blonde hair curved around her face. When she flashed a smile, she was beautiful, but Athena didn't smile easily. They'd been married eight years. No children.

"Thanks, babe. It started out as evangelism," Miros said with a grin, "but he got offended." Athena shook her head and went back inside.

Miros took a long swig of lemonade and then said, "Let's sit down before the neighbors see us. They might call the police." After we sat and Oliver climbed into my lap, Miros continued. "Look, I'm just telling you about the old person I was. I just thought what I thought about Black people. No one told me anything about you."

"So you were prejudiced for no reason."

Miros put his hands up. "It was what I saw from my father and uncles when I was growing up. It wasn't my worst problem, because I could hide what I thought about people pretty easily. My worst problem was with women."

Miros sank deeper in his lawn chair, and his voice became much quieter than normal.

"Only a couple of years ago, I would ride around the plant and be hung over or drunk or high, thinking about women. My eyes were full of adultery. To me, women were just pieces of meat. I had no regard for them. It was all I knew, and it ruined me."

"You did that crap while you were married to Athena?"

Miros got up and waved me to go further into the backyard, away from the house, to a fire pit where we sat in Adirondack chairs. "Tension would build up in me, and I would just need a release. After work, I would go home and eat dinner, and then I would tell Athena I was going out with a few of the guys. I would go to a tavern alone, drink, chat with the bartender, and keep an eye out for a woman drinking alone, a barfly. Barflies hang around bars and get drunk alone."

"You were a barfly too, right?"

"No," Miros groaned. "A barfly is a *woman* who gets drunk in a bar alone, usually broken-hearted, wanting affection and attention."

I smiled inside that Miros refused to identify himself as the barfly he had been.

Miros continued, "I wanted to take advantage of the barfly. If I got lucky, I would go home with her and have sex. Then I would stagger home to Athena. I was ashamed, but that didn't stop me."

"Why did Athena put up with it?"

"Good question. I have no answer. We both came from alcoholic families, so maybe craziness seemed normal to her. I was really a screwed-up piece of work, but I'm grateful now for my second chance."

Even after two years of living right, Miros got emotional when he contemplated his past.

"I heard a sermon once—the preacher called it the 'Fourth Song of the Suffering Servant' from Isaiah 53. That servant's song is a description of what really happened when our Lord Jesus was crucified ... an innocent man, tortured and beaten beyond recognition. Jesus was despised, forsaken, stricken, smitten, afflicted, pierced, crushed, and scourged." Miros's face was ashen, haunted, drained of color, as if he'd seen a ghost. His chin quivered as he spoke. "It was painful and deeply shameful. God did this to him, and Jesus accepted it without even opening his mouth in protest."

"Jesus was God's son, right?" I said. "Why would God do that to his own son?

"Because of my sins." Miros pounded a fist against his chest.

"What do you mean by because of your sins? Jesus died just for you?"

"Not my sins alone, but I felt my sins added to the suffering he felt. That was why I had to change. There's a verse in the sixth chapter of Hebrews—it made me feel that by my willful sins I was crucifying Jesus over and over again. I brought continual shame upon Jesus. When I understood that, I knew I had to change."

"You felt your sins were adding to the suffering Jesus felt that day. I get that. But how could any father allow his son to suffer like that? It makes me sick just to think about it."

"You're missing the point. God is an absolutely righteous judge. Our sins—" Miros swung his fingers back and forth to indicate the two of us, "—our sins had to be paid for. God allowed Jesus to be a guilt offering for our sins, so God exalted Jesus because of his great sacrifice. It's the only reason any of us can be at peace with God. Our good deeds are worthless to solve our problem. We needed a savior."

"So Jesus bore my sins as well?"

"Absolutely. Jesus has already paid for the sins of all people past, present, and future. But you still have to trust and believe in Jesus, or his sacrifice will do you no good." Then Miros turned the tables on me with a question.

"Billy, God is calling you, inviting you to come to him through Jesus. You've seen what Jesus has done for me. Why don't you accept the invitation and believe in him?"

Miros's conviction touched my emotions, but not enough.

"I reject the invitation, because I think your whole system doesn't make any sense. I don't need Jesus to die for me. What I really want is my day in court with God, so I can present my case and prove how God has done me and my family wrong."

"My friend, you don't understand the offer God is making. God doesn't owe us an explanation for every bad thing that's happened in our families. My father was the meanest man I ever met, and I haven't gotten a reason why I had the misfortune to be his son. I only know God is my good Father who's provided all I really need to have, and all I need to know."

I stood up and pointed at Miros.

"Right there is the problem, because God *does* owe us an explanation. Can God fairly judge his own conduct? If God is honest, fair, and just, I'll be found to be an innocent man because of all the good I've done, despite all the suffering God has sent my way. I'll be worthy of the same reward you expect to receive in eternity."

CHAPTER 19

Week 1—Thursday

I spent most of the day Thursday lost in memories of Rose, Sharon, and Miros, and when I reached the end of that journey and fully returned to the present, I cringed under the glare of an unseen interrogator's spotlight.

Darkness filled my living room except for the bright beam of a parking lot light shining on me through the window. Exposed and ashamed, I quickly yanked the lever of my recliner, breaking the quiet with a ratcheting clunk. I got up and closed the blinds, curtains, and draperies in all my rooms. When I'd shut out all the light, I felt safe.

After a few moments, however, the light's glow crept around my window treatments, creating ominous shapes of bodies, gallows, and claws across my walls, plants and bookshelves. I flipped on several lamps to dispel the gloom. Exposed again under the lamp's light, I began hearing the voices of my accusers. I couldn't tell where the voices originated, but they kept intruding as I tried to think about all the things I'd done wrong and formulate my next steps. Different voices kept piercing my conscience, and their delight at tormenting me was plain.

"You rejected God first. You turned away from him. You earned that tattoo."

Until that day, just a few days after my surgery, I couldn't recall ever saying I rejected God's offer or I didn't need Jesus. Ezriah was correct—people reject God before he rejects them. It shamed me to be included in that number.

"You're as guilty as hell," another voice said, with quiet satisfaction and contempt.

Murder someone?

Never. Not me. But a murderous spirit did reside in me. With Eddie, it had come out without warning. At the Fields family reunion, it became clear my murderer had lurked within, waiting for an opportune time—waiting for my better self to break down and yield to the ravenous beast who hungered for destruction more than it desired pleasure.

"There is nothing good in you. Miserable and ruinous is what you are." Something seemed to breathe on my neck with hot hatred.

In the case of Eddie, fear drove me, combined with Eddie's refusal to do what I told him to do.

Why didn't he just kill the snake like I told him to?

The reason was simple—because Eddie loved animals. He would never randomly take an animal's life, even if one of his best friends wanted him to. Back then, for me it felt like a matter of survival. But that was a mistake. My brain completely misfired, and the god of this world tricked me.

"You're already dead to God, for you do not fear God," another voice said. "Alexander said as much. Go ahead and die now. You are not worthy of life. Yes, go ahead and die right now."

Rose had hurt my pride. She didn't see me or want me the way I wanted her to, yet I never really tried with Rose. I'd given up, figuring she'd never see me as an equal or as a lover, so I couldn't remain friends with her.

TRUE STATUS

Sharon wanted to give our relationship another try and asked me to forgive her, but such magnanimity was beyond me. I couldn't let her consider me her fool. I guarded myself with a hard, unyielding spirit.

Even if we never got back together, I should have been more kind.

The memory of the sun setting over the lake in Admah closely matched my vison of the sea in my nightmare parable. The nightmare's disastrous results came quickly, but my real-life choices set me on a slower, inevitable path to hell. My sojourn into the past revealed in me a small heart full of violence, fear, self-pity, pride, selfishness, and condemnation, with no forgiveness. A pretty résumé it was not. My accusers were correct in their denunciation.

Remorse and regret overwhelmed me. I'd always been skilled at solving complex problems, but the solution to my current predicament escaped me. I needed to atone for my wrongdoing, but my next step was unclear.

Why would Alexander lead me into a dead end with no way out?

Fatigue crashed on me all at once. I could barely move from my recliner. I dragged myself to the bedroom and fell into bed without bothering to take my clothes off. Nothing mattered anymore.

Someone's voice spoke with glee.

"Yes. Give up, because you are one worthless piece of crap. God could never love you. Such a shame. Such a pity."

Such a shame.

CHAPTER 20

I stood at the edge of a broad thoroughfare, peering through fog. The tumult of a crowd, the sounds of heavy breathing, and the pounding of feet grew as the mist gradually cleared. A throng of people ran in the road—some fast, others slow and struggling. Everyone moved in the same direction, like a strong river's flow. The road was rough, sometimes gravel and sometimes dirt, and it curved uphill and down. A noisy throng of spectators lined the road, witnessing every step of the race.

While I stood there trying to figure out what this vision meant, someone pushed me and a young man's voice spoke.

"Get in the race, Billy. This is your life. Do not listen to your accusers. They are not of God."

So I ran too, fast and hard. Light, thin strands of fiber ran from me to other people. Some strands consisted of multiple fibers braided together, and others were a single thread. I pulled at the strands and they stretched easily, but I couldn't break them. A permanent connection existed between me and everyone around me. Some of the fibers tugged me back, and some pulled me onward.

A few people ran right in the middle of the road on a narrow strip that seemed to be lit by reflectors. They must have been able to see better. I tried to jump onto the narrow strip, but with each attempt I ended up on the other side of the strip. It was unfair.

Why should they have more light than me?

I purposely rammed some other runners. Seeing them stumble warmed my heart for a few seconds, but regret soon followed.

I knew some of the people who ran nearby. My brothers, sisters, and parents were all there, but they didn't respond to my shouts of recognition. I became discouraged and decided to stop. I stepped over the curb and sat on the edge of the road, in spite of some of the spectators' pleading for me to keep running.

I wrapped my arms around my knees and leaned forward, but it was as if my arms, legs and chest had lost all feeling. Weights encircled my arms and my legs, and a heavy jacket encased my torso. The weight of the jacket squeezed my chest, back, and shoulders, making it hard to breathe. Something like Velcro held the jacket and the arm and leg weights in place.

When I tugged at the jacket to pull it off, my heart raced, and nausea filled me. I put the jacket back on tight. I tried to remove the loads from my arms and legs, but as with the jacket, every attempt made me terribly afraid and sick. I began to panic and whimper. The people told me to get back into the race or else the gatherers would come for me.

"Can't you see?" I said to everyone and no one. "I can't run with these weights on me. I don't want to run. It's too hard."

Then someone touched my shoulder and said, "I love you, Daddy. You have to keep running."

I turned my head to one side. "I don't have any children. Why are you calling me Daddy?"

"You never knew about me," the person said. "I love Momma too, but she never told you about me."

TRUE STATUS

I stood and spun, feeling the heat rising in me. "I don't understand what you're talking about. I don't know who you are."

I took a step back and almost fell into the road when I saw him. It was like looking at my own reflection, just like the man who'd appeared in the mirror at home.

"I know you don't," he said. "You were both drunk when it happened. My life was very short and no one ever met me, not until I got here. They call me Benotenn, Benotenn Yates. I wish I could have gotten into the race and breathed the air for even a few minutes, but I am comforted here."

"I don't know what to say to you. I don't remember, and I don't know you." I waved my weighted arms in frustration. "I don't understand any of this. It isn't my fault."

"I've known *you* since you were in high school," Benotenn said. "I've been watching you ever since. You never loved Momma. She needed your help, and you didn't even give her a thought after you were done with her. She's still in the race."

"Who's your mother?"

"Momma's name is Millie St. Vincent, but you knew her as Sandy. She was two years younger than you. She looked up to you because you were so smart. Do you remember her now?"

"I'm very sorry, but I don't remember her. What is it you want from me?" I was trembling so much I could barely speak.

But even as I denied Sandy's memory, I began to recall her and saw her face. My description of her had once been, "Gorgeous, but not too bright." In thinking of her, as sick as it seems, old lust rose up in me. I hoped Benotenn couldn't read my mind.

Benotenn said, "What's on your hands?"

I raised my hands and looked at them. They dripped with blood.

Heat rose behind my eyelids and burned my conscience. "I'm not a murderer. I've never killed anyone." I shook my hands and wiped them on my clothes. "How can my hands be covered in blood? And I asked you before—what do you want from me?"

"I want you to get back in the race."

Benotenn shoved me back onto the road. Blood covered my clothes. My fellow runners were bloody too. Some were wounded, dripping with their own blood.

Did we fight each other, unaware of the wounds we inflicted? Mindless gladiators?

At one point, a thick forest of trees blotted out the light, and in deep darkness, a profound loneliness and foreboding overtook me. I envisioned a giant fist crashing down on my head. My knees turned weak, and I moaned as dread filled my mind. Time seemed to drag endlessly on. Finally, the darkness lifted, and I was able to continue.

Several times, I stepped to the side and sat down on the curb. Each time Benotenn met me.

"How did this blood get on me?" I asked. "Why does everyone have blood on their hands?"

"Not everyone has blood on their hands. I don't," Benotenn said, holding his own hands out.

"Well, you never lived," I roared. "You don't understand what it's like."

"I never lived because you never cared enough to find out if I existed."

Benotenn spoke quietly and with an unwavering eye contact that I could not meet.

"I was an afterthought in life, and now I'm an unknown that Momma can never forget. She feels guilty every day.

How can you not understand why there is blood on your hands? You are not innocent."

"How could I have known? Why is there blood on me?" I cried, my chest heaving in my struggle to breathe. "I'm not perfect, but I didn't intend to hurt people, I always wanted to help them. I couldn't have known about you."

"Are you sure about that? You knew what alcohol does. You knew what sex does. You should have found out about me and Momma. You should have let her know you would help her take care of me. If just one person had helped her, I might have lived. It should have been you. Fathers are made to protect their children."

"You know what, Benotenn? I never said I was perfect." I pounded my chest and shouted. "But I'm better than ninety percent of the people out here. Why do you condemn me?" Even though I tried to defend myself, the thought of all my combined sins convicted me. I was lying to Benotenn and myself.

"The whole world is sin-sick. You are not a hero. Your ignorance was and still is willful," he said. "Being better than ninety percent means nothing, but I don't condemn you. I want forgiveness for you, but you have to stop lying to yourself." He pointed a long slender finger in my face. "You could have taught me so much. I would've been your best friend by now."

Benotenn turned away. Strangely, I was afraid he would leave me alone. I wanted to justify myself before him more than I wanted forgiveness. I wanted him to know it was not my fault, but I didn't know what else to say.

It struck me like a beanball on the noggin that I'd destroyed my own dreams. In my ignorance, I'd let my deepest wants escape and flow through my hands like sand.

"Tell me, Benotenn, why do I have these strings all over me? I'm in a spider's web. I'm trapped. I can't get free from this prison."

"It isn't a spider's web or a prison. It is a blessing. It is life. They are not strings—they are threads. Think of them as threads in a piece of fabric."

"Fabric ... you mean like the fabric of a shirt, or a tapestry?"

"Yes, woven together. You need to make the threads stronger."

"I don't know how," I said, shaking my head.

"You've got to try, and you've got to stay in the race," Benotenn said. "It would be very bad for you to leave the race now. Also know this—many here love you. Not just me."

"What about these weights all over me?" I tugged at the burdens I carried. "They're killing me, but it hurts so much. It makes me sick to pull them off."

"They *are* killing you. You need to take them off."

"I can't take them off. They're part of me ... they *are* me. What are they? It's miserable whenever I begin to take them off."

"They're your sins. It's only natural you love them, otherwise they wouldn't be yours. But they're not you. They're just what you do and don't do."

"I can't take them off!" I wept, and my body trembled. "You don't understand. I'll die without them, but they are killing me. Please help me, Benotenn."

"I can't help you. Maybe if you love something more than them, you'll be able to take them off."

"Why can't I run on that narrow strip in the middle? The ones who do can see more clearly. This isn't fair."

"That is the way. The Lord's church. You have to be placed in the way by the Lord. You can't get there on your own."

"Will someone please help me?"

"You've got to call upon the Lord."

"How do I do that? How do I call the Lord?"

TRUE STATUS

I began to run again and sobbed with each step. I crumpled to the ground and got back up and stumbled off the road again. My sins encircled me, and they were all I could see.

Though daylight had turned dark and my eyes could no longer see, I felt Benotenn's arms encompass me. "Daddy, you've got to get back in the race. Please live for my sake."

Benotenn's words did not penetrate my heart.

"I can't. I didn't know it before, but now I know for certain I am unworthy. There is no hope for me."

I woke up still fully dressed, drenched in sweat.

CHAPTER 21

Week 1—Friday

I stayed in bed for an hour, dwelling on how I'd failed Benotenn, my son. He was real, but he was dead—yet he was alive somewhere. I yearned to see Benotenn again. There was something wonderful about seeing a part of me who looked so much like me. We would've been good friends.

But I was certain I'd never see him again.

Bright sunshine pressed against my window panes, wanting to come in. I kept the draperies shut, preferring the darkness. I wished I'd never met Alexander. What good was it to recognize my sins? What good lay in realizing there was no way to atone for them, because my wrongdoing was too great?

My conclusion was that looking back on my life had been to show me my unworthiness to be alive, so I would finally understand God hated me for good reason and had rejected me justly.

I knew what I needed to do, but feared what awaited me after death.

My final act of defiance? Or surrender?

Surely, in death Eddie would know what I did to him. I feared that confrontation in life, but the thought of God,

Eddie, and others shaming and haranguing me forever in eternity was worse. Perhaps there was no escaping my consequences.

Footsteps and muffled voices from the apartment above intruded on my solitude, as well as the roar of car engines readying for the morning commute. I got out of bed and stumbled to the kitchen, and although it was still morning I retrieved a beer from the refrigerator and drank it. I rarely drank—never in public, and never alone. When I did drink, I would just sip a beer with guests in my home, and only if they were drinking.

I downed three cans of beer in less than an hour and with each swallow my conflicted thoughts coalesced on my only acceptable course of action. The plan would be carried out in my garage workshop, so I grabbed the rest of the six-pack and tramped outside. Sunlight blinded me when I emerged from my apartment building.

At the back part of the property was a long row of connected single-car garages. As I approached the unit that served as my workshop, a car pulled into another of the garages. Moments later Edmund Landes and his dad, E.J., emerged. E.J. drove his power wheelchair and gave me a wave and a nod as they moved toward the building.

I tapped the garage door code keypad several times before I finally put in the correct code and the door rattled open. I stepped into my workshop quickly and pressed the button to close the door. As the door came down, Edmund and his father observed me until the door blocked their view. They were probably wondering why I would shut myself into the garage.

After a few minutes, the opener light went out and semi-darkness engulfed me, not quite matching my mood. The air—warm, dry, and filled with the sweet aroma of pine sawdust—made me feel right at home. My workbench sat at the center of the space where I'd spent many enjoyable hours hovering over it, fashioning all sorts of furniture for my friends and family.

I'd never been in the garage with the door closed, but light from a small back window crept into the garage, so instead of turning the light on, I walked to the workbench and leaned back against it. I drank the fourth beer, crushed the can, and threw it. The empty can clanked against the wall and skittered across the floor, followed shortly by the fifth can.

I climbed up on the six-foot-long workbench, stretched out on my back, and looked up into the gloom. With my arms folded on my chest and eyes closed, the soothing image of death as peaceful sleep crept into my mind. Eternal rest with no consequences. Someone banged on the garage door, but they got no response from me. Several minutes passed before I got up and flipped the light on.

I scanned the workshop and spied some rope. I retrieved it and returned to the workbench. The rope was an inch in diameter, hard and rough with tiny spines sticking out like a prickly pear. I laid the rope on the workbench, made a loop, and tried to wrap the rope around the top of the loop. The rope was very tough and difficult to wrap around, and the spines cut into my hands. It was as if the rope had a will of its own, resisting being formed into such a deadly device, but finally I completed the knot and loop.

I climbed onto the workbench and tied the free end of the rope to one of the rafters that supported the loft, putting the noose at eye level when I stood on the workbench. I examined the setup and reached for the rope, planning to pull on it to test that the rafter would hold my weight, but before my fingers touched the rope my cell phone rang. I froze.

After several rings, I reached for the phone, but a familiar voice said in my ear, "Stop. Don't answer it. You're not long for this world, so it doesn't matter."

The phone continue to ring, but it soon stopped. I remained motionless until I recognized the voice in my ear as one of the accusers from the day before.

Benotenn had said, "Do not listen to your accusers. They are not of God."

I pulled the phone out of my pocket. My father had called and left a voice message.

I played the message and heard my father's baritone. "Son, when are you going to come home?" After coughing and clearing his throat he added, "I'd like you to come for a visit soon, if you can. Give me a call back."

The rumble of my father's voice had always had a mesmerizing effect on me. As a child, I could sometimes ignore my mom, but never my dad. At that moment, my foolish thinking and my drunkenness were clear to me. In addition, the memory of Benotenn begging me to live for him broke through my dross-covered heart. How could I end my life? Certainly I needed to live for my parents. I opened the garage door and stepped out. Instead of calling my father, I texted a message that I'd be home late that same night.

The garage door slid shut, and I leaned against the garage and took several deep breaths. I'd been suffocating in my workshop without realizing it. The pavement rocked back and forth like the deck of a storm-tossed ship. I crossed the parking lot slowly, planning each step to keep from falling, and after much effort, I made it into the building. When I got near the laundry room, I stumbled to the floor and couldn't get back up. All my strength had departed.

Even as unworthy as I was, my life had to go on. I needed to discover how I was going to live with myself.

CHAPTER 22

I am Alexander, angel of God. Billy's angel.

I have watched over Billy since his conception. I petitioned the Lord for permission to intrude directly into Billy's conscious life with five revelations.

The Lord said, "If this man will not listen to my word, will he be persuaded by your revelations?"

"Lord, you know all things."

My heart sank. I was certain my request would be denied, but the Lord said, "You may provide for Billy the five revelations which you have requested, but then you must return to your regular ministry to him." Then the Lord added, "How often I have longed for him to come home to me, but he has not been willing."

Then, I dared to question the Lord.

"Lord, will you permit the enemy to audibly communicate with Billy again, perhaps even make their presence felt?"

"Mighty Alexander, do you fear the devil and his angels? You must perform your ministry and trust my wisdom, power, and goodness, for Satan has requested a little more time."

"Yes, Lord."

Then to my dismay, the Lord asked me, "What spirit resides in him? That of Job? Or Balaam?"

"Only you know, Lord."

My goal for Billy was godly sorrow, repentance, forgiveness, and a new life in Christ. Instead, Billy chose worldly sorrow, unrelenting shame, and death. Yet, I was determined to continue my work as the Lord commanded. I stood by Billy, watching, helping, and fighting to protect him. It was an honor to do this, a labor of love.

Faithful saints like Lancaster Yates and Joseph Pullman contributed to my work. I urged Lancaster Yates to call his son when he did. Joseph's angel had prompted him to do his laundry a day early, so Joseph would be in position to soon encourage and revive Billy.

★★★

We angels have observed God with wonder and awe since our beginning, and we have longed to understand God's plan for you. As time passes, we learn more, and we see more clearly the Lord's wisdom, even though there is still much we do not understand.

I will here share some of what God has revealed to us about himself. Much remains mysterious and unknowable, even for us. My expression of these things will fall short of complete accuracy, but I will do my best to express it.

They are the Trinity. They share the same nature, knowledge, power, and purpose. There will never be anyone else like them, for they are each timeless, without beginning or end. The knowledge they have of each other is complete and satisfying, and makes the love they share perfect. They alone understand the treasure of being completely known and understood. They are one, but they are also distinct in that they each have their own will and preferences. There is no competition between them, as each yields willingly to the others.

The first is the visionary, planner, and protector. The second is the creative power, the one who upholds every created thing, and the third binds the first two in a relationship of deep and limitless love, with a desire to fill everything with his sanctifying power. The desire of the third is also to bring the plans and work of the first two to complete fulfillment. You know them as the Father, Son, and Holy Spirit. They are one God, in three distinct but equal persons.

When the Lord breathed into man the breath of life, we saw immediately the difference between man and the other creatures. The man knew he was created to love and honor God, just as we do—just as the Father, the Son, and the Spirit love and honor one another. We saw the marriage relationship of the man and the woman and realized they were more like God than even the angels. Marriage mimicked and represented the relationship of the three who are one, whom we worship continually.

Angels are spiritual beings created to carry out the will of God, to worship God, to care for God's creation, and especially to minister to the children of God. The number of angels is too many to count. To understand the scale of our magnitude, envision all the planets and stars in the universe, and know the number of angels far exceeds that number.

In many ways, we are superior to you—stronger, faster, and more intelligent. However, God did not make us in his image, so we can never be like God in the same way you can.

Some angels rebelled against God. You know them as Satan and his angels, or the devil and his demons.

★★★

After meeting with the Lord, I began an anxious return to Billy's side, but a bright white streak came at me like a missile. The streak struck me and sent me spinning under the stars between earth and heaven. Pain erupted throughout my being.

A voice boomed in my ears. "You do fear me, because you know my power is great and my cause is just."

"Why did you strike me?" My ire burned uncontrollably for a moment. When I righted myself, our ancient foe prowled around me. He appeared as a bejeweled white lion whose monstrous belly revealed the terrified countenances of men. Their faces pressed from the inside out in silent shrieks. "I know who you are. What do you want, you old serpent?"

I averted my eyes from his horror.

"Are you squeamish about them? I will soon spew them out into the outer darkness, where there is weeping and gnashing of teeth."

I shook my head. "What do you want? Why have you accosted me?"

"I only seek what is right. Step away from Billy. He deserves hell."

"What motivates your heart, Satan? Why did you rebel? Was it jealousy, because humans are the pinnacle of all creation?"

"I seek justice. You lowly guardian angels do not understand the role I, the most glorious of all angels, play in the service of God."

"You are the enemy of God. You hate everything God created."

Satan circled me in a furious flash of rage and roared his words out.

"I do the will of God. I bring trials to separate the worthy from the unworthy, as the wheat from the chaff."

"All could have been made to stand as righteous, but for your tactics of confusion and deception." I had often wondered why God granted Satan so much freedom. Satan would now surely try to deceive me. "You tempt humans so they sin. Then you accuse them before our God, crying for their condemnation."

"It is the will of God," Satan said, with his lying tongue.

"No. God offers mercy and forgiveness. He restores."

"Alexander, God is playing you for a fool. Billy's place in the lake of fire was foreordained by God himself."

"No, the lake of fire is for you and your demonic angels. There is hope for Billy, by the blood of Jesus Christ."

Satan shuddered at the name of Jesus Christ.

"I will escape punishment," he screamed, "for you underestimate my role and my power. But you know many humans destined to burn, don't you?"

"Ones you beguiled with your lies, until for them it was too late."

"Why does God allow it, if it is not his will? I know you become weary of all the souls you have lost. You have lost more than you have saved."

"The ones saved are each worth my life's labor."

"We can argue," Satan snarled, "until eternity comes. I say to you, step aside from Billy, that you may guard one who is more worthy."

"While Billy still breathes, there is hope. I will never abandon him. Now get behind me, Satan, and oppose me no more." I continued my journey back to earth.

Satan shouted after me as I left him.

"I only seek to spare you the continued waste of your efforts."

***

God does not direct the activities of Satan, but he sets boundaries Satan cannot cross without specific permission. If you resist the devil, he will flee from you, at least for a time. We angels all wondered why the Holy Spirit led Jesus into the wilderness to be tempted by the devil. Yet Jesus showed that a faithful person can resist the devil through prayer and the word of God.

Long ago, the first human pair rebelled and fell from life into death. In so doing, they disrupted the natural process of transformation that occurs as humans walk intimately in the presence of God. In Jesus, anyone who is willing may pass out of death back into life.

I, Alexander, give daily testimony to the recorders regarding everything Billy does and says.

One day Billy will answer to the Lord for the life he lived.

CHAPTER 23

WEEK 1—FRIDAY

"Billy, what's wrong? You sick?" Joseph Pullman came out of the laundry room as fast as he could, limping on his cane. There was fear in his voice. My appearance must have been awful.

"Yeah, I'm sick."

"Your clothes is filthy. What happened to you? What was you doin'?" When Joseph bent down to help me up he must have gotten a whiff of the mixed stench of body odor and beer. "Whew, you been drinkin'. You ain't a drinkin' man, Billy, and it's still mornin'."

Joseph helped me into my apartment and settled me at the kitchen table.

"It's dark in here," he said. He set about opening all the blinds and drapes in the kitchen and living room. "There, that's a lot better. Sunshine will make you feel better. It always makes me feel better."

"Thanks, Joseph."

"Have you ate anything?"

"No. Wasn't hungry."

"Skinny guys like us got to eat."

Joseph rambled around my kitchen, busying himself, until he served me a breakfast of bacon, a cheese omelet, toast, and grape juice. It was amazing to see Joseph whip up that meal.

"I didn't know you were a cook." I devoured the food and washed it down with the juice, surprised at how hungry I was.

"Sometimes Mom didn't feel like cookin', so I had to learn. Got to take care of Mom, you know?"

"That breakfast was fantastic. You're a good son and a good friend."

"You know what? You been a-drinkin' and now you is a-stinkin'." Joseph chortled at his rhyme. "I guess you gonna live. You need to take off them dirty clothes and clean yourself up." Joseph turned to the sink and set to work washing the pans and utensils and racking them up to dry.

I sniffed myself, and Joseph was right. My body reeked. Bits of sawdust clung to my clothes, the same clothes from Thursday which I'd also slept in.

"Why you been drinkin'?" Joseph stood drying his hands with a towel.

"Well, I recently realized I've made a lot of bad mistakes in my life, and it made me kind of depressed. So I had a few beers."

"I know what you mean. I get depressed a lot too. But drinkin' don't solve nothin'. It makes things worse. I keep tellin' you, what you need is Jesus. He'll forgive all the wrong stuff you done. Jesus died for our sins, you know?"

"Joseph, I promise you I will consider Jesus more seriously than I ever have in my entire life." I intended to keep the promise, even as I wondered what kind of justice system punished an innocent man like Jesus in place of the guilty. My doubts abounded that such a swap could be an effective antidote for my sins.

"That's good, my friend. Let me know if you want to talk about it. Right now I've got to get back to my clothes washin', dryin', and foldin'." Joseph gave me a pat on the shoulder and ambled to the door. He added with a song in his voice, "I guess you gonna live, yeah, I guess you gonna live, but I will check you later."

"I'm going to my parents' house today, so I'll be gone a couple of days."

"All right. Have a good trip."

Before reaching the door, Joseph spun around and pointed a finger at me. "Hey, you ever find your Bible?"

"Yes, I did. I found all three of my Bibles."

"You been readin' 'em?"

"Only a little bit. I read some of the parables in Matthew."

"Well, that's good. I love the Gospels." Joseph turned to go.

"Tell me, Joseph, do you have a favorite book of the Bible?"

"I love it all, but 'specially the Psalms and Acts."

"A friend of mine said I should read Romans. What's it about?"

"I guess—hmm, I guess it's about the Christian system, I'd say. Yeah, it explains the Christian system."

"The Christian system? Okay, well, what about Psalms and Acts? What do you like about them?"

"Psalms covers all my feelin's. You know—sadness, happiness, being afraid, and anger, all the things I feel. Psalm 23 is about confidence in God no matter what happens. And Acts explains how the church got started, a great book for knowin' how things happened. You know, like history."

"Thanks, Joseph. That gives me some idea of what to be reading. Thanks a lot."

After Joseph left, I took his advice and peeled off my clothes and threw them in the hamper. I took a shower and examined my tattoo once again in the mirror. I felt it, rubbed it, and tugged at it, but it remained unchanged. My admission of guilt and shame hadn't made any difference to the tattoo. It wasn't going anywhere. My rejected status was unchanged.

The hope of another appearance by Benotenn made me linger in front of the mirror, but my son did not show. My life couldn't end by my own hand. Joseph had raised my spirits, and Alexander had caused me to recognize my own blindness and wretchedness.

Yet my blindness remained. I didn't know how to continue to live with myself, and the way forward was not clear. Out of nowhere came a clear message that I ought to pray. So I said, "Jesus, help me."

I rested until that afternoon and then began to read the New Testament book of Romans. I looked forward to spending a couple of days with my parents. I hoped to discover the truth I needed, and a path toward peace with myself.

I doubted I would find it.

CHAPTER 24

WEEK 1—FRIDAY NIGHT AND SATURDAY

The five-hour drive from Louisville to my parents' home in Frankfort, Illinois, flew by, and I soon found myself pulling into their driveway. Their ranch house, covered with a sand-colored brick exterior, contained twenty-five hundred square feet of living space and sat on an acre of flat land in a subdivision that had once been a cornfield.

Multiple times every year for the previous twenty years I'd made the trip back home, but all that had transpired in the last four days since my surgery made this visit different. The porch light welcomed me like a beacon at eleven o'clock in the evening—well past my parents' bedtime—but I knew they'd be up and listening for my arrival. I tapped on the front door and then let myself in with my key. Mom and Dad greeted me with hugs and kisses and went off to bed.

In my old bedroom, I threw my overnight bag onto the bed and went to the window to look out into the back yard. Tall Tower stood strong, bearing witness to Dad's workmanship and his great job of maintaining it for the last thirty-seven years. A long series of nieces and nephews had grown up playing on Tall Tower. Had any of them had the sanctity of *their* playtime invaded by the god of this world?

The trees behind Tall Tower were silhouetted against a charcoal sky. The wind cut through them, bending them as if beckoning to me to come out and enjoy the night. I grabbed my coat, zipped it up to my neck, and pulled on a cap to prepare for the April night chill. I went out, shivered, and pulled my hood over the cap and tight around my head.

I stood in the lower level of Tall Tower just like all those years ago, when I'd foolishly accepted the challenge from that unearthly, ungodly voice. My hope was that the voice would speak to me again. My intention was to defy whatever suggestion the voice made, to show I was prepared and not to be tricked anymore. So I stood there, and patrolled back and forth around Tall Tower, and marked time in the dark. After forty-five minutes I didn't hear any voice, so I went back inside to bed.

I guess the devil only shows up when you're not ready for him.

I got up at nine o'clock Saturday morning. As I entered the kitchen Mom was heading out the door, but she stopped when she saw me.

"Did Alexander make another appearance? Did anything else unusual happen since I was at your place?" Mom struggled with bags and boxes of brochures and other papers.

"No and yes. Need some help with that stuff?" I went over and took the materials from her, then followed her out to her car.

"Thank you, baby. Are you okay?"

"I'm fine," I said, not mentioning I was on pins and needles.

My mind persisted in whirling back over all the mystical events of the week. Everyday objects, even the air itself, couldn't be trusted. Anything might conceal a trap, a rebuke, or an otherworldly attack, ready to spring at any moment. Every creak and squeak of the house put me on high alert. My legs wobbled as I walked. My psyche was shot.

But I couldn't tell Mom all that.

"I've got to emcee the ladies' day event today," she said. "It starts at ten. We'll talk this afternoon, Billy." She looked at me, her eyes augering into mine. "I want to know about everything that's happened."

She backed the car out of the garage and waved goodbye.

I finished breakfast and found Dad in his office recliner, reading his Bible and shaking his head. Dad sported a black and silver beard and a glistening bald head. Certificates, plaques, and awards decorated one of the walls. Photos, African masks, and a 2005 Chicago White Sox World Series Championship poster adorned another wall. Two bookshelves I'd made for him held religious books along with a menagerie of wooden animals.

"Good morning, son. Have a seat." Dad motioned to the desk chair. "Sleep well?"

"Yes, sir. I stayed up for a while last night thinking about things, but when I finally went to bed, I slept like a baby. Best sleep I've had all week." I spun the chair slowly and looked around Dad's office. "You've filled every square inch of space in this room."

"Yeah, there's a lot of good memories in these things." Dad sat up in the recliner. "But I want to know what's happening with you. Your mother tells me you've been having some bad nightmares."

"Ever since my surgery. They've been terrifying at times, but I wouldn't call them nightmares. They're more like visions sent to me by God."

I got up and paced around the room.

"Dad, brace yourself, because this is going to sound completely crazy. I've been chastised by a giant angel, seen souls burning in hell—even my dead son rebuked me."

"Your dead son?" The coughing fit that grabbed Dad practically rolled him out of his chair. "You never told me I had another grandson."

"I didn't know either. He was revealed in a vision. He said he'd been aborted, and he blamed me for not saving him, except I never knew he existed. But he was right. I should've found out about Sandy. I should have never gotten her pregnant. I completely forgot about her."

"Wait a second, wait, wait. Who is Sandy?"

"I knew her in high school. Her name was Millie St. Vincent, but everyone called her Sandy. I didn't even know her that well. It happened at a party. It was the only time I've ever gotten drunk."

"You've got to be kidding. I *know* Millie St. Vincent. She still lives in the area. I know her family."

I was dumbfounded. One more person accusing me of wrongdoing, one more person whose life I'd ruined. Sandy had suddenly become real.

"She's the store manager at the Super Walmart in Orland Park," Dad said. "I've seen her there on weekends."

"I've been to that Walmart many times when I come home. I'm going to be sick."

"Son, you should go and see if—"

"No, Dad, let's talk about something else. What were you doing just now, before I came in?"

"All that can wait. You don't want to talk about Millie? Then tell me about my grandson."

"Well, his name is Benotenn—"

"Benotenn?"

"Yes, and he looked just like me. He was on my case to accept responsibility for my sins, especially concerning himself and his mother. He was angry with me, but said he loved me and his mother. During that vision, the weight of my sins suffocated me. I was dying. It was horrible, but Benotenn encouraged me to keep running."

"Why were you running?"

"It was like we were running a long, hard race, and all the dead people were spectators."

"Oh, yes, those who had gone on before. A great cloud of witnesses." Dad nodded as if he understood the image of a race.

"You couldn't stop running for long," I continued. "Not running meant death, and the gatherers would come get you. I met a gatherer in my nightmare parable, and he was awful."

"Nightmare parable?"

"Another bad dream. It was something right out of the Bible. The gatherers were throwing people into hellfire, and they were burning."

"Oh, my Lord."

"It made me sick. Just like I am right now." My stomach churned. I was ready to vomit. "Benotenn was the only good thing in those visions." I went to the kitchen, got some water, and returned to Dad's office. "Let's talk about something else. What were you doing when I first came in?"

He ignored my question and pursued his train of thought. "Don't you think Millie would want to know about Benotenn?"

"She'd think I'm crazy. She probably hates me." I sat again in the desk chair. "When I came in here, you were shaking your head. I interrupted you. What were you focused on?"

Dad hesitated, wanting to talk more about Sandy and the visions. He apparently decided not to push me right then. "I was sitting here thinking about a Bible passage I'd just read. It's an example of unbelievable cruelty and evil."

"What is it?

"I was reading in the second chapter of Matthew about the birth of Jesus. The Magi from the east were searching for the baby Jesus to worship him. King Herod heard about it, and called together the chief priests and the scribes of the Jews and asked them where the Messiah was foretold to be born, and they told him Bethlehem. Herod then called the Magi to his court and told them when they found Jesus to return to him and let him know, under the pretense he wanted to worship Jesus too. Actually, he wanted to kill Jesus, because the Messiah would be a threat to his power. The Magi did find the baby Jesus, but they were warned in a dream not to go back to Herod. Let me read verses thirteen through eighteen of Matthew 2."

He ran his finger down the page and began to read.

"Now when they had gone, behold, an angel of the Lord appeared to Joseph in a dream and said, 'Get up! Take the Child and His mother and flee to Egypt, and remain there until I tell you; for Herod is going to search for the Child to destroy Him.' So Joseph got up and took the Child and His mother while it was still night, and left for Egypt. He remained there until the death of Herod. This was to fulfill what had been spoken by the Lord through the prophet: 'Out of Egypt I called My Son.' Then when Herod saw that he had been tricked by the Magi, he became very enraged, and sent and slew all the male children who were in Bethlehem and all its vicinity, from two years old and under, according to the time which he had determined from the Magi. Then what had been spoken through Jeremiah the prophet was fulfilled: 'A voice was heard in Ramah, weeping and great mourning, Rachel weeping for her children; and she refused to be comforted, because they were no more.'"

While Dad was reading, the back door opened and closed. I thought perhaps Mom had returned early from her event, but I didn't hear anything after the door closed and didn't go check to confirm who it was.

"Now, that's a part of the Christmas story no one ever talks about," Dad said. "Can you imagine the anguish of those parents whose baby boys were slaughtered?"

"No, I can't. It makes me sick. Why does God allow such evil to happen?"

"Think of the little boys and girls who watched their baby brothers being murdered," he said. "I wonder about the impact on those families. And the soldiers—did they feel any remorse in carrying out such orders?"

"You know, Dad, I still hope to become a father someday, and if anyone harmed my child, I'd kill them. I'd be so angry and bitter no one would be able to stand me." I took a family picture from the shelf, one taken of all of us when I was a baby, and held it up. Mom and Dad were beaming in the photo. "If anyone had hurt any of us, you would've killed them, if you'd had the chance."

Dad shook his head.

"Maybe when I was younger, but not with what I know now. What good would my bitterness do? What good would revenge do? It wouldn't bring the baby back. What if one of the soldiers was sorry and repented of murdering the babies? What should God do with that soldier?"

"I have no idea. What would God do? What if the soldier went and apologized to the families? What should they do?"

"We all need forgiveness, so we all should be willing to give forgiveness, but it might be really hard and might take some time." Dad picked up his Bible and patted it. "This book says any repentant person who believes in and obeys Jesus will be forgiven of their sins, and Jesus adds them to his church. Even murderers. Son, we all need that. Not just the murderers—all of us need Jesus. He died for all of us."

"That makes no sense to me. What kind of justice system allows an innocent man to take the punishment of the guilty?"

The question silenced Dad for a few moments before he answered.

"That's a good question, and I'm sure I can't explain it. But that's the system God has set up, at least as far as our sin problem goes."

He thought another moment.

"Maybe this will help." He held up a hand and began ticking off points on his fingers. "If the law requires you to pay a fine, or you owe taxes and you don't pay up, you could eventually go to jail. But if someone pays the fine or the taxes for you, you're in the clear. The Bible often describes our sins as a debt we owe God that's too high for us to pay, because the payment requires a sinless life. So in a sense, our sins held us for ransom until Jesus gave his life and paid off our debt. We just have to have faith in Jesus and accept what he's already done for us."

"Sounds great, but where does faith in Jesus come from? That's my struggle." I tapped my forehead with both hands.

"I know where faith comes from, so that's a question I can answer. Romans 10:17 says faith comes from hearing the word of Christ, the Bible. That's why I was so glad when your mother said you were starting a class about Jesus and the Bible."

"Yeah, that starts on Tuesday. Plus I started reading Romans yesterday on my own, but it's going pretty slow. I'm still on the first chapter."

"Dwell on it, son. Approach it with an open and sincere heart, and the word of God will do the rest. It's powerful."

"So, Dad, how do *you* deal with it when it seems God has let you down?"

Dad leaned back in his recliner. "Hand me that picture you were holding."

I did.

"You see this family? I didn't always have it, but God blessed me with a wife and all these children. I'm mindful of what God's given me, and what he's brought me through. Then, I remember the promise of an eternal future with God will be better than anything I've enjoyed on earth. So if God doesn't do what I think he should do, I can accept it."

I sighed, got up, and looked out the window. There stood Tall Tower, my safe place, where as a child I'd always felt the spirit and love of my father. I realized how blessed I was to still have my father with me. It was a miracle he'd survived the accident. I'd always been bitter at how he'd been so badly hurt, but at that moment, I understood God had spared his life. Time and the accident had begun to break Dad down, but Tall Tower stood strong as a symbol of both his original physical strength and the inner strength he'd developed through his trials.

The voice that had invaded Tall Tower's sanctity and challenged me to take a foolish risk echoed in my mind.

"Dad, we have an opponent, don't we?"

"What are you talking about, son?"

"I'm talking about the devil. I've started believing in the devil even if I'm not so sure about trusting God. At one time, I didn't realize we had persistent opposition, but now I'm sure of it."

"Not just an opponent," he said, and raised a forefinger to make his point. "We have a cunning enemy that wants to destroy us, and who hates every good thing. Also be on guard against yourself, Son, because sometimes the devil finds a willing partner in us. At times, our flesh will rise up in us and try to take over our lives again, tempting us with lust, pride, and pleasure. You need to trust in God and Jesus. They're our best help."

The floor creaked in one of the nearby bedrooms and spurred me to action. "I'm going to see who that is."

"I didn't hear anything."

The repeating tap of soft footsteps led me down the hallway toward the living room. I went past the living room, then the dining room, and stood in the kitchen, but heard only silence.

Then a whisper.

"Come in here, Billy Goat Billy."

My beloved oldest sister Dolyana was the only one who still called me by my alter ego name, but the voice didn't sound like hers. Dolyana, twelve years older than I, was the best and the smartest of all of us.

I peered around the corner into the laundry room, but didn't see anyone. Off the laundry were three adjoining rooms—a small bedroom, a half bath, and a humongous family room. I went to the family room entryway and peeked in.

"Dolyana, is that you?"

I held my breath and strained to decipher the meaning of each noise of the house. As I was about to step into the family room, I felt two hands reach out from behind me, one on each side of my waist, and poke me. "Boo!"

"Ow, Dolyana." I squirmed and twisted around. "You crazy thing." I was terribly ticklish, and the pokes in the sides made me jump more from the tickle than from being surprised.

"Ha, ha." Dolyana howled and clapped her hands. "You sounded like a little girl."

I hugged my big sister. "What are you doing creeping around like that?"

"I was just listening to what Daddy was telling you about the Bible and the church." She sighed and looked down. Her smile was gone.

"Why didn't you join us?

"I just don't believe that stuff anymore. I can't believe it."

Dolyana had always been slender, but after giving birth to three children, she'd finally begun to gain weight. We went into the family room. Dolyana sat on the couch, and I sat on the floor.

"What happened?" I asked. "You were always right there with Mom and Dad, getting all of us ready for church. I was the only skeptic."

"I know. I loved church. I put so many hours in at the church teaching and watching kids, mine and other people's. I worked hard for the church for years, you know, really a lot of time and effort, but it was all for nothing."

"Why are you saying that? I've started reading my Bible and I'm starting to think there may be something to it. What went wrong for you?"

"After the New Year—" Dolyana slumped back in the couch and covered her face with her hands. "After the New Year, I found out Reginald was seeing another woman. I even caught him looking at porn." She lowered her hands and stared at them. "My wonderful Christian husband is a cheater."

I sat next to Dolyana and put my arms around her. "I'm so sorry, Dolyana. What did they say at the church?"

"They act like they don't believe me, and some of the church women act like it's my fault. Reginald lied about it, but I showed the elders and the preacher the text messages and porn on his phone."

"What about counseling? Maybe counseling would help you two."

"Reginald acts like it's my problem. I've always prayed to God that I would be a good wife and that Reginald would love me, but God's abandoned me. He's not hearing my prayers anymore. I've prayed so hard for so long. I would have been better off if I never believed in Jesus. I wasted so much time in the church."

"Have you told Mom and Dad what's going on?" The muscles in my neck and shoulders tightened. I was at a loss for how to comfort my sister.

"Yes, they know. They've been praying for us, but it's not helping. I can't feel God anymore. I always admired Reginald so much. I couldn't believe he'd betray me and toss me aside. I don't know what I'm going to do."

Dolyana went back to one of the bedrooms to rest. She'd been staying with my parents for the last few days. My head ached. I stood and took several deep breaths and stalked around the family room, then returned to the couch and stretched out.

Dolyana had gone deep into the wilderness of despair, and not long ago I would've followed her there. Instead I focused on how Dad and Mom and Mrs. Heaviland had handled their tragedies. They didn't blame God when inexplicable trouble happened. They trusted him anyway and continued to do what was right. Truth and right could not be based on our moment-to-moment feelings or circumstances, yet such had guided my life. I wanted to change, even if it meant facing my fear of condemnation by a forgotten friend.

Dad was right. Sandy would probably want to know about Benotenn. She'd think I was nuts, but I needed to take a trip to the Super Walmart anyway.

CHAPTER 25

WEEK 1—SATURDAY

I arrived at the Walmart early Saturday afternoon to find it packed with shoppers. I made my way to the service desk, and when it came my turn to speak to the clerk, I asked if I could speak with store manager Millie St. Vincent. The service manager asked if he could help me, but I declined and told him I needed to speak with Millie herself.

Another clerk behind the counter, an older man, spoke up.

"You're lucky to catch that girl, 'cause after today she's moving up to district manager and she'll be all over the whole region. Smartest little thing we've ever seen. Ain't she, Hank?" He nudged the service manager, who only grunted. "Yes, sirree. She started right here during high school, and I helped train her. So proud of that little girl."

About fifteen minutes later, Millie appeared. She was an attractive Black woman—petite, barely five feet tall, with olive skin and sandy brown hair pulled back in a ponytail. She wore a dark blue pencil skirt suit. How I'd forgotten her was beyond my comprehension.

"Hello, I'm the store manager, Millie St. Vincent. How can I help you?" She stood with her hands at her sides and spoke without smiling.

"Hello. My name is Billy Yates. Would I be able to speak to you privately for a minute?"

"What is this concerning?" She folded her arms.

"You may not remember, but we knew each other in high school."

Her face contorted as if she'd tasted something bitter.

"Oh, yes, Mr. Yates, I remember you. In fact, you've been in this store many times over the years, and we've actually spoken a few times, but you didn't remember me."

Beads of sweat formed on my forehead. "I'm sorry about that. I wish I had been a better friend. But today, I need to tell you something."

Millie spoke into a small radio. "Keith, would you meet me at my office? Yes, right now. It won't take long. Thank you." She lowered the radio. "All right, come with me."

Millie led me through the store to an office area. A broad-shouldered security guard met us when we arrived.

"Keith, I need to meet with this customer. Please wait out here while we go into the conference room."

Keith nodded. "Understood."

Millie closed the door and turned toward me with one hand on a chair and the other on her hip. "What in the world is this about?"

I took a deep breath. "I just learned this week I got you pregnant back in high school."

The color drained from her face. She silently pulled out the chair and sat with her elbows on the conference room table with her head in her hands. After a minute, she spoke.

"It's impossible for you to know. I never told anyone. No one at the clinic would have told anyone else."

"Why didn't you tell me?"

Millie gave me a sour look. "How in the hell did you find out this week, twenty-five years later?"

I repeated my question. "Why didn't you tell me?"

She leaned back, blew out some air, looked at the ceiling and then swiveled to fix her eyes on me.

"Because you were a jerk. I was only fifteen, and I thought it meant you loved me and you were so nice and smart, but you turned out to be a frickin' jerk. After the party, I thought you'd be my boyfriend, but you acted like you didn't even know who I was. How could you be like that? So—so heartless? You treated me like trash, and that's how I felt. But I never was trash."

I sat at the table a few chairs away from Millie and winced at her final assessment of my behavior.

"I apologize for my thoughtlessness. I was seventeen, and that was the first and only time I ever got so drunk. I'm sorry for what you went through."

Her eyes turned hard. "You weren't drunk the next day—or the days or weeks after that."

How often I'd envied friends who'd married their high school sweethearts and who'd been together for over twenty years by their early forties. Millie could have been the high school sweetheart I never had, but back then I was consumed with shame for being drunk and out of control that night.

How often had I ambushed my own hopes so stealthily that I was unaware of it?

"When I found out I was pregnant—"

Millie stopped, got up, and opened the door. "Keith, this may take a bit longer than I thought. You can go. It'll be all right. Thanks for coming."

"Okay. I'll check back every few minutes."

She sat again, but this time she focused on her hands folded in her lap. Her voice was pitched higher, as though she was much younger.

"When I found out I was pregnant, there was no way I was going to you for support. And I wasn't going to tell my parents, because of how they reacted when my sister got pregnant. I was all alone. I made a decision on my own, a decision I regret every day." She reached for a tissue to wipe her eyes. "My baby, Bennie, would have been twenty-four years old now."

"You call your baby Bennie?"

Did heaven influence her, or did she influence heaven in the naming?

"They told me I'd be able to get on with my life right away, but I couldn't, I was so sad. I didn't even know whether my baby was a boy or a girl, but it helped me grieve when I named the baby Bennie after my grandfather Benjamin. I didn't want to think of my baby as an *it*."

"He was a boy. In heaven, they call him Benotenn."

"So you've been to heaven? That explains everything, doesn't it?"

She laughed, and the boss in her returned. She looked at me with flinty eyes. "Why don't you just tell me how you found out, and why you're here? What's the point of your coming here anyway? It's not going to change anything."

"It's unbelievable, but this week visions starting coming to me, and I have no idea why. It began when an angel urged me to examine my past, and he mentioned you. I'm ashamed to admit I didn't recognize your name."

Her face was opaque, devoid of emotion as she studied me. I turned my gaze away from Millie, closed my eyes, and kept talking.

"Later, I saw tortured souls burning in a hellfire furnace. The hot sulfur stench of hell made me physically ill. And in the last vision, I was dying, suffocating in heavy garments woven from my own sins. I was too weak to take them off, even though they were killing me. I was unwilling to disrobe from my sins because letting them go made me sick. But Benotenn was there, the only good thing there. It was Benotenn, our son, who told me I was his father and you were his mother."

I shrugged my shoulders. "How else could I have known? I had no idea he even existed. He was angry with me for not being there for you and for him, because he wanted to live. The reason I came here was to let you know he said he loved me and he loved you too. Benotenn called you Momma. He's forgiven us, and my hope is that message brings you some comfort. Last, I'd like to ask your forgiveness for how poorly I treated you. I'm truly sorry."

I observed her light brown eyes and waited silently for her response to my request. I yearned for her forgiveness, and even hoped she might like me just a little.

Millie stood and regarded me with a pitying stare.

"Mr. Yates, I can clearly see you are certain of the supernatural events you described, and I appreciate your intention to share with me the comfort you've found. Is there anything else?"

I supposed she figured I'd learned about her and the baby by some reasonable means, but had lost that truth in my deluded mind. She wouldn't try to understand something that was impossible to accept without also accepting inexplicable, otherworldly things.

"No," I said. "I did what I came to do."

"Good. I have to get back to work." She dashed out of the room, and I plodded out following her. Heaviness filled my body.

Millie was apparently not in a forgiving mood that day, but I surprised myself after maneuvering through the aisles and shoppers, because when I reached the exit, lightness had returned to my step. I was certainly guilty, but no longer ashamed. I had no fear of being confronted by Millie or anyone else regarding my treatment of her. My behavior had been bad, but I'd admitted it and asked her forgiveness. I could let go of the shame.

Still, my guilt generated fear, but my fear then was of the judgment of God. I needed to figure out how to escape that judgment. I went to church with my parents the next day, but the sermon didn't provide the needed answers. After the service and lunch, I returned to Louisville.

★★★

That night, I read the first chapter of Romans again and found it discouraging. It seemed to condemn everyone who wasn't religious. The eighteenth verse kept ringing in my mind.

> For the wrath of God is revealed from heaven against all ungodliness and unrighteousness of men who suppress the truth in unrighteousness.

I wasn't sure about continuing to read Romans, because the ungodly certainly included me. However, I looked forward with excitement to the 'Jesus in the Old Testament' class which would begin Tuesday evening. Ezriah would be surprised at my newfound motivation.

CHAPTER 26

Week 2—Tuesday

Ezriah picked me up Tuesday for the class, and since I hadn't spoken to Ezriah for almost a week, I filled him in about Benotenn. We rode with the car windows open. The breeze carrying April's flowery scent of spring was cool and comforting as I told my story.

Ezriah mulled over my tale for several minutes as he drove.

"It sounds like a takeoff from Hebrews 12," he said, "where the writer describes Christians as being in a race surrounded by a great cloud of witnesses. I always think of the witnesses as Christians who have passed away and are watching those of us who are still alive. You know that passage also talks about throwing off things that entangle us."

"Like my heavy garments of sin?"

Ezriah glanced at me. "Yeah, it says something like that."

"So that vision was right out of the Bible, just like my nightmare parable. Guess that makes me some kind of prophet."

"Except for the part about Benotenn. Do you believe that was real?"

"It was real." My fists pounded into my knees and my neck grew hot. "Sorry, I didn't mean to yell. I met Benotenn's mother this weekend while visiting at home. I didn't even remember her, but my father knew her. She still lives in my hometown."

"You met the mother?" Ezriah's eyebrows and the pitch of his voice went up at the same time. "What was that like?"

"Bad. She hates me, but it was a relief to get the meeting over with." We pulled into a parking space at the seminary and started walking. "It just confirmed to me that these have been truthful visions."

"So now what?" Ezriah threw an arm around my shoulders and shook me. "You gonna believe in Jesus now?"

"I want to believe, but I've never developed faith in Jesus. My dad says faith comes by hearing the word of God, so for maybe the first time, I've been seriously reading my Bible. And I'm taking this class, so we'll see what happens. How's the family?"

Ezriah stopped walking and rubbed his forehead. "Deanna and the girls are fine, but our oldest, Lucian, quit his job."

"Didn't he just start a new job? What happened?"

"He said his boss insulted him the first week on the job, and Lucian felt he couldn't succeed with a manager like that."

"What did his boss say?"

"Lucian's boss said, 'Most Black men are either too aggressive or too passive. You seem like you're going to be too passive.' How could he make a judgment like that the first week on the job? Lucian reported it to Human Resources and resigned the next day. He couldn't stand to work for someone with such a negative attitude."

We resumed walking. "I'm sorry to hear that," I said, "but you know prejudiced people have all sorts of preconceived ideas. What's Lucian going to do now?"

"I don't know, but he should've found another job before he quit." Ezriah tapped his lips with an index finger. "He may have to come back home. That will send our stress level through the roof."

"Nothing says you have to let him come back home." I patted Ezriah on the back. "Lucian's a smart kid. I'm sure he'll be back on his feet soon." I took in our surroundings. "It looks like we've arrived."

The campus was tree-lined and park-like, a typical college campus in an urban setting. We stood in front of Wesley Chapel, where we located our classroom on the building's second floor. The walls were blue-green, and the floor was covered with a light gray and plum carpet. A large monitor hung above several dry-erase boards at the front of the room, and soft lighting created a comfortable environment. Six round tables were arranged in an arc around a podium. Ezriah and I took seats at a table with two other students and introduced ourselves. Our table mates were Lawrence Lessons, a slender man in his twenties from the West Virginia mountains, and Hugo Mason, a big-bellied man who appeared to be in his early fifties—about Ezriah's age.

I scanned the room like I always did in public spaces to count the Black faces. I found three—Ezriah, a young woman named Ariun Christian, and me. Ariun bore a remarkable resemblance to my sister Dolyana, or at least a younger version of Dolyana.

An assortment of mostly middle-aged women and men were present, and we all gradually settled in for what I hoped would be an interesting class. According to my count there were twenty-five participants plus the professor, Harlan Stanley, who appeared to be about seventy-five. When Professor Stanley arrived he made quite a stir when he opened several boxes and loosed the aroma of warm cookies. Most of us accepted his invitation to help ourselves to the unexpected treat.

The gathering had the feel of a mid-week Bible study from my childhood, even more so when Professor Stanley asked if anyone had something they wanted the class to pray about. Lawrence eagerly asked for prayer for his parents back in West Virginia, and Hugo sighed and tapped his fingers impatiently as several others added their requests. Professor Stanley then led the class in prayer for the specific requests and for God's blessings on the class and the participants. It was very different from the 'Bible as Literature' classes I'd taken in college, which most students viewed as just another English class and not a time to commune under the blessing of God.

Professor Stanley stood at the lectern in a gray suit, white shirt, and blue tie, his snowy hair gleaming.

"The entire Bible took fifteen hundred years to complete. About forty people wrote it, and they lived at different times and in different countries, so most of the writers never met each other. Yet the Bible tells one coherent overarching story."

Professor Stanley gave a thick handout to each of us. The first sheet included two passages of Scripture he asked us to read silently.

> But know this first of all, that no prophecy of Scripture is a matter of one's own interpretation, for no prophecy was ever made by an act of human will, but men moved by the Holy Spirit spoke from God. (Second Peter 1:20–21)

> And He said to them, "O foolish men and slow of heart to believe in all that the prophets have spoken!" Was it

not necessary for the Christ to suffer these things and to enter into His glory?" Then beginning with Moses and with all the prophets, He explained to them the things concerning Himself in all the Scriptures. (Luke 24:25–27)

"So, my friends, the apostle Peter proclaimed the Old Testament scriptures were written by prophets under the direct leading of the Holy Spirit. Luke quotes the resurrected Jesus as saying he was going to show his doubting and discouraged disciples how those same prophets wrote about his life and cruel death in advance. In this class, we will take the same mental journey Jesus took with his disciples. We will see how the work of Jesus the Messiah was completely foretold in the Old Testament scriptures hundreds of years before Jesus was born. I am excited to make this journey with each of you, and I hope it will strengthen your faith."

For the next ninety minutes, Professor Stanley led us through a fascinating discussion. I was looking forward to questioning Ezriah about it.

Professor Stanley concluded that first session with a preview of the second.

"Next time, we will learn about how God's covenant to one man, an ancient promise made four thousand years ago to Abraham, demanded the coming of Jesus as a fulfillment of that promise."

Our assignment for the next week was reading to learn about the term 'covenant.'

When we stood and gathered our things to go, Lawrence said, "I'm starving. Y'all want to join me in getting something to eat?"

Hugo said, "Now that's an idea I really like."

I looked at Ezriah, and he nodded, so I said, "We're in. What did you have in mind, Lawrence?"

"It's a place called Josh's Grotto. They specialize in Italian food, but they have a wide selection. It's not too expensive, and they give you really big portions."

"Yes, we've been there," Ezriah said. "It's nice, and not too far."

Lawrence checked his phone and added, "Uh-oh, I forgot. My girlfriend took my car. Can I get a ride?"

Hugo beckoned Lawrence with a wave. "Sure, come on. Ride with me."

★★★

The restaurant was less than five minutes away. Wonderful aromas met us as we entered the dining room through what appeared to be an ancient sandstone brick archway. Josh's Grotto had a warm, old-world feel, and the cobblestone flooring, potted plants, and flowing fountain gave diners the sense of being outdoors.

After the server brought warm bread, Lawrence said, "I enjoyed the class today. I've been in Bible classes my whole life, but not so much from the Old Testament. But I learned a lot. I'm studying so I can become a preacher one day. What did y'all think of the class?"

Hugo grunted.

Ezriah looked up from the menu.

"It reinforced some things I already knew, but I liked it," Ezriah said. "Professor Stanley seems like a nice guy. Knowledgeable."

My phone vibrated, but I didn't recognize the number and let it go to voicemail. Then, I said, "It was a good class. I do have a few questions. Like, if the Old Testament prophets spelled out Jesus's life and work so completely, why didn't the people and the Jewish leaders recognize Jesus when he showed up?"

A waitress named Amalea took our order.

"I'd say it's not really all that clear," Hugo said. "It seems to me Jesus's followers were stretching the meaning of the Old Testament scriptures to fit the narrative they wanted to be true."

Lawrence almost choked on his water at Hugo's words.

Ezriah said, "No, they weren't stretching the meaning. We have to remember sometimes the prophecies had double meanings, one relevant to the prophet's time and one pointing to Jesus. Also the prophecies are not all together in one book. They're spread throughout the Old Testament, which makes sense. Like the professor said, the prophecies were written by prophets in different times and regions."

"The ordinary people didn't have a problem seeing Jesus as the Messiah," Lawrence said, "especially when they heard him teach and saw his miracles. The religious leaders were the problem. Most of them were blinded by jealousy of Jesus and—"

Hugo waved his hands and said, "Look. These were ignorant people, superstitious and easily persuaded by the stories they were told."

"The people were expecting a king that was a great military or political figure," Ezriah said, "one who would overthrow the Romans, so there was confusion about what the Messiah would do."

Servers brought our food, and for a few minutes the debate ceased as we dug in. Ezriah had lasagna. My salad and lemony, caper-topped chicken piccata with angel hair pasta looked and tasted wonderful. Lawrence had spaghetti and meatballs, and Hugo's meal included glasses of wine, soup, grilled steak, and assorted vegetables.

After a convivial silence while we ate, Ezriah spoke.

"The people of Jesus's day were not ignorant. They were a lot like us. They were eyewitnesses to what happened, and when they saw Jesus die on the cross, they thought their movement was over. Some went into hiding, fearing for their own lives. Others left town. Their leader was killed, so they thought they'd lost their fight."

I said, "If that's true, how do you explain what happened to change that?"

"It was right there in the passage," Ezriah said. "—in the second passage we looked at today. The resurrected Jesus appeared to his disillusioned followers and proved to them he was alive after having died. That made them bold and fearless, willing to preach the gospel of Jesus and to die for it themselves."

Hugo shook his head. "That's your opinion, but it's not proof."

Lawrence jumped in. "It may not be proof, but it's logical and reasonable. They saw Jesus's dead body, and they were afraid. Christianity should have ended before it got started, but it didn't, because Jesus's followers saw him alive *after* they saw him die. More than five hundred people at one time saw him alive."

I raised my hands. "Hey, guys, we should be discussing some of the Old Testament prophecies Professor Stanley talked about, like the passage in Micah about the Messiah being born in Bethlehem."

Lawrence said, "And Psalm 22 described the crucifixion before the practice was even invented."

"And Isaiah spoke about the virgin birth," Ezriah added, "and also a graphic description of Jesus's punishment and death."

"None of the passages name Jesus," Hugo said. "Isaiah just describes a man's execution. It could be anyone."

I began to have some doubts. "Ezriah, how *do* we know Isaiah was talking about Jesus?"

"Isaiah identifies him as God's suffering servant. Isaiah says he died not for any wrongdoing of his own, but for the sins of the people, and through his death the people were healed. Isaiah provides a description that fits no one else except Jesus."

I turned to Hugo. "That sounds pretty compelling, if Isaiah gives the manner and purpose for the death seven hundred years beforehand. How do you explain that?"

Amalea had been standing nearby listening to our debate. "Are you all preachers? I think the Bible is fascinating, but sometimes it's confusing."

Hugo snickered, "Because it's full of contradictions and nonsense. That's why it's confusing. And no, we aren't preachers. Just friends sharing our opinions."

Lawrence asked, "Uh ... Hugo, what church do you belong to?"

"I don't belong to any church, and I've never been a believer in the Bible. My parents taught me to think for myself, logically and critically." Hugo leaned forward in his chair and shook his finger. "In fact, I'm concerned about the detrimental impact the Bible's had on people's lives."

I said, "I'm a critical thinker as well, but I wouldn't say Christians are illogical. Professor Stanley seemed quite reasonable and rational."

Lawrence's eyes narrowed as he looked at Hugo. "Why are you even taking the class, if you've already rejected the idea of Christianity?"

"I'm taking the class because my daughter recently married. She and her husband have become born-again Christians and moved to upstate New York." Hugo paused and then continued speaking in lower tones. "I don't mean to insult any of you, but my wife and I are very concerned that our daughter and son-in-law have been attending a Bible-believing church. I'm learning more about the Bible so I can empathize with my little girl, and also show her the Bible's fallacies and dissuade her from this path."

Lawrence smiled. "The Bible is the truth, my friend, not a fallacy."

"I have two daughters," Ezriah nodded toward Hugo, "so I understand you're worried about this unexpected change in her beliefs. What do *you* believe in?"

Amalea brought us our checks and again stood nearby, listening.

"I believe we're the development of an undirected, self-existent natural universe. I believe there's no—"

"What do you mean by 'self-existent universe'?" Lawrence interrupted. "Are you saying the universe always existed?"

Hugo fixed his gaze on Lawrence.

"Yes, it always existed, with no creator. There is no God, no one for us to look to for purpose, meaning, or direction. No supernatural activities. I believe in the capability of human beings to solve their problems through logic, scientific inquiry, and compassion for one another. Have you ever thought about all the atrocities committed in the name of God, and especially in the name of Jesus, not to mention the hypocrisy of Christians?"

"I admit there's been a lot of violence done in the name of Christ." Ezriah leaned back and crossed his arms. "But I would argue even greater wrongdoing has been done by atheistic regimes throughout history. Wherever you have people, you'll have hypocrites, and not just in the church."

I added, "Hugo, a self-existent universe would mean the universe itself had existed forever, but most scientists now believe the universe had a beginning. The only thing—"

Lawrence interrupted. "Does that mean 'In the beginning God created the heavens and the earth' is completely consistent with the big bang theory?"

Amalea edged closer to ask a question. "If God could be eternal, why can't the universe be eternal? Why does it have to have a beginning?"

Ezriah said, "Yes, the big bang theory is consistent with the first sentence in the first book of Genesis."

"Many scientists believe the universe is very old," I added, "most say almost fourteen billion years old, but scientific theory also says it can't have existed forever because it would have experienced heat death, the loss of usable energy, and none of—"

Lawrence rubbed his forehead. "Heat death? Billy, fourteen billion years seems way too old to be biblical. If that's the age of the universe, how old is the *earth* supposed to be?"

"Most scientific sources I've Googled think it's about four and a half billion years."

"No way." Lawrence shook his head. "I can't go along with that. I'm a believer in a young earth."

Ezriah said, "I believe the Bible is true, but Lawrence, you can't date the age of the universe or the earth from the Bible. That's not the purpose or design of the Bible."

I tried to complete my thought. "Anyway, that's what scientists think would have happened by now. Heat death. So if the universe was eternal, none of us would be here now. The only thing that could exist forever would have to be outside space, time, and matter, which sounds a lot like what we understand God to be. It seems reasonable to me to believe God has existed forever, and therefore God is the one that created the universe and us. The thing I've struggled with is the nature of God's character, mainly because of some of the same things Hugo pointed out, but I'm certain God exists."

Amalea took our credit cards and cash and returned a short time later.

Hugo shook his head. "I simply disagree that God is necessary. I'm good without God. So many ideas attributed to God are atrocious, especially the one about eternal punishment if you don't believe in Jesus."

Ezriah tapped his fingertips together. "I agree with you in that we need to be applying science and looking at the evidence. Good science and good theology go together. But there are limits to scientific inquiry. Logic and evidence suggest there's a creator, and if there is a creator I guarantee you he is not only smarter and stronger than we are, but he's also more righteous, just, and equitable than we are, even if we don't like all his ideas."

We left the restaurant, and Ezriah turned to Lawrence. "Do you need us to drop you somewhere?"

"No, thanks. My girlfriend will pick me up shortly. Our place isn't far from here, and she's already on the way."

We all stared at Lawrence for a moment and processed his comment. Then Ezriah said, "All right. See you next week."

We moved on to the parking lot, and Hugo said, "Good Christian man, obeying the good book?"

Ezriah said, "Well, it doesn't—"

"Don't get me wrong. I don't care about the choices the young man makes, but isn't it a little hypocritical to profess devotion to Jesus while he lives with his girlfriend?" Hugo chuckled. "My friends, don't you call that the sin of fornication? Christians are just like everyone else, but they profess to be so much better."

Ezriah said, "We don't claim to be better than anyone else. We all have our struggles, we all have problems. We trust in a perfect savior *precisely* because we fall short."

We parted ways at the parking lot and Hugo waved at us. "Good night, gentlemen. It's been a pleasure."

In the car, Ezriah said, "Whew. I wasn't expecting all that back-and-forth. Sorry you had to hear all that."

"Don't worry about it."

Hugo was right about Lawrence, and I was sure Ezriah felt the same also, but I didn't feel like talking about it right then. "Let's get out of here."

★★★

After Ezriah dropped me off, I replayed in my mind the class and the dinner discussion that followed. There was some truth in what all of us had said that night, and at one time I would've agreed with much of what Hugo had said. But reading the Bible and listening to Professor Stanley and Ezriah was beginning to have an effect on me. Life and truth were more complicated than I'd previously thought. I needed to be more open-minded and careful in my thinking before drawing conclusions for or against Christianity. Human failings and difficult-to-understand ideas did not necessarily mean the Bible was false. As Ezriah said, God was surely a lot smarter than me. The things God did could have been correct, and my wisdom was insufficient to see it.

That night, I read another chapter in Romans and found where, in the second chapter, the apostle turned the tables on the religious people and hit the self-righteous worshippers of God right between the eyes. They said when the self-righteous were judging the people who didn't know God, they were actually judging themselves, because they'd done the very same things.

> But do you suppose this, O man, when you pass judgment on those who practice such things and do the same yourself, that you will escape the judgment of God?

How would Lawrence respond if someone pointed out he was a Christian who was living the same sinful lifestyle as many unbelievers? My old girlfriend Sharon Fields turned away from the same sin after Miss Hannah confronted her. What would it take for Lawrence to give up his sins? My takeaway from Romans 2 was everybody in the whole world, religious and irreligious, was under the condemnation of God. Not very encouraging, so I didn't continue on to Romans 3 that night.

Just before bed, I checked my phone and saw I had a voicemail. I played the recording and the lovely voice of a woman enraptured me.

I couldn't believe it. Angeline, my surgical nurse, had called me back and left her phone number.

CHAPTER 27

WEEK 2—THURSDAY

I called Angeline back on Wednesday morning. We decided to meet Thursday for lunch in the cafeteria of the hospital where she worked. I arrived thirty minutes early and found a place called The Café on the second floor, an airy dining area overlooking a lush green atrium extending from the first floor to the high glass ceiling. The smell of delicious, healthy food was everywhere.

A small table next to a clear low wall provided a nice view of the indoor garden. The prospect of seeing Angeline excited me so much that I forgot she'd probably ask about the mystical, terrifying spiritual journey I'd mentioned in the card. My excitement faded and my stomach flipped as I recalled what I'd written. If I told her the truth about what had happened, Angeline—the woman of my dreams—would think me delusional. Not a good first impression. How could I make her believe all that had happened to me had really happened?

When she entered the dining area, she didn't see me at first. Tall and well built, her curves were like an hourglass, with hips a little wider than her shoulders. When she turned and spotted me, she smiled. Her deep-brown, clear skin and oval face were just as lovely as I remembered.

Angeline strode toward me in her navy blue skinny scrubs that consisted of a short-sleeve, V-neck shirt tucked into fitted drawstring pants. I stood and took a few steps toward her.

"Hello, Mister Yates—I mean hello, Billy. Nice to see you again." We shook hands.

"Hi, Angeline. Great to see you as well."

"I'm hungry. Let's get something to eat."

Angeline led me into the kitchen area. Her glossy black hair curved into loose curls and springy coils, with a couple of strands hanging like bangs on her forehead. She gave me a tour of the options available which included pizza, whole grain sandwiches, soups, salads, fresh fruit, and grilled foods. Angeline selected a sandwich and a fruit salad, and I had a sandwich and chips. We paid for our food and returned to the table.

"Were you surprised to get my card?"

"We get notes and cards from patients every now and then, so the card wasn't too surprising. But most cards don't ask for a meeting." Angeline looked up from her salad with a twinkle in her eye and added, "What's really unusual is for me to meet with a patient for lunch. That's different. I don't do that."

"Why did you call back?"

"I was curious about your tattoo, your children, and the spiritual journey you said you were on." She fixed her dark eyes on me. "I've been on a spiritual journey myself recently."

Your children?

My attempt to hide my surprise was not successful. "My children. What do you mean?"

How did she know about Benotenn?

"Tell me about your children. Are they away at college?"

"I don't have any children," I said. "Why did you think I did?"

"While you were under the anesthesia …" Angeline paused, as if making sure she hadn't mixed me up with someone else. "One of the things you said was, 'My children are at school, but I want them at home.' There was such longing and sadness in the way you said it, and you said it more than once. It was very touching."

My face became hot. "So I was telling you my secrets. Did I say anything else?"

"You also said, 'I'm on my own,' and 'You're my angel.' I hope I didn't embarrass you. What does that mean about your children? I actually identified with the feelings you expressed, because I long for my child as well."

"I think of my students as my children, but I've always wanted children of my own and to teach them everything I know …. That's probably what I was talking about. What happened with your child?"

It seemed Angeline left me for a moment as her gaze turned inward. "Seven years ago, I lost my baby girl to a miscarriage."

"I'm sorry to hear that. It must have been very hard."

"Well, one day maybe I'll tell you more about it." Angeline pulled her chair up and leaned toward me. "For now, tell me about the spiritual journey you've been on since we first met. You said it was mystical and terrifying."

I decided to tell Angeline the truth just as it happened. I hoped she wouldn't think I'd lost my mind. My heart raced.

"Angeline, when you were talking to me before my surgery, you mentioned demons. And you said you pray for your patients, so you must believe in spiritual things that can't be explained logically. Is that correct?"

"You know what? I try to understand the facts and draw conclusions based on facts," she said, as she placed her hands on the table and made unwavering eye contact with me, "but having worked in the healthcare field for close to fifteen years, I've seen things happen that no one could explain. Things that couldn't be anything else but miracles. I also believe in God, prayer, and the existence of angels and demons. So, yes, you're correct."

"I'm thankful you believe in supernatural things, because there's no natural way to explain the things that happened to me. At the same time, I'm certain the visions have been truthful." I told her only about my experience with Alexander at the hospital. Then I waited for her response.

Angeline leaned back and played with one of her earrings. "It's possible on that day you were stressed and worried about the surgery. The stress combined with the anesthesia could cause your mind to play tricks on you."

Tension gripped my neck muscles. I didn't know what I could say to make her believe me. The lunch hour was almost over. If Angeline returned to work on that note, I'd probably never see her again. Then I remembered Alexander's riddle—the riddle Alexander had told about Angeline. The meaning wasn't clear to me, but if it meant something to her, then she'd have to wonder how I knew about it.

"Before you dismiss me completely," I said, "let me tell you what Alexander said about you. It's a riddle I don't understand, but hopefully it will mean something to you. He said, 'One day ago, she took her life and plunged it into death, yet now she truly lives. How can that be?'" I gazed at her lovely eyes. "Does that mean something to you?"

Angeline stilled for a long moment, and then she smiled. "Alexander told you that, on the day of your surgery?"

"Yes. He appeared when I was checking out of the hospital."

"That's very interesting, because the day before your surgery, I was baptized into Christ."

"What does being baptized have to do with being plunged into death?"

"Huh … that's amazing." Angeline shook her head. "I can't believe it. Maybe Alexander really was an angel, and maybe you're a prophet."

"Could you explain it to me?"

"When you're baptized, you're completely submerged in water." Angeline motioned with her hands like she was pushing something down. "It's like being buried in water. The preacher said I was being baptized into Christ's death. The old sinful person I used to be remains buried, and I was raised up out of the water with my sins washed away to live a new life, just like when Jesus was resurrected. That's in the book of Romans, in the Bible."

"Really? I'm reading Romans, but I didn't get to that part yet." I laid both my hands palm down on the table. "So you see, that was something I had no way of knowing that you did. I am *not* crazy. Right?"

"I never said you were crazy." She tapped my hand. "But I have to get back to work."

"Angeline, there's more to my story, and there's a lot more you haven't told me. Do you have some time Saturday morning? We could just go to the park."

We made a date for Saturday morning.

★★★

Back at home, I read the third chapter of Romans with more motivation, because I wanted to find the part Angeline had mentioned about baptism. I didn't find it, but at the start of the chapter I found a lot more of the condemnation I'd seen in the first two chapters, only much more graphic. It compared our throats, tongues, and lips to the rottenness found in the grave of a decaying corpse, full of cursing, poison, violence, misery, and death. It summed up humanity by saying we had no fear of God, but at the end of the chapter there was finally something hopeful.

> But now apart from the Law the righteousness of God has been manifested, being witnessed by the Law and the Prophets, even the righteousness of God through faith in Jesus Christ for all those who believe; for there is no distinction; for all have sinned and fall short of the glory of God, being justified as a gift by His grace through the redemption which is in Christ Jesus; whom God displayed publicly as a propitiation in His blood through faith.

The mention of the law and the prophets was intriguing, because the whole point of Professor Stanley's class was to show the Old Testament—the law and the prophets—foretold the existence of Jesus. My understanding of the bottom line was that my redemption was only possible through faith in Jesus. Redemption was what I was searching for.

To be honest, I still wanted a love relationship with Angeline more than anything. If that wasn't possible, nothing else mattered. That was probably how my classmate Lawrence felt about his girlfriend too. I thanked Alexander for the riddle of Angeline. Saturday, I would seek to unravel the mystery of her lovely scars.

CHAPTER 28

Week 2—Saturday

On Saturday morning at ten o'clock, Angeline and I met at Pope Lick Park, one of four huge parks that make up the Parklands which circle the city of Louisville. Pope Lick Park had miles of paved paths for bikers, joggers, and walkers, as well as unpaved trails for hiking through the gentle rolling hills of Big Beech Woods. We stuck to the paved paths that wound through a prairie preserve, where the strong scent of cedar and blooming wildflowers greeted us. The temperature was seventy degrees with a light breeze, and Angeline wore sneakers, blue jeans, a T-shirt and a light jacket. I was dressed similarly—with the addition of a denim cap.

"Do you remember before your surgery you said you didn't have any tattoos?" she asked. Our shoulders brushed as we walked.

"Yes. I remember you asking me about it. It seemed like a joke. It didn't make sense, because I've never gotten a tattoo. The first time I saw it was two days after the surgery."

"Where did it come from?"

I shrugged and held my hands palms up. "I have no idea, except to say it's a message from God to confirm my state of rejection."

"So strange."

"Strange is exactly what my life has been since my surgery."

Angeline leaned lightly into me with her shoulder. "What else happened to you?"

I explained about the nightmare parable, the man in the mirror, and the vision of Benotenn. I left out the haunting by my invisible accusers. My intent was to tell her, but the words wouldn't come out. Their demonic condemnations had held no hope or pity, and I couldn't bear to repeat them. The funny thing was their denunciation matched much of what the first three chapters of Romans had said about the sins of humanity, yet Romans offered the hope of redemption while the demons urged me on to utter despair and death. I shivered.

Angeline shook my arm. "Hey, Billy. Snap out of it."

"What is it?"

"You went silent on me after the part about Benotenn and that miserable marathon." We'd stopped walking, and Angeline clutched my shoulders and looked deep into my eyes. "What were you thinking about just then?"

"Well ... I was reliving feelings of hopelessness and fear."

"What was the most terrifying part?"

"The first vision when I was thrown through the air toward a burning oven was scary, but it was just a nightmare. Probably the most terrifying part was the vision of the miserable marathon, as you called it, when I couldn't take off the weights. They were painful, but I couldn't stand to take them off. I was going to suffocate and die encased in my sins. That was truly awful."

"It sounds awful."

"You know what? Being humbled was probably worse than my fear." I looked away from Angeline and added, "I was helpless and weak. Like Benotenn said, I was no hero."

TRUE STATUS

"You found out you had a problem you couldn't solve on your own. Jesus is the hero."

"Yeah. A lot of my family and friends have been telling me the same thing for a long time." I laughed and pointed to myself. "But *I've* always wanted to be the hero."

A corner of her mouth quirked upward in a half-smile. "If you play your cards right, maybe you can be my hero."

"That's been my plan all along." I took her hand in mine, and we continued walking the pathway on its large loop around the park. I wanted to press Angeline close to me but decided against it for the time being.

The warblers harmonized with the gentle prairie breeze in a song of spring, of new beginnings. Angeline—tender, gentle, and kind—would be mine soon enough.

"How did you get these scars?" I pointed to the scars below Angeline's left eye and on her hands.

She grimaced. "Now you want me to recall the worst time of my life."

"It's really none of my business," I admitted. "I understand if you don't want to talk about it."

Angeline took a deep breath. "I got married at nineteen. I was so stupid. It didn't take long before it was obvious Junius, my husband, hated everything about me."

"I can't believe that. You're such a lovely person. You're a dream to me." We sat on a park bench.

"You're sweet. But Junius was crazy with jealousy and didn't want me to have any friends. He was mean. Sometimes, he hit me. He was a drinker." Angeline squeezed her eyes shut and pressed them with her hands. "Some days, he threatened to kill himself, and other days, he threatened to kill me. He was pitiful. He'd cry and apologize afterward, but he always did it again. I took it for nine years. I finally divorced him after he attacked me with a knife."

"You stayed with him nine years?"

"Everyone said I should. I wanted to do the right thing."

"What set him off the last time?"

"I started attending church, and he didn't want me to go. One day, a friend of mine from church, another young married woman, came over to our house to study the Bible with me. Junius came home, and I could tell he'd been drinking, but he didn't say anything until my friend left."

"He waited until the two of you were alone?"

"Yes. He accused me of plotting to leave him, and he came after me with a knife." Angeline clenched her fists and starting sobbing softly. I put my arm around her. "I was pregnant. I lost my baby girl."

"I'm so sorry ... I wish I could—I'm really sorry."

"He chased me into the yard, and I ran to a neighbor's house. They called the police."

"Did Junius go to jail?"

"Yes, but he got out last year."

"Has he bothered you?"

"I heard he returned to Louisville, but he hasn't contacted me. Thank God for that. I hate him. God forgive me, but I hate that man so much. He ruined my life." Angeline jumped up and started pacing back and forth. "That was seven years ago, and I haven't dated anyone since then. I just started going back to church a couple of months ago. Before that, I watched online services and read my Bible almost every day."

I was silent for a moment before I spoke. "But life *can* be good again, right?"

"Yes, I think life can be good again." She smiled and held out her hand, and we continued walking. We departed from the paved path and walked arm in arm down a hard-packed dirt path. The warmth of Angeline's body seeped into mine, and the fragrance of flowers and shrubs close to both sides of the path carried us along. We stopped and watched hundreds of bees, butterflies, and other insects buzzing and flitting from flower to flower.

Angeline said, "Isn't it funny these plants and creatures just know what to do? Sometimes, I agonize so much over even small things, and big decisions can be really hard for me. I don't want to repeat the mistakes I've made before."

"Maybe it's because we imagine what could be, or what might have been. We see too much. We remember the mistakes for too long."

We resumed our walk, and the path led us to an open area. There was a little playground with swings, slides, and a merry-go-round, but there were no children playing.

"Billy, do you ever think about Benotenn?"

"Yes. I think about Benotenn all the time."

"You're confident he really exists? He wasn't just a dream?"

"He was real. I saw him on two different occasions. Benotenn exists, just not in this life. He's as near as the air we breathe."

"I think about my baby every day too. I named her Dahlia. Have you ever heard of the National Memorial for the Unborn?"

"No. What is it?"

"It's a memorial in Chattanooga, Tennessee. It provides a way for parents and families to honor children lost due to abortion or miscarriage, and it helps the parents heal. I have a paver stone for Dahlia with her name and due date on it, and another's there at the memorial. It allowed me to do something to honor Dahlia and to remember my child. I'd like to visit the memorial one day. Maybe you'll want to do something for Benotenn."

"I don't know. It's weird to know *he* knows what's going on here. I wonder if doing something to honor him here would add to the happiness he feels there."

"Maybe honoring Benotenn would help you to heal."

"Do I need healing? Do I deserve healing?"

She patted my chest. "I think there's a lot of guilt and wounds in there that need healing. I need it." Angeline laughed and added, "Whether we deserve it or not is another matter."

My mind wandered. I looked down the footpath we had just traversed and examined the passersby.

Were we being watched?

I kept thinking about Junius and the possibility he might start stalking Angeline, especially now that I was in the picture to stir his jealousy. "It's after noon. The time's flown by."

"We've talked about some terrible things today, but this is a beautiful place," she said. "I've enjoyed our time together. I guess it's been cathartic, because I feel better now than I have in quite a while."

"My apartment is filled with plants. It's like a miniature garden paradise. And I have a huge collection of books, which I consider my tree of knowledge. You'll see it sometime."

"I'd like that. Why don't you come to church with me tomorrow?" Her eyes glowed as she touched my arm. "The people are really nice, and the teaching is great."

"I'll come with you one day. At present, I'm taking an Old Testament class, and I promise you I'm reading in the New Testament on my own. I think I'm getting enough Bible for right now."

★★★

We parted ways and each went to our respective cars, but Angeline's invitation to church was a sign she wanted our relationship to grow. Our romance would thrive, just like the plants I'd nurtured for so long. Angeline was the woman of my dreams, just like I knew she'd be from the very first time I met her at the hospital and heard her say, "Hello, my friend, I will be taking care of you."

After that day in the park, I returned to my apartment and read Romans 4.

I was happy to read about more good news, about the blessing of having your sins forgiven. That sounded really great. What I didn't understand was what it meant about circumcision and Abraham being credited with righteousness. I remembered Professor Stanley had mentioned God had made an important promise to Abraham thousands of years ago. This passage was comforting.

> "Blessed are those whose lawless deeds have been forgiven, and whose sins have been covered.
>
> "Blessed is the man whose sin the Lord will not take into account."
>
> Is this blessing then on the circumcised, or on the uncircumcised also? For we say, "Faith was credited to Abraham as righteousness." How then was it credited? While he was circumcised, or uncircumcised? Not while circumcised, but while uncircumcised.

So I had great anticipation for the class coming up on Tuesday.

Could even my lawless deeds be forgiven, covered, and forgotten?

CHAPTER 29

Week 3—Tuesday

Ezriah picked me up again for the second class session. In the car, he said, "How did Saturday go?"

"Great. I'm going to marry her." My chest swelled at my proclamation.

He snorted with laughter. "Planning the wedding already, are you?"

"Well, I haven't told her about the wedding yet." I shrugged, held my hands up, and thumped my chest with my thumbs. "How could she resist all this?"

"Yeah, you're all that, but maybe you should wait until after the third date and after you propose and after she accepts." Ezriah shook his head as he drove. "Do you think you're getting a little carried away? Being impulsive can get you into a lot of trouble."

"Maybe so, but I can't stop thinking about Angeline. And the third date was yesterday."

"I guess that means you didn't do your homework."

"Actually, my homework is done. I read all about covenants. I'd never thought about the Old Testament and New Testament actually referring to an old covenant and a new covenant. And I never really knew the biblical meaning of a covenant before."

Ezriah said, "It was pretty interesting. God's covenants are why he does what he does."

"Doesn't God just do whatever he wants to do?"

"I guess so, but I think it's more accurate to say God does what he promised to do in his covenants with people, even if it required his only son to suffer and die."

I tilted my head and looked at Ezriah. "You're going to have to put that all together for me."

"We'll talk about it."

While traversing the campus with Ezriah, my spine tingled with an awareness that someone—or something—overflowing with hatred tracked us. We were not alone.

We entered the room before the start of class. The room already buzzed with my fellow learners, sharing with each other the gems they had discovered in their study of covenants. I looked carefully at their faces to discern if anyone seemed to be focused on me. I imagined the faces of those that might have malice toward me for reasons known and unknown—Millie, Eddie, Mr. Ubel. The faces of Rose and Sharon—and that strange man in the power wheelchair, E.J. Landes—materialized.

Did they remember me? Hate me? And those I hurt and never even knew it—what about them?

I searched for a menacing scowl, pitiless eyes, smiling teeth hiding treachery. Prophetic visions had been given to me, and at that moment I wished for the power to see beneath the veil of human faces. Such was not granted me. Thankfully, however, the energy of the class sank into me, and my uneasiness subsided. I'd returned to work the previous week, and the intellectual fire that drove my classmates' self-discoveries was the same as that I tried to create in my own students. Lawrence and Hugo were engaged in heated debate when Ezriah and I arrived, and we took our seats with them at the same table as the prior week.

"When Jesus died on the cross," Professor Stanley said, "he inaugurated the new covenant. The new covenant was really the fulfillment and renewal of a covenant God had made with Abraham two thousand years earlier. Abraham's story is explained in the Old Testament book of Genesis, and our study of it will help us understand how it defined the work of Jesus in the New Testament."

Professor Stanley walked around the classroom as he said, "Let me ask you all a few questions about your understanding of contracts. First, what's the typical relationship between parties that enter a contract?"

Several hands flew up, and one man shouted out his answer. "They're business associates."

Another added, "Or maybe a consumer and a retailer."

Professor Stanley said, "Okay, they're business associates in some way. Why do they enter into a contract?"

Ezriah said, "Mutual benefit. One wants to get paid for performing a service, and the other person is willing to pay for the service."

"Yes. It could be a contracted repair service, or it could be to purchase some item like a car or a house. There is mutual agreement and some benefit on each side, so each party voluntarily enters into the agreement. When does the contract end?"

Hugo said, "At some specified date, or when the obligations of each party are completed."

"So, at some point, there is a specified termination of the contract. What happens if one party doesn't fulfill the contract?"

I said, "There could be a withholding of the payment, the product, or the service."

Ezriah, the attorney, added, "Or someone might take legal action by suing the other party."

"Very good. Now, based on your reading, how were the covenants of the ancient Near East different?"

Again hands sprang up. Professor Stanley pointed to one of them. "Yes, sir, what do you think?"

"Usually one party was more powerful than the other, and things may not have been completely voluntary on the weaker party's part."

I said, "Failure to fulfill the obligation might mean the failing party would deserve to die, which I assume the more powerful party could impose on the weaker party if he wanted."

Lawrence said, "It was really interesting that the covenant made the two parties like blood relatives rather than business associates, and it was based on a desire for an intimate personal relationship and love between the parties. That was pretty cool."

Ariun said, "Yeah, the stronger party offered love and protection, and the weaker party offered love and loyalty." Her voice rose as she continued. "It was scary though, like being in a gang, or paying protection to mobsters— especially the fact the covenant had no ending. The obligation went on forever. I wouldn't have liked that."

Professor Stanley grinned. "I suppose if you were in a covenant with the wrong person, it could be a really scary thing." He looked back up to the group. "How are contracts typically entered into? The parties usually put their signatures on the written contract, but covenants were entered into with a blood ritual, a kind of ceremony. They would cut up animals—"

"That part was gross, cruel, and barbaric," Hugo said, shaking his head.

A middle-aged man responded. "You should see what they do to pre-born babies sacrificed on the altar of convenience. We need to be more concerned about people than animals."

Several students groaned. "It's not that simple, and we're not even talking about that," someone said. "Can we stay on the subject?"

Ariun wrinkled her nose and added, "Still, just think about all that blood. And they had to touch it. Eeew." She shivered.

Professor Stanley continued. "And they would line the animal parts in two rows, and the two parties would walk between the rows, through the blood of the animals that pooled in the middle. The animals signified the party that violated the covenant would pay with their lives."

The professor stopped and leaned against a table. "What is most interesting is that God ratified his covenant with Abraham with a ceremony with the slaughtered animals, but only God passed between the animal pieces. Scholars interpret this to mean God did something that would never have been done in the ancient Near East—he was committing to keep *both* sides of the covenant. So if Abraham and his descendants didn't keep the covenant, God committed to taking the punishment himself, which explains why Jesus died for the sins of the world."

I asked, "Why would God make a covenant like that, where God pays the price for a human's failure?"

"Good question. I'll let each of you figure out your own answer, but I'll tell you this—my answer to that question changed my life."

We spent the rest of the class discussing Abraham and how the covenant with Abraham led to Jesus establishing the new covenant.

The professor returned to the lectern to make his final remarks.

"God made several wonderful promises to Abraham, including a son, many descendants, land, and great honor. But God called Abraham to walk before him and be blameless, meaning Abraham was to be God's representative to his children and descendants. God didn't define for Abraham what it meant to be blameless. That didn't come until hundreds of years later when God gave Israel the Law of Moses, which includes the Ten Commandments. It was the greatest expression of God's expectations for moral, societal, and legal behaviors the world had ever seen. Within the Law of Moses are many illustrations of the work of Jesus Christ. We'll examine the Law of Moses next time."

***

After class, the four of us returned to Josh's Grotto and ordered dinner, and I addressed our little group.

"Guys, I finally understand something that never made sense before—" I had to stop for a moment. I felt like dancing and exploding. "It never made sense to me that God would design a legal system where an innocent person would take the place of a guilty person, but now I see why Jesus's death makes sense. God was fulfilling the commitment he made to Abraham in that ancient covenant ceremony. God took responsibility for both sides of the covenant, so when the humans failed, God stepped in to take our punishment."

Lawrence said, "Why did God do that—take that responsibility?"

Hugo said, "Because of God's love for humanity." He cackled and added, "I guess he knew we were hopeless on our own."

We all stared at him.

With eyes wide, Lawrence asked, "Hugo, are you a believer in God so soon?"

"No, sorry, but I can follow a good story. I just don't think it's a true story. I have a big problem with the awful

224

behavior of God's people. And God often seems so unfair and unreasonable, especially if you're not one of the chosen."

I said, "I know what you mean, because the bad behavior of Christians—"

Just then Ariun Christian, the woman from our class, walked into the dining room alone. She was slender with caramel skin, long straight black hair, red fingernails, and a lovely smile with gleaming teeth. We all stared and then invited her to join us, but she declined and continued to another table. She said she'd be joined by a friend shortly.

Lawrence said, "Guys, how old do you think Ariun is? I'd say she's in her thirties. She's gorgeous."

Hugo said, "A little older. A timeless beauty. Wow."

"Boys, put your eyes back in your head," I said, and continued my previous thought. "The bad behavior of Christians always put me off too, plus I never understood why God allowed so many bad things to happen. I always believed God existed. But now having learned more, I think I've misjudged God."

"The people God chose to use were not good people," Hugo said. "Abraham had slaves, you know, and he had sex with his wife's slave, Hagar, and got her pregnant with Ishmael. So Abraham had at least two sons, but only Isaac inherited the promises of Abraham—Ishmael was left out. Isaac had twin sons, Jacob and Esau, but only Jacob and his descendants got the blessings of the covenant. God rejected Esau. Jacob was a liar and a cheat, a real scoundrel. It seems to me the Bible promotes the worst kind of discrimination between people."

I said, "Kind of makes you doubt the wisdom and goodness of God, huh?"

"It goes back to what Hugo said earlier," Ezriah said. "God knew all of humanity was hopelessly sinful, not just the people God chose. All humanity really is hopeless without God. None of us are righteous on our own. Genesis says Abraham believed God, so God credited Abraham with righteousness he did not have."

I said, "I just read about that. The fourth chapter in Romans really emphasizes the part about crediting Abraham with righteousness."

"That corresponds directly to us today," Lawrence commented. "That's why we're saved through belief or faith in Jesus, not because we're so good. Abraham didn't deserve the blessing he was promised, and neither do we." Lawrence looked around at us before settling his cool blue eyes on Hugo and added, "I know I have sins I need to let go of." Hugo looked away.

I said, "Romans also talked about circumcision and uncircumcision. What was that all about?"

Ezriah said, "That was the sign God required for Abraham and his descendants. The males had to be circumcised to be included in the covenant promises, and the uncircumcised were excluded. The parallel to circumcision for us today is baptism."

"More rituals?" I asked.

"Deadly serious requirements."

Lawrence said, "Hugo, you're also overlooking the fact that God didn't leave Abraham and Jacob where they were. God used life experiences over the years of their lives to make them much better men than when they started out. That's what I'm hoping for."

"It would be a lot more convincing," Hugo responded, "if we didn't have so much moral failure among Christians." Hugo pointed to Ezriah and me. "Surely, as Black men, you must know the extent to which slave owners in this country used the Bible to justify slavery— how they manipulated the Bible to propagate an unjust and immoral system to subjugate your people."

"Just because people misuse the Bible doesn't make the Bible untrue," Ezriah said. "And remember, abolitionists were also Christians who risked everything they had to end slavery. You can't judge God and Jesus on the basis of people's performance. You have to look at the wisdom and the truth of what is revealed in the Bible, and what eyewitnesses of Jesus recorded. Jesus's life is an established historical fact."

I said, "Hugo, you have to admit the Bible lays it all out there. It presents the good, the bad, and the ugly. Nothing is hidden. It's pretty amazing Abraham's character grew so much that now he's revered for his faith by Muslims, Jews, *and* Christians."

Hugo sighed. "Like I said, a good story. Sadly believed by millions."

The servers brought our food in the midst of our discussion, which continued for some time with no resolution. Still, things were becoming clearer to me.

***

After Ezriah dropped me off at my apartment, I opened my Bible and read another chapter in Romans. The fifth chapter was a good one, and very encouraging. It explained Jesus sacrificed for us while we were his enemies. I supposed it meant Jesus died for his enemies with the expectation some of us would become his friends and followers. This verse seemed to sum things up.

> But God demonstrates His own love toward us, in that while we were yet sinners, Christ died for us.

I continued on to Romans 6 and found the passage Angeline had mentioned about baptism, death, and resurrection.

What shall we say then? Are we to continue in sin so that grace may increase? May it never be! How shall we who died to sin still live in it? Or do you not know that all of us who have been baptized into Christ Jesus have been baptized into His death? Therefore we have been buried with Him through baptism into death, so that as Christ was raised from the dead through the glory of the Father, so we too might walk in newness of life.

I reflected on the beautiful logic of why Jesus took our place on the cross. It made perfect sense.

But why did he do it?

Professor Stanley had said, "My answer to that question changed my life."

I bowed my head, tears of shame streaming, I had heard the answer my entire life and it had never before sunk in.

For God so loved the world.

Goosebumps covered my body.

Please forgive me, Lord.

I raised my head in repentance and gratitude.

I felt lighter, as though my past blinders had fallen away. All I'd studied became very clear. I understood, and I wanted to be freed from my sins and start a new life just like Angeline had. I thanked Jesus for bringing Angeline into my life. She was all I needed.

"I believe this, Lord, and I'm ready for a new life. I finally get it. I repudiate my sins, and I'm sorry for them."

What would a new life be like?

"I'm going to be baptized."

When I said those words, an immediate chill swept through my apartment. The malevolent demonic accusers who earlier had almost hounded me to death were furious at my newfound conviction. They must have been the ones tracking my steps.

TRUE STATUS

I should've been afraid. I wasn't. I bounded and danced around my apartment looking for a sign of them but found none. I believed myself safe.

I was wrong.

Before bed, I repeated my nightly ritual, consisting of stripping off my clothes and standing in front of my bathroom mirror with my left arm raised. Before raising my arm, I would always pray the tattoo would be gone and Benotenn would again appear to me. Each night, disappointment met me on both counts. That night was no different.

I touched my reject label and felt only my skin. The label was certainly part of me, and I wondered if I'd ever be rid of it. I lingered, looking at myself in the mirror. How deep were my sins? What was the extent of my violations of God's rules? In my vision of the race, I saw and felt my sins' weight, and knew they were killing me. But observing myself in the mirror, I now looked fine, with no visible sign of sin's ravages except my tattoo.

How much and for how long had my sins secretly affected my thinking, decisions, and behavior? When I tried to do good, what insidious effect did my sins impart, and what harm did I do?

Some things I recalled upon reflection of my past, but there was no doubt much beyond my ability to assess.

Jesus took my place on the cross, because four thousand years ago, God, in the covenant ratification ceremony with Abraham, agreed to pay the penalty for Abraham's and his followers' failure to be blameless.

If Jesus took care of everything for us, what was the point of God handing down the Law of Moses and the Ten Commandments hundreds of years after the covenant with Abraham? What was the point of the Law of Moses, if our problem had already been solved long before?

CHAPTER 30

I drove myself to the third session of the 'Jesus in the Old Testament' class. After the class, I planned to pick Angeline up and spend the evening at a week-long street festival called Taste of the Town. I arrived at our classroom and joined Ezriah, Hugo, and Lawrence at our usual table just in time to hear Professor Stanley begin asking questions.

"How would you characterize the behavior you'd expect from a good and moral man or woman?"

Hugo straightened his posture and pulled his shoulders back. "I think each person should make decisions to do the most good and cause the least harm."

"Mr. Mason, that is certainly an admirable goal," Professor Stanley nodded. He pointed to another student. "Yes, Miss Heath, go ahead."

"A good person treats others fairly or equitably. Everyone should be treated with respect and compassion."

Lawrence waved both hands. "Going back to what Hugo said, how could you know what choices result in the most good? That seems like an impossible goal. Plus, who gets to determine what's good? The rich educated elite? The smart people? There could be a lot of disagreement about what's good."

Hugo crossed his arms. "It's not elitist. Guided by compassion as Miss Heath said—compassion, reason, and informed experience—people of good will can determine what is good."

"Who can determine what's good?" Ariun grinned, revealing her sparkling teeth. "In some circumstances, doing wrong might be the best choice for those you love. Remember Rahab's lies that she told to protect the Israelite spies from the King of Jericho?"

An elderly woman shook her head. "It's never right to do wrong. We should just follow the Golden Rule. Do to others as we would have them do to us." She chuckled and added, "Surely, we can understand that."

Professor Stanley said, "That's what Jesus said, and he added that the Golden Rule summed up the Law of Moses, which included the Ten Commandments and more than six hundred other rules. Most people in the world today would probably agree the Ten Commandments are an excellent standard to live by."

I said, "So that's the answer to your question. A good and moral man or woman should follow the Ten Commandments so they can be saved."

"No. We're saved through faith in Jesus, but the Ten Commandments are a reflection of God's perfect moral standards. And in the many requirements of the Law of Moses, we can see the work of Jesus Christ."

"So what's the point of the commandments?"

"They reflect God's character, and they teach us what's right and wrong. We practice the Ten Commandments to honor God, and to make the world a better place."

Lawrence said, "The law defined what good behavior is. Otherwise we wouldn't know what's moral or immoral."

Ezriah added, "Jesus taught we should keep the letter and the spirit of the law."

I tapped Ezriah's shoulder. "What does that mean?"

"It means we don't commit murder or any of the things that lead up to it, like hatred or name calling."

"So you're saying calling someone a fool is as bad as murdering them?"

"No, it's not as bad, but they're both sins. Murder starts somewhere in our thoughts of devaluing or hating a person. Murder is the worst-case end result of a sinful process that begins in the mind."

A middle-aged man added, "So that's why Jesus said lust for a woman was sinful, just as committing adultery is sinful, but he didn't say lust was as bad as committing adultery."

We spent the remainder of the class discussing the Law of Moses and how Jesus was represented in the entire system of animal sacrifices that went along with the Law of Moses. At the conclusion of the class, Professor Stanley said, "Next time, we will discuss the unconditional promise made to King David that one of his descendants would reign on David's throne forever. That descendant is Jesus Christ."

After the class Ezriah, Lawrence, and Hugo again went to dinner, and I went to pick up Angeline. I anticipated an out-of-this-world night with my winsome girl, but I was running a little late. I looked forward to the next class, but that night's turn of events made the class on the Law of Moses my last one.

I never saw Professor Stanley again.

CHAPTER 31

Week 4—Tuesday

Angeline and I had seen each other three times in the first few days after we met, but due to clashing schedules we'd not been together in more than a week. I was starving for her presence. Since she didn't work the next day, and I didn't have a class until late Wednesday afternoon, I expected we'd enjoy the Taste until late into the evening.

I emerged from the cool air of Wesley Chapel into the blast-furnace heat of May and sprinted across campus to my car. I didn't want to be late in picking up Angeline. My backpack beat against my body as I dodged strolling pedestrians and whizzing cyclists, and somehow I managed to reach the parking lot with no collisions.

As I approached my vehicle, I tripped, stumbled, and crash-landed on the asphalt. Stinging pain pierced my hands and knees, and my forehead burned where I skinned it. I jumped up, limped to my car, and barreled out of the parking lot, headed to Angeline's apartment.

She lived on a street near the festival area, and of course her street and several others were closed to outside traffic. I lost more time driving around, looking for a parking spot close to her apartment building. Finally, I parked three blocks away and walked.

The evening temperature was eighty-five degrees—with a warm breeze. Only a few years earlier, the average temperature in Louisville in May was just seventy degrees. The new normal was summer-like weather in the spring and scorching temperatures of over one hundred degrees during the summer months, which was why street festivals were now frequently held in the spring.

Sweat trickled down the center of my back. My khakis were ripped at both knees. I swiped at the moisture on my face and found my forehead was bleeding. I chuckled and winced at the same time. My knees ached, but I dragged onward.

I approached Angeline's house from the side where it sat on the corner amid a noisy throng of revelers. A tall, thick evergreen hedge surrounded the property, with the house number on a small sign nestled among the branches. I looked for the entrance into the yard but didn't see one. When I'd passed the corner, I turned and went back, this time looking more carefully at the hedge.

A narrow indentation revealed an entryway formed by a second overlapping hedge behind the first, with a small gap between the two. I slid between the hedges and discovered a black wrought-iron gate with metal palm tree silhouettes. The gate chirped as I swung it open and stepped into a brightly lit courtyard.

The crowd noise faded as I walked toward the house, while the burbling song of running water grew and mist cooled my face. Bright beams from a lampstand in the middle of the courtyard made me blink, while another large light was mounted on the house above the porch. Together the two lights illuminated the entire area.

Lilies, roses, and other flowers of purple and white decorated the yard and sweetened the air with their fragrance. The walkway passed between two fountains containing koi and other fish. The house, a Victorian mansion built in 1896, had been renovated and divided into six apartments, and Angeline lived in one of them. Her dwelling place's exterior was old, but with classic nineteenth-century elegance.

I rang the bell for Angeline's apartment, and she buzzed the outer door open. I found her apartment door and knocked.

Only thirty minutes late. Could've been worse.

The door flew open, and she immediately fussed. "Why didn't you return my call or my—" Her eyes widened as she took in my appearance, which was apparently terrible. "What happened? Are you all right?" She pulled me into the apartment. "You look like you've been in a fight. There's blood on your face—and on your clothes."

My shirt was indeed stained with blood. Apparently I'd touched my head wound and spread the blood to my shirt.

"It's nothing. I was running, and I fell." But my sides were not drenched in sweat, giving me the minor consolation that my surgery of three weeks earlier had been successful.

"Come with me. I need to look at your injuries." Angeline led me into the bathroom, where she cleaned my head wound. I pulled up my pants legs to reveal scraped knees, which she also attended to.

I smiled at the tender care Angeline provided. She wore blue jean shorts and a loose white blouse. Her long black hair fell to her shoulders, held back by a hair band adorned with semi-precious stones. Her earrings matched the hair band.

"Seems like you know what you're doing," I said. "Are you a nurse or something?"

She squinted at me, her eyes twinkling. She left the bathroom and returned with a cold pack wrapped in a wash cloth. "Put your hands on this. It'll help the stinging and burning. Why were you running? Was someone chasing you?"

"Why would someone be chasing me?"

"I've just been worried about Junius showing up again."

"That guy has us both spooked, because I was thinking the same thing. But no one was chasing me. It was just me being late, and I ran to try to make up time getting here."

"You should've called and told me you were going to be late. Being on time is not worth getting hurt." She leaned over and hugged me. "Did you think I'd take off on you for being a few minutes late?" She laughed. "I called you and texted you."

"I always silence my phone for the class. I forgot to turn the ringer back on."

She eyed me for a moment before she spoke. "Do you still want to go to the festival? We could hang out here if you want."

"Let's go to the festival. I'm starving."

Right after I spoke, I wished I'd chosen to spend the evening curled up with Angeline at her place. Who knows where things might have gone? Angeline was a new Christian, and I didn't want to mess up her faith or make her think all I wanted was sex.

Lawrence living with his girlfriend came to mind. I was serious about Angeline—my plan was to marry her—so I was perplexed about how to take things to the next level.

"Okay, but we're going to have to buy you a new shirt." With a smirk, she added, "But ripped khakis are a thing, you know."

Before we left the courtyard of Angeline's home, I turned back to look at the old mansion. "This seems like a really nice place. Do you like it?"

"I absolutely love it. It's beautiful, and I feel safe here. It's as if someone designed it just for me. There are so many little touches that make this feel like home. Did you notice the palm branches embossed on the front door? They symbolize victory and life."

"I didn't know that, and I didn't notice the door, but I saw the palm trees on the gate."

"I'm glad the entrance to the courtyard is hidden. Otherwise all sorts of strange people would stop by to enjoy the garden."

"Yeah, I could barely find my way in here." I looked around the yard and at the mansion. "So this is your hiding place."

Angeline stopped and pulled me toward one of the fountains. "Let's talk for a minute."

"What is it?"

We sat on a bench, and I peered into the water. Two fish came up to greet us, but they worked their lips at me and flipped back under the water, their tails splashing a message of either disapproval or disinterest.

"After my divorce, I was in therapy for years, and for a long time my world was home and work with occasional trips to the grocery store." Angeline clicked and picked her fingernails. "I'm a little anxious about the festival crowd. I do better in controlled environments."

"We can skip the festival."

"No, I really want to go. It'll be a good test for me."

"We don't have to stay long. I wanted to show you my place. You'll like it. Lots of plants. And I have a huge library. Over six thousand books. It's my tree of knowledge."

"Your tree of knowledge? That's what got Adam and Eve in trouble, you know." She stood and held out her hand. "Let's go."

We pushed through the hedges and joined the joyous tumult of the crowd headed to the Taste of the Town festival. We turned onto Broadway, the main street for the festival, where hundreds of booths were set up. Mingled aromas of ribs, grilled chicken, and pierogis encircled us. I was ready to eat, but Angeline insisted on first getting a new shirt for me, and we found a booth selling University of Louisville gear.

"This is what you should buy. Do you like it?" Angeline handed me a cardinal red short-sleeve jersey that buttoned up the front. "This will look nice with your complexion."

Of course, I bought it and put it on.

"That's much better," she said. "It covers all the stains from your wounds." I basked in her approving gaze. "Now we can eat."

We parted ways briefly, because my mouth was set for a jumbo turkey leg and Angeline wanted ribs. We met in the middle of Broadway after we purchased our food. I had the turkey leg, freshly fried thin-sliced potato chips, and a soft drink. Angeline had pork ribs with coleslaw and fries.

Her eyes narrowed when she saw me. "What? No beer or wine? No alcohol?"

My body stiffened. "I never drink. Is something wrong?"

Later, I was sorry I'd said never, because I didn't mean to deceive.

"That's good to hear," she said, "because my ex-husband's love of the bottle almost got me killed." She paused for a moment. "But you're a better man than he was. I guess I'm skeptical of men. I'm sorry."

Soft rock music filled the air, and we followed the sound to a side street where tables were crowded around a band on a stage. We spotted an open table in the back, away from the stage, and sat side by side. I reached for my turkey leg, but Angeline grabbed my hand.

"Let's bless our food first." She bowed her head, and I did likewise. "Dear Lord God, heavenly Father, we thank you for this food which we are about to receive for the nourishment of our bodies. We thank you too for allowing us to enjoy this festival together. We ask this prayer in Jesus's name. Amen."

"Amen. That was good," I said. "My parents always pray before eating, but I've gotten out of the habit."

"I never heard my father pray."

We relaxed, sampled each other's food, and enjoyed the music, as comfortable together as if we'd known each other for years.

Angeline's gaze drifted over the crowd as she ate. "Has there been any change in your tattoo?"

"No. I check it every night, and there's no change at all. I guess it sums up the most important thing about me, a fitting epitaph. Here lies one rejected by God."

"Don't be so morbid. That doesn't have to be your life. No one who comes to Jesus in faith will be rejected by God."

Angeline's conviction was admirable.

"You know, last week I decided I wanted to be baptized."

"That's *great*." Angeline pumped her arms and drummed her feet on the concrete. "How did you come to that decision?"

"I've been reading Romans, and everything Jesus did finally made sense. The class also helped a lot."

"Once you decide, you shouldn't delay. You need to wash away your sins."

Her excitement made me smile. "I'm going to called Ezriah tomorrow and see if he can baptize me."

"Let me know when and where. I want to be there. What was your class about today?"

"The topic was the Law of Moses. Did you know there were over six hundred laws the Jews were supposed to follow?"

"They had lots of laws we don't have to follow anymore. Like dietary rules, and doing all the animal sacrifices."

I put my food down and turned to her. "But we're supposed to still keep the Ten Commandments, right?"

"I think the Ten Commandments are repeated in the New Testament, so I would say so."

"Last week in class, we learned about the stupendous and unconditional promises God made to Abraham and to his descendants. God keeps his word, so we know God was going to fulfill the promises made to Abraham no matter what. And we get to be included in the promises, just because of our faith in Jesus." I grimaced and shook my head. "I don't like that."

Her voice rose. "Why? Sounds good to me. What's the problem?"

"The problem is, we don't have to do anything to earn it. If the good stuff is guaranteed, where's our motivation coming from? I want to do something, and not let Jesus do all the work." I rolled my shoulders and shuddered. "Abraham made some really bad decisions, and he put his wife at risk to protect himself, and his grandson Jacob was really a dirty rotten liar."

"How about the love of Christ as our motivation?" Angeline leaned forward and elbowed me. "I think from God's perspective we're all dirty rotten liars. None of us are good."

That brought me back to my reading in Romans— everyone was filthy, like the decaying rot in an open grave. "I actually know that, but it's hard to accept. It seems too easy."

"The Holy Spirit helps us to do good things. We just can't contribute to our own salvation."

"What was the point of making conditional promises under the Law of Moses a few hundred years after the unconditional promises made to Abraham? Did the Law of Moses supersede the earlier promises?"

"You're giving me a headache." She raised a hand to her head. "We have to have faith in Jesus and God. Abraham came first, and he's still our model of faith. Forget the Law of Moses."

"Forget the Law of Moses? Isn't that like forgetting the Ten Commandments?"

"The Ten Commandments teach how we should behave, but good behavior alone can't save us. It's all about faith. You criticize Abraham, but over time his faith grew to the point that he was willing to sacrifice his son just because God told him to do it."

"Really? I must have missed that part. Did Abraham kill his own son?"

"No. He was about to, but God stopped him. It was a test." She stared at me. "If you lost all the things you treasured most, would you still trust God?"

"How could I ever answer a question like that?"

"I've been through that test for the last seven years."

"And your answer?"

"I can finally say yes."

The lights were low and the music was sweet. I leaned over and kissed Angeline on the cheek. She turned to me, and I kissed her mouth. The curve of her mouth and her soft full lips stoked a fire in my chest that threatened to burn through my clothes. She reached one hand under my shirt and ran her warm fingers up my spine while her other hand, also under my shirt, pressed against my chest and then slid to my side. I pulled her closer and we caressed one another with tender, desperate kisses.

We got up from the table and moved into the shadows between two buildings for a little more privacy. I leaned back against one of the structures with one arm wrapped around her waist and she leaned her head against the side of my face and her hand again wandered slowly over my chest and belly.

"I'm never letting you go. You know that, right?" I said. I expected her to say something similar, but instead she held my face and kissed me again with toe-curling hunger.

Angeline paused and her hand came to rest on my belt.

"I want you to know I have completed my medical exam and have determined you are quite fit, well built. What's your secret?"

The compliment put a big smile on my face. "I hope you don't examine all your patients like that. I might have to report you to the nursing board of professional ethics."

"I don't discriminate. All tall handsome Black men with full beards named Billy Yates get exactly the same treatment. Now what's your secret?

"Probably my genes. My dad is pretty lean and muscular, and before my surgery I ran almost every day, but I haven't done any aerobic exercise in over a month now."

My thoughts went back to my vision of the race, and the condition of our fellow festival-goers who had no idea they were in a desperate race observed by unseen spectators who either mourned or cheered for them. The road in my vision seemed endless, but it would end for each of us. What would be waiting for us, a loving eternal Father or an angry God? I didn't want to think about the coming judgment.

"Let's go back to my apartment."

"Okay," she said. "I've always wanted to see the tree of knowledge."

When we got to my car, I found a ticket stuck to my windshield for parking in a no-parking zone. The fine was $100. I resolved to worry about it later. We hopped onto Interstate 65 and headed for my apartment, only ten minutes away.

Smoke spilled like oily gray ink across the black night sky well before we got there.

When we arrived at Bethesda Apartments at midnight, ambulances, fire engines, and police cars were everywhere. My neighbors ran back and forth screaming, while others stood around holding each other and staring at the fire that had swallowed the wing of the complex where I lived.

Or had lived. My apartment, along with my pictures, shelves, plants, and my beloved books—everything was gone.

It was the beginning of a journey through hell.

CHAPTER 32

WEEK 4—WEDNESDAY

A powerful gust of wind blew poisonous air in our faces, even though I'd parked away from the fire. The fumes attacked our senses with the acrid scents of burned plastic, wood, and chemicals, searing our eyes, throats, and lungs until we retreated to the car.

As we gasped for air, Angeline said, "Smoke like that can cause respiratory or cardiac failure."

When the wind died down we tried again, moving toward the small crowd of residents comforting each other. The fire roared, cutting its way up and out like a blowtorch, immersing the roof in flames. With each gust of wind, orange and white flames shot higher into the sky, endangering the next building over. Gray and black smoke billowed out in noxious clouds. Through the windows we could see the glow of the building's heart as the blaze consumed it from the inside, leaving the brick exterior intact.

"Where's your apartment?" Angeline asked.

I pointed to the bottom of the inferno. "That was me, down there. All gone."

She clutched my arm. "I'm so sorry."

"Someone wanted me dead."

"Why are you saying that?"

"I've had an awful feeling lately that someone—or something—is after me."

"Something?" She leaned closer. "Like what?"

"Something heartless, without pity. Sadistic."

"How do you know that?"

"In the last few weeks, I've been able to feel them. Sometimes, I can hear their voices."

Firefighters wet down adjacent buildings to contain the fire. The heat turned the water to steam, sending great white plumes to mix with the black smoke. The fire chatter—the hiss, crackle, and popping of the blaze—was horrible background commentary to the agonized wails of my weeping neighbors and the moans of the injured. A reporter from a local television station spoke to a camera.

"So far, there are three confirmed dead. Nine others have been taken to area hospitals. Several residents are still unaccounted for. "

I searched for someone I knew. E.J. Landes was there, but I didn't recognize him at first, because he appeared to be standing. His broad and thick shoulders towered above the crowd, and then I realized his power wheelchair held E.J. upright inches above the ground with straps at his knees, waist, and chest. I approached him. His face lit up when he spotted me, and he waved and shouted.

"Hey, everybody, look who's here!"

A few people clapped and cheered. "The fire commander asked for an accounting of family members and neighbors," he said. "We were afraid you were toast, like Ubel."

"What happened?"

"Pool chemicals."

"What do you mean, pool chemicals?" My head pounded. His words didn't make sense.

"Swimming pool chemicals. The firefighters suspect that's how it started. Ubel was doing something with them. Looked like the chemicals detonated in his face and led to all this."

"Ubel's dead?"

"We saw them carry him out. They tried to revive him, but he was burned bad. Real bad."

"Anybody else hurt?"

"We saw paramedics treating Mrs. Pullman and Joseph. They took them to the hospital. There were more, but I don't know who."

"Oh, no. I need to find out about the Pullmans." My stomach burned and churned. Either of them would be lost without the other.

Firefighters approached us. "Folks, please move back. It's not safe for you here."

Angeline and I pulled back. I led her to my garage workshop to watch from there.

"Why," I said, partially to myself, "would our maintenance man be working with pool chemicals so late at night?" I tapped the code into the garage keypad and then turned my eyes back to our burning building.

"Does sound strange."

"Ubel *was* strange. The guy always gave me the creeps." The door shook and slid open and I stared back at the burning building, pondering whether I might have been the target.

Angeline gasped and moaned. "I think I'm going to be sick. Someone really is trying to terrorize you."

"You might be right. I don't know. Hard to believe."

I turned from the fire to Angeline, who stood staring at the hangman's noose I'd left dangling there three weeks ago. I hadn't been in my workshop since then. My heart failed.

"Look, someone's been in here drinking." She pointed at the crushed beer cans scattered on the floor. With the other hand she rubbed her forehead.

"I ... I did that."

"What do you mean? You lied to me? You told me you never drink."

"It was when all those visions happened. I was losing my mind. And the guilt—I finally saw my sins and I couldn't take it. I didn't mean to lie. I rarely drink."

"You were going to kill yourself? You're *suicidal*?" Her eyes grew wide as she watched me. "You're just like Junius. Charming one day, then the next day he'd threaten to kill me, and the next he'd say he was going to kill himself." She started backing out of the garage. "No. I can't live like that."

"I'm not suicidal. It was just that one time. Angeline, wait. I'm nothing like Junius. You've got to know that. I would never threaten you. I was just overwhelmed then."

"It's starting all over. I hate the drinking, and I hate the lies."

"Listen, listen. I'm not a liar. I'm not a drinker. We're perfect for each other."

"I have to get out of here."

"I'll take you home. We can take it slower. You'll see."

"No. I'll call a ride-share. Do *not* follow me." She waved me off. "Leave me alone. I can't take this."

Then she was gone.

I came out of the garage and followed her with my eyes as she ran weeping into the moonlight. I wanted to pursue her, but it would only make things worse. I decided to try later when her anxiety subsided.

I went back to the workshop and sat on the floor in the front corner. I kicked myself for not cleaning up the mess I'd made. As I watched the smoldering ruins, my strength was sapped and heaviness filled my limbs. I'd lost everything.

I crawled across the floor, climbed up on the work bench, and took hold of the rope, still hard and prickly. I untied the rope and slammed it against my homemade wooden storage shelves, sending cans of paint and wood stains crashing to the concrete floor. A can of cherry red paint lost its lid in the fall and spilled its contents across the floor, and as the paint spread so did the smell of rotten eggs, much like the stench from the soul-burning furnaces in my nightmare parable.

I picked up the rope and the empty beer cans and tossed them into the trash bin and returned the unopened cans of stain and paint to their correct places. I put the lid back on the cherry red paint and dumped the can in the trash as well, because the rotten odor indicated it had gone bad. I attempted to clean up the spilled paint with rags, but couldn't do a good job. I got some of the paint on my hands and tried to wipe it off, but I wasn't successful at that either.

The sounds of sobbing and misery suffused the apartment complex until it permeated the surviving structures. They too seemed to mourn for their lost sibling and its inhabitants. Fine ash from the dead and destroyed floated in the air, and we either breathed it in along with the diluted poisonous gases, or it settled on us in a delicate layer for one final embrace. Even my workshop tools understood. The hammers, saw blades, router and drill bits grieved for their lost handiwork.

My heart was heavy, and soon exhaustion overtook me. The stickiness of the paint had the same feel of the blood on my hands in my vision of the race. I returned to the front corner of the garage and slumped against the wall, again watching the smoking remnants of my home, until finally I fell into restless slumber. It was three o'clock Wednesday morning.

***

The soft pattering of footsteps woke me, and something touched my leg. I opened my eyes and saw Mr. Fluff, Joseph Pullman's cat, riding on Patches, Joseph's dog. Mr. Fluff's paws were wrapped around the sides of Patches's head, and it seemed both were satisfied with the arrangement. Patches was a tall, coffee-colored goldendoodle with several gray spots, and Mr. Fluff was a ball of black and gray fur. Patches climbed into my lap, and the three of us rested there while I stroked their soft fur. We were comrades in shock. Having them as company helped me relax and plan what to do next. The list included a call in to work, see if Miss Dianne could take Mr. Fluff and Patches, find out how the Pullmans were, and call my insurance agent.

At eight o'clock, I called my department head, Eugene Edwards, to let him know I wouldn't be coming in to work for a few days.

"Bill, I'm sorry to hear about your loss. I'm glad you're okay."

"Thank you. It's really staggering. Hard to believe your home and all your stuff—*everything*—is just gone." I trembled as I spoke.

"I hate to add to your stress ... but I have more bad news. You know the college has been struggling financially, right?"

"Yes, but I thought—"

"We all thought the board had secured the necessary funding, but the deal fell through. The college is closing at the end of the semester."

We talked a few more minutes, but I was no longer listening.

TRUE STATUS

My life had turned inside out in less than a day. I couldn't believe how quickly things could change. I'd come to believe in Jesus, and my life had taken a terrible turn for the worst. I banged the back of my head against the garage drywall multiple times, and Patches, who rarely barked, gave several sharp disapproving yelps. This had to be another nightmare from which I'd wake any minute.

I prayed.

"Jesus, I promise not to take my own life, but I can't take this." My head throbbed and my chest grew tighter by the minute. "Give me strength or take my life now. Please help me, Lord."

Patches looked at me with sympathetic oval green eyes as he put a warm paw on my shoulder and licked my face. Mr. Fluff stretched his body across my chest as if to give me a hug.

I stood up and held Fluff in my arms.

"Okay, guys, let's see if Miss Dianne can take you in. I've got stuff to do today."

Dianne Davis and her husband, Robert, were a Black couple in their late seventies, married for almost fifty years. She was petite, about five feet three, and he was built like me, thin and over six feet. Both were full of vigor and strength that belied their ages. The pair were the unofficial parents or grandparents to the apartment residents, so when I knocked on their door, I was happy to find them unharmed by the fire.

★★★

Mr. Robert answered the door.

"It's Billy Yates, honey ... come on in, son. You look like you've been through it, but we're glad to see you're okay. We've been praying for you."

Miss Dianne came in and threw her arms around me in a generous hug.

"Thank God. We thought you might have been trapped in the fire. We thank God for protecting you. We knew you were unaccounted for last night. Where were you?"

"I was at the Taste late last night. Normally, I would've been home asleep when the fire broke out. I spent last night in my garage."

Mr. Robert said, "That's God's protection over you. It's a blessing. Do you know that?"

"Yes, sir." I hadn't previously thought of it as God's blessing. "Can you keep Mr. Fluff and Patches? I've got to get going to the hospital—to check on the Pullmans."

Miss Dianne said, "Of course. And you should have come here last night. That garage is not a safe place to be at night. You don't know who might be lurking around."

Mr. Robert said, "Fluff and Patches are like family members here, but you can't rush off like that. You need to get cleaned up first. Have you eaten?"

"No, sir."

Miss Dianne said, "Take this young man so he can get a shower. I'll fix your breakfast. You like bacon, eggs, waffles, coffee?"

"Yes, ma'am. No coffee. Thank you."

Mr. Robert led me away to the bathroom and gave me fresh towels, "I've got some clothes that should fit you just fine. They'll be laid in the guest bedroom when you come out."

Before and after entering the shower, I visited with my tattoo. It was relentlessly consistent and unchanging. I longed for it to be gone. Along with everything that had happened, my reject label was wearing me out. I couldn't stop looking at it, and every time my heart ached at the sight of it.

TRUE STATUS

After showering and eating, I was refreshed and thankful to have neighbors like the Davises.

Mr. Robert said, "Now, Billy, I must tell you—Mrs. Pullman didn't make it last night. Smoke inhalation. The paramedics couldn't revive her."

"And Joseph?"

"They took him to University of Louisville Hospital. I don't know his condition."

"Do you think Joseph knows about his mother?"

"Don't know 'bout that."

"Mr. Robert, where is God at times like this? The Pullmans were good Christian people."

"Good and bad happens to everybody, but God is still right there with his people, giving strength, comfort, and teaching us so we can help somebody else. Jesus knows what it's like to suffer as a human being. The Bible says Jesus learned obedience through suffering, and his pain qualified him to be able to help us. You a believer?"

"Yes, I'm planning to be baptized."

"That's good. Don't delay. You've got to wash your sins away."

"Yes, sir, Mr. Robert."

I intended to head off directly to see Joseph, hoping I'd be able to bring him some comfort. Instead, something within me dragged me back to where my beloved hole in the ground had been. I clenched my fists and jaw when I stood before the soggy mess that had been my beautiful refuge. A burned-plastic chemical stench stung my eyes and nose.

I dropped to my knees with my head in my hands. Someone's pitiful sobbing that echoed in my ears annoyed me in my grief, until I realized the cries were my own. I closed my eyes and hoped this was another miserable vision, and that soon I would wake and find nothing had happened. But of course, when I opened my eyes the fire's reality was evident. There was nothing to salvage.

"Dear Lord, please help me and my neighbors. All this is too much for me to take."

I arose with aching knees and made my way to my car.

From my car, I called Ezriah and told him I was ready to be baptized. I had to hold the phone back from my ear as Ezriah gave a mighty shout and whoop of praise to God. He was tied up in court, but we scheduled him to baptize me at noon the next day. After the call with Ezriah, I texted Angeline.

BILLY: You get home last night ok?

After a few minutes her reply came.

ANGELINE: Yes, I'm fine.

BILLY: Can we meet somewhere?

ANGELINE: No, I can't.

BILLY: Okay, I'm going to be baptized tomorrow at noon. I hope you will be there.

I included the name and address of the church, but she didn't reply. I shrugged. In my mind there was no way Angeline was not coming back to me. I could not, would not believe she was not coming back.

My next move was to visit Joseph at University of Louisville Hospital.

CHAPTER 33

WEEK 4—WEDNESDAY

I parked in the hospital parking lot and grabbed my backpack with my Bible in it. Joseph might take comfort in having the Scripture read to him. The thought of seeing Joseph with terrible burns gave me pause, but as it turned out, he wasn't badly burned. He'd been hospitalized due to smoke inhalation that had put his life at serious risk.

When I edged Joseph's hospital room door open, fearful shrieks emanated from inside. I flinched, lost my grip on the door handle, and then opened the door again and peered inside.

"Hello, Joseph?"

There was no reply. His hospital bed was set upright like an oversized recliner, and the scary cries emanated from the television. The suspenseful old classic about a monstrous shark—*Jaws*— was playing, but Joseph was in anguished sleep, uttering gut-twisting moans interspersed with bursts of weeping. His wild, curly silver hair was splayed across the pillow, and his smart bed cradled him and tracked his vital signs with built-in wireless sensors.

A monitor at the foot of the bed reported the results. A clear oxygen mask covered his nose and mouth, and a tube from the IV stand nourished and hydrated him with intravenous liquids.

Two wall sconces stood guard over the bed, giving comfortable lighting that was not too hospital-bright. The bed looked like a sort of vehicle, a space shuttle ready for transport. I envisioned protective shields closing over Joseph, and the bed carrying him down a runway for blastoff to the outer heavens.

I'd known Joseph for fourteen years. At first, I'd been put off by the lumps on his face, his herky-jerky movements, and his manner of speech, but his persistent quest for my friendship won me over, and we became friends. Since his mother had passed away because of the fire, Joseph would need support in a way he'd never needed before. I took my Bible out and flipped the thin gold-edged pages, considering what to read to him.

I'd last consumed the sixth chapter of Romans, so I silently devoured Romans 7 to decide whether I'd read it to Joseph. The chapter was tough to digest—its author, the apostle Paul, spoke about his terrible turmoil between wanting to do what was good and the realization he didn't have the ability to actually do good. My mind swirled with recognition of the truth of Paul's writing, because I'd been one who always asserted that I did good. But since I'd been overtaken and lectured by Alexander, how sinfully short I'd fallen was obvious. Paul concluded the chapter by declaring Jesus Christ had rescued him from his dilemma. The same salvation from my own poverty of personal power to do right was my hope.

Romans 8 transitioned from the previous chapter's frustrating struggle to exultant expressions of hope and victory, so I read the eighth chapter aloud, hoping Joseph would hear it. My voice cracked as the words challenged my own feelings over my losses. I prayed Joseph, who'd suffered more than I, would be encouraged. I stood shakily to deliver the chapter's concluding verses which resonated so much with me.

> And we know that God causes all things to work together for good to those who love God, to those who are called according to His purpose.
>
> What then shall we say to these things? If God is for us, who is against us? He who did not spare His own Son, but delivered Him over for us all, how will He not also with Him freely give us all things? Who will bring a charge against God's elect? God is the one who justifies; who is the one who condemns? Christ Jesus is He who died, yes, rather who was raised, who is at the right hand of God, who also intercedes for us. Who will separate us from the love of Christ? Will tribulation, or distress, or persecution, or famine, or nakedness, or peril, or sword?
>
> But in all these things we overwhelmingly conquer through Him who loved us.

Even as I read the words, believed them, and was encouraged by them, doubts and questions surfaced.

How could they be true?

I'd heard Bible teaching my whole life, first from my parents, and then from others like Mrs. Heaviland. I searched Joseph's face for signs he'd heard me.

A faint smile appeared on his face. It grew, and he nodded his head ever so slightly. He fumbled for his oxygen mask and lifted it.

"Amen."

I had to lean close to his face to hear him. "Yes, amen," I responded.

"Billy?" A bigger smile widened across his face, revealing the surprise of handsome teeth with no gaps or stains. "That you?"

"Yes, it's Billy."

"Thank God." Joseph dropped the mask to his face, sucking oxygen for a few breaths. "Thought ... you ... was ... burned up. I ... banged on ... your door ... no answer."

"I was at the festival last night, so I wasn't home."

"Mom is gone. She ... didn't make it." Joseph let the mask fall back on his face and he looked at me with bloodshot eyes which silently became overflowing puddles of tears.

"I'm so sorry, Joseph."

After a moment of searching for something else to say, I collapsed back into the chair and reflected on the Scriptures I'd read.

Could God really use the stupidity, incompetence, or evil intent of Mr. Ubel to bring about good for Joseph? Was Joseph, as he lay there almost too weak to lift his mask, truly an overwhelming conqueror? And if he was, how?

And what was it that he conquered?

"Lord," I said, "help me believe and understand."

I struggled to stay awake, but soon, sleep overcame me, and I dozed off.

Soft whirring and clicking, stopping and starting again, aroused me from my nap. E.J. Landes had positioned his wheelchair to my left, directly between me and the door, and when I woke he seemed to be studying me. I snapped my head back at the sight of him, my hands and feet became cold, and a vein in my neck throbbed.

"E.J., you startled me. What are you doing here?"

"Same as you." He narrowed his eyes at me. "Visiting my neighbors injured in the fire."

"Oh, of course. Sorry." My face and neck grew hot with embarrassment. My tone suggested E.J. had no right to be there. "What do you think Ubel was up to last night?

"I have no idea about what he was doing or who might have influenced him. Based on my dealings with him, I'd say Mr. Ubel was a foolish man with no moral compass."

"What do you mean?"

"He took shortcuts in his work. And he doubted God's goodness, wisdom, authority ... maybe even God's existence."

"Ouch. By that standard, I've been pretty close to that most of my life. Was I a fool?"

"Hmm ... maybe." E.J. gazed at me and smiled. "But it looks like you've changed course."

"What do you mean?"

"What's that you're holding?"

I clutched my Bible and raised it up and slowly shook it.

"Yes," I said. "I suppose I'm at a crossroads."

"We all need to reach the point of decision. Ubel chose bitterness, pride and self-importance."

"My pride has certainly been punctured recently. Maybe there wasn't much difference between me and him."

"I once told Ubel God's intelligence and righteousness were obvious from the natural world. and he said 'the world's a craphole,' along with a few choice modifiers. You couldn't tell him anything."

"I understand bitterness. I lost my home, my girlfriend, and my job, all in one day." Heaviness filled my body, and my throat ached. "If one more thing happens, I might be right there with Ubel. Did your place burn too?"

"No. Our apartment was not affected."

Joseph woke again and ended our dialogue. "Anyone ... seen ... Fluff and Patches?"

"Yes," I said. "After the fire, I was asleep in my garage unit, and Mr. Fluff came in riding on Patches, and they woke me up. Mr. Fluff riding on Patches's head was the funniest sight."

I laughed at the memory of Fluff's paws wrapped around the sides of Patches's head. E.J. smiled faintly.

Joseph said, "They always do that ... good friends."

"I took them to Miss Dianne and Mr. Robert. They're safe."

"Thanks ... I was ... worried they was hurt." Joseph put the oxygen mask back on, fell silent, and sank again into sleep.

"Joseph loves his pets," I said to E.J.

"I've always loved animals as well. When I was a child, before my accident, I especially loved catching turtles, lizards, and frogs at a pond near where we lived." E.J.'s smile grew, and his eyes sparkled at the memory. "Animals fascinated me, and I spent all my time back then learning about animals. I had no interest in anything at school that didn't involve some sort of critter. I didn't do well in school as a young child, because it didn't interest me. I spent so much time down at the pond that I earned the nickname Frogman."

Frogman.

Eddie Frogman.

Cold waves of shock and nausea washed through me.

I wanted to escape from the room. For an eternal moment, the dread of punishment for my sins hung over my head, as it had during the darkest part of my vision of the race. I stared at E.J. Landes, and instead of seeing the worn-out wrinkled face and long white hair and beard, I saw the childhood best friend I'd injured so grievously, a friend who seemed to have no memory of what I'd done.

I poked around to verify what I already knew. "Where did you live back then, and what kind of accident did you have?"

"I was born in Frankfort, Illinois. When I was in second grade, I slipped backward off a huge rock near a river. I had a traumatic brain injury and a broken neck." E.J. tilted his head to the side. "Why do you ask?"

Perhaps fear and guilt had suppressed my memory of pushing Eddie off that rock. Since my recent remembrance of that terrible deed, I'd trembled at the thought of being confronted about my treachery and betrayal of my friend. I had no intention of telling E.J. the truth.

"No reason. I was just curious." I stood up and prepared to excuse myself from the room, and E.J. silently tracked me with his eyes.

Then a voice called to me—one that paralyzed me—speaking to my spirit.

Tell him.

Ask him for forgiveness.

Where that voice came from, I never learned. Perhaps from Jesus. Or perhaps from Alexander or my own conscience. I resisted, but eventually I slowly lowered myself back into the chair.

"Eddie ... isn't that what they used to call you?"

"Yes, a long time ago."

"Eddie, I have a confession to make. I was one of your best friends. Remember Billy Goat Billy? Me, you, and Sammy were the triplets." I couldn't control my tears, and I choked on my words. "You don't recall your accident, but you didn't slip off that rock."

"Tell me what happened."

"I pushed you. I'm so sorry, but I pushed you."

"Why?"

"You were holding a snake. I was afraid of it. I wanted you to kill it, but you wouldn't. I was so angry and afraid when you let it go, when you threw it. For a second, I wanted to kill you. So I pushed you."

"Why were you so afraid?"

How could I explain that part without sounding crazy? I couldn't think of a way to do that, so I told the truth. I leaned in close to E.J. He looked bewildered.

"This is hard for me to explain, and I didn't know it then, but I've come to believe I encountered the devil that day. He filled me with fear. I thought the snake was sent by the devil to come get me. That sounds nuts, and it's no excuse for what I did to you. I'm sorry. Can you forgive me for all the suffering I caused you?"

"I forgave you a long time ago, but I've always wondered what spooked you. I remember the terror in your eyes."

My mouth fell open. I leaned back in my chair in silence.

Eddie did remember what happened, and he's already forgiven me.

I sent up wordless thanks to God before I spoke. "I thought you had no memory of it."

"Let me give you the condensed story of my life since the accident. That's what I believe it was—an accident. An accident, okay? You didn't know what you were doing."

I nodded, grateful.

"After my injury and during all the years of therapy, I met lots of amazing doctors, nurses, and therapists who inspired me to want to recover and learn. When I was finally able to go to school again, I poured myself into my studies, and for the first time, I was a really good student. I'd hated school from my time in kindergarten, so discovering I *could* excel at school shocked me.

"I went to college to study animal behavior, but the lure of a lucrative career won my heart. I ended up getting bachelor's and master's degrees in business and finance. My first job after college was in banking, and soon I got involved in investment banking. I met my wife—"

"There's a Mrs. Frogman?" I snorted out laughter. "I always thought your last name was Frogman."

"Other people did too." Eddie grinned. "I spread that tale myself."

"Is Edmund your only child? I've seen only the two of you here."

"I have two younger children. They're back home with my wife in River Hills, Wisconsin."

"Investment banking? So you're rich, right? What are you doing here?"

"I made an insane amount of money in just a few years. Have you ever heard of the Edmund J. Landes Sr. Foundation? We provide scholarships to students pursuing animal-related science degrees. Ten years ago, I realized I no longer enjoyed my work, so I returned to my first love, which was researching and teaching about wildlife."

"You're an educator too? You've had a good life?"

"Yes, I've written twelve books, both fiction and nonfiction. Two became bestsellers. None of these things would've happened if I hadn't gotten hurt. The way I see it, what you did to me turned out to be the best possible thing for me."

"That's unbelievable." I meant the words as I said them. "Totally unbelievable."

Maybe Ubel worked for E.J. Maybe E.J. wanted revenge. My heart thumped louder and louder as the feeling of being stalked on the seminary campus returned. Maybe E.J. had had me followed. "What are you doing here? Still married?"

"Happily married. We go home every weekend. When I began writing fiction, my memories of that day at the river began to surface. The images of you pushing me off the rock and the look on your face became stronger and clearer." E.J. closed his eyes and leaned his head back.

"Did you ever want to get even?"

"At first, anger gripped me. Then hatred, then obsession. I decided to find out everything I could about you. You were easy to find on social media, and I hired a private—"

"What were you going to do?"

"I don't know, but my attitude made me a murderer before God, and I couldn't stand that. So I repented and sought counsel with a therapist and with my preacher. They helped me to see God's good hand has been all over my life, and he's blessed me."

"That all took place years ago, right? You moved into Bethesda Apartments just a couple of months ago, but you still live in Wisconsin. Why move here?"

"You are unrelenting." E.J.'s eyes glittered. "My desire for revenge ended, but not my obsession with you and your motivation. Remember, I'm an extremely wealthy writer and a student of animal behavior. Sometimes, I focus on the human animal." He shrugged one shoulder. "I suppose I'm doing research for what may become another book—a memoir, a mystery, who knows. I wanted to know the man who almost killed me when we were both little boys. What was he thinking back then? And what did he become?"

"What conclusions have you drawn?"

"What I am prepared to say is that I apologize for spying on you, and I would like us to be friends again." E.J. reached out his left hand to me.

I hesitated and swallowed, but I grasped his hand and shook it. "Apology accepted. It would be my pleasure to renew our friendship."

I didn't know E.J.'s heart, but if I was to be a Christian, I needed to trust God's people, and to have confidence in God's provision for the times when people betrayed my trust.

I stood to leave, but Joseph stopped me, even as he still slept.

"Listen." I motioned to E.J. as I leaned over the bed. "What's he humming?"

"It sounds like 'Jesus Loves Me.'"

"Ah yes, I remember. Jesus loves me, this I know, for the Bible tells me so."

"That makes all the difference." He shifted in his chair. "Tell me one thing. What was going on about four weeks ago, when you closed yourself up in your garage? Edmund and I thought that was a strange thing to do, and we were concerned. I had Edmund bang on the door to see if you were okay, but you didn't answer."

"Let's just say it was a low point in my life. One day, I'll tell you about it, but right now I need to get to a hotel and get some rest. I haven't really slept in about thirty hours. Let's hope I don't fall asleep at the wheel before I get there."

We shook hands again and I left.

Did Jesus really love me?

Did he protect me in the garage that night?

Does he still love me, even now?

CHAPTER 34

Week 4—Wednesday

When I left the hospital, all my material possessions hung on my back. I proceeded on an expedition for clothes, toiletries, food, snacks, and other supplies. But my heaviest possession was loneliness, and I lingered in the aisles, conversed with strangers in a cozy coffee corner, and chatted with the checkout lady.

I longed for connection with Angeline, but she didn't respond to my calls or texts. The front desk at Wilderness Extended-Stay Hotel greeted me at around two p.m. Soon thereafter, I scarfed down two premade sandwiches and stretched out under the covers in the suite's king bed.

I hoped for the respite of immediate sleep. Instead, my mind rehashed recent events, while the sounds of racing, giggling children vibrated through my hotel room's ceiling.

My treasured, irreplaceable possessions were all ashes. My one book, the Bible, was my complete library. Lost were more than sixty-six hundred books along with their custom-made bookshelves. The only job I'd truly loved would soon come to an end, Angeline was gone, and Joseph might die. I wanted to sleep and not wake up.

How would I be able to bounce back from it all? What would be the resilience elixir for me? How do human beings move forward with confidence and hope, free of bitterness after their lives are decimated?

How did E.J. traverse from a place of hatred to wanting to renew our friendship?

How did Joseph sing 'Jesus Loves Me' while fighting for his life and mourning his mother?

Could Angeline learn to trust again, after the one who vowed to love her tried to kill her? How long would the process take?

Angeline's struggle had not been on my mind until that afternoon, and I wanted to help her, but doubted I'd get the chance. My prayer was that Angeline would learn to trust and love someone again, even if that someone was not me. I prayed for all my neighbors, and for more strength to believe in the promises found in the book of Romans.

Just as I had exhausted myself with all my questions and sleep descended on me, my cellphone shattered the silence.

It was my sister.

"Hello, Dolyana."

"Where are you right now? Are you driving?" She spoke in low, rapid-fire tones.

"I'm in an extended-stay hotel."

"What are you doing in a hotel? What happened?"

I filled Dolyana in on my ordeal of the previous couple of days.

"I'm sorry about the fire," she said. "I'm glad you're okay, but I have more bad news." Her deep breath came through the phone. "Mommy and Daddy are in the hospital. They—"

"What happened?"

"They were in a car accident. Daddy was driving, and he had a stroke while they were on the road." She paused, then went on. "We're all at the hospital. They're in the

ICU. You need to come home, but it sounds like you aren't in any condition to drive tonight. You need to get some rest and come in the morning, okay?

"Okay."

"I'll see you tomorrow."

I texted Ezriah and told him I had to leave town in the morning, so we rescheduled my baptism from noon to eight o'clock the following morning, before Ezriah had to be in court. I texted Angeline the time change, but she didn't reply.

I prayed for my parents through the heavy hollowness in my chest. Emptiness overflowed and drowned my soul. I pulled the covers over my head and tried to sleep, but rest did not come. I got up and took off my shirt and looked upon my rejected tattoo, my secret moniker. Only Ezriah and Angeline knew of my shameful label. I'd known about it for only a month.

How much punishment would I receive? And how much would my loved ones suffer to satisfy my debt of sin? I'd thought Jesus paid for my sins, but if that was true, why did the sanctions upon me seem endless? I'd lost everything. Why did God allow it?

My skeptical thoughts were wrong, but they felt comfortable, like cherished bad habits. Still, I prayed for understanding and read Psalm 23, one of the Scriptures Joseph had recommended.

> Even though I walk through the valley of the shadow of death, I fear no evil, for You are with me; Your rod and Your staff, they comfort me. You prepare a table before me in the presence of my enemies; You have anointed my head with oil; My cup overflows.

My Bible identified that psalm as 'A Psalm of David.' Professor Stanley said God had made King David great and unconditional promises. I supposed those promises sustained David when he faced terrible times under the shadow of death. I strained to remember the promises God had made to me, but my brain failed me.

I put my clothes on and dragged myself to my car with the intention of returning to my garage workshop. The only part of my home that was left would be a comfortable refuge for a couple of hours.

★★★

I arrived at seven-thirty the same evening and tapped the code on the keypad to open the garage door. The daylight faded fast as scudding black and gray clouds darkened the sky.

When my new apartment was ready, I'd need some bookshelves, so the planning process for rebuilding a few items began. I pulled my project notebook from a storage shelf, but I recoiled and dropped it at the sight of what looked like a glob of blood on the spine. My skin crawled as I bent down and examined the notebook as it lay on the garage floor. The glob was only a congealed clod of red paint, left over from the recent spill.

Relieved, I found a rag and wiped my hands. I cleaned up the notebook and examined the area of the spill. I'd done a terrible clean-up job, leaving smears of red everywhere.

I moved to the workbench with the notebook and flipped to a clean page. Heat radiated from the concrete floor, and sweat dripped from my forehead. The evening was calm—no breeze to provide relief—and an unusual quiet surrounded the complex. Miss Dianne's warning against being in my workshop at night flashed into my mind as I eyed the assortment of crowbars, hammers, wooden mallets, screwdrivers, and saws hanging from the workshop's walls.

TRUE STATUS

I was surrounded by deadly weapons.

The driveway in front of the garage was deserted in both directions, holding only the gloom of shadows. It was as if everyone else except me had received a notice to get out of town in the face of some oncoming dreadful occurrence. I returned to the workbench, and in the silence my breathing echoed. My heart pounded against my chest as if it would break my ribs.

Something bumped the back window. I spun and stared, but saw only darkness. My senses shifted to high alert. A low scraping sound began, and I looked around frantically to locate its source, only to discover the sound was my fingers clawing the edge of the workbench. I took some deep breaths and tried to calm down.

Soft footsteps sounded outside. I peered into the dark driveway, hoping to see Patches and Mr. Fluff, but no pets were there. The footsteps stopped.

I was ready to make a mad dash for my car when a figure shrouded in black appeared in the parking lot, directly in front of my garage. After a moment, the figure got down on all fours and slunk onto a low wall before disappearing into the shrubbery.

Abruptly it reappeared, sitting among the bushes and gazing directly at me. I couldn't tell what—or who—it was. I backed up, away from the front of the garage. The door operation button was to my right, and I jumped for it to shut out the thing.

I was already too late.

Just before I hit the garage door button, still focused on the unmoving thing in front of the garage, a tapping noise sounded from behind me. I whirled to find Ariun Christian from the 'Jesus in the Old Testament' leaning casually against my workbench, a smile on her face and a mallet in her hand.

"Hope I didn't startle you, Billy Goat Billy."

I trembled at the sight of her. "What are you doing here? How did—? Where did you come from?"

"I slipped in while you were distracted." She pointed toward the front of the garage, and when I looked, there was nothing to be seen. The figure outside was gone.

"Who was it?" I wanted to rip the mallet from her hands and beat her with it.

"No idea." Her tone was offhand. "I saw you staring out there, but I didn't see anything." She picked up a bag from behind the workbench and extended it toward me before depositing it on the edge of the workbench. "I brought you dinner."

She pulled up another bag and retrieved a monstrous burger and fries. She immediately sank long, unnaturally white teeth into the burger.

"Mmm ... so good. Juicy. Here, help yourself." She flicked my bag with her fingers. "Water's in there too." She pulled out a bottle and set it down next to the bag.

Condensation dripped from the water bottle, tempting me. I hesitated, then grabbed the bottle and sipped the cold water which helped settled my nerves. My body and mind began to relax. I was glad to no longer be alone, even though Ariun was uninvited.

Did I hear the crack of the seal being broken when I twisted the cap of the water bottle? Or had it already been broken?

I put the bottle down and paced the small area of garage on my side of the workbench.

Ariun was dressed casually in white slacks and sandals. Her pink short-sleeved blouse and matching earrings were a nice accent to her brown skin. Her hair was tied back into a ponytail, with short strands floating around her face. The highlights in her hair shimmered as if electrified—tiny sparks even appeared to shoot off the loose strands. Ariun's perfume sweetened the air. The overall effect was hypnotizing.

Her resemblance to my precious sister Dolyana was eerie, except for the sparking hair.

I leaned toward her. "Your hair ...it's ... so strange, but captivating."

"How sweet." She patted her belly and smiled. "I love captives."

"What's that supposed to mean?" I pushed back from the workbench.

"Calm down. I was just joking. Anyway, I commend you on your decision," she said, in between licking ketchup off each of her fingers.

"What are you talking about?"

"Your decision to rebuild the old shrine that burned. You're smart." She tapped my notebook of bookshelf designs. "You should repopulate it with all the wisdom of the world, just like before. Just think—you can have your old life back, only much better."

"What are you talking about—the old shrine?"

"*Your* shrine. The shrine to human wisdom and accomplishment, of course. The monument to the work of your hands."

"How did you know about the fire?"

She waved a dismissive hand. "What does that matter? I have my sources. Besides, it's hard to miss a burned-out building, along with all that smoke." She cocked her head and gave me a knowing smile. "Maybe I work for E.J. Landes. He hired a private investigator to follow you."

"I already know about that."

"And *I* know all about *you*, but it doesn't matter how I know. And you're right to be skeptical about the Bible."

"Actually, I've started to believe it and in Jesus and his promises."

Ariun waved her hand in front of her face. "Please. Not that name."

I stopped pacing in front of my meal bag. The aroma tempted me, and I pulled out the burger and fries and set them on the bag. I silently gave thanks to God for the food—praying before eating was a new habit I was working to develop. I prayed too to be able to remember the things I'd learned from the Bible. I took a big bite of the sandwich and gobbled down some fries. It was all very tasty.

"Good? It's medium-well, just like you like it." She brushed the stray hair from her face, and a shower of glittering points of fire followed her hand. Seeing them, I suddenly wondered if Ariun herself had set the blaze.

"You know Angeline's not coming back to you," she continued, "even if you do get baptized. She's done with you. But there are plenty of other women."

"That's not the reason I'm getting baptized. You don't know anything about me or Angeline."

"Oh, but I do. Like I said, I know all about you, and I know all those"—she made air quotation marks with her fingers—"'true believers' aren't protected. Just look at your parents and Joseph. Their lives are hanging in the balance. Has your God ever protected them from suffering? The answer is no, and you know it. That's why there are so many miserable Christians. They're getting no return on their investment."

"Who are you?"

"Someone who can reward you with what you deserve." She took a long drink from her bottle of water. "You've met my kind before. Alexander and I are made from the same stuff. We're just on opposing sides."

"You're an angel?"

She shrugged and ignored my question. "I've known you since the day of your conception."

"Big deal. What do you want?"

"I want to give you gifts. Let me show you."

We stood at opposite corners of the workbench—about six feet apart—yet somehow she reached her right arm out and touched my left temple with her index finger. She moved so quickly I didn't have time to react. I flinched and swatted at her hand, but too late. My head spun.

"I just expanded your vision," she said, "so I can show you the gifts. First, a desirable companion for you." A group of beautiful women immediately appeared. "You just need to pick one, or maybe two. Whatever you like."

"Ohhhh ...." I was breathless, and leaned forward as if it were possible to draw closer to the women in the vision. One of them could be the love of my life.

"She'll give you the children you long for and much more. Okay, moving along here. Second, a career destination suitable to your talents."

I saw myself teaching at a prestigious university among adoring students and admiring faculty.

"I love my current school," I murmured.

"But it's closing," she said with a sour smile.

I imagined bragging to my friends and family about the plum job I'd landed.

"No more teaching at a podunk community college for you," she said. "And third—fame, wealth, and luxurious living."

In my mind's eye, talk-show hosts interviewed me before hordes of fawning fans, about my best-selling memoir and my numerous awards for contributions to the field of mathematics.

I pulled in a deep breath and swelled up, taller and bigger. "Yes, I deserve recognition for my exceptional talent."

"Fourth, and finally, full recovery for your dear parents and Joseph."

"Wow. All those things are so amazing and wonderful. But what does it cost?"

"Billy, Billy. There is no cost. All you have to do is show proper respect and appreciation to your benefactor." Ariun's piercing eyes held me captive.

"What's the proper way to show appreciation?"

"Simply fall down on your knees right now. Give your loyalty, praise, adoration, and worship to the prince of the power of the air—the god of this world—and all these things will be yours."

A sudden wave of nausea overtook me, and I turned and paced again. I'd trade all the women in the world to have Angeline again, but she was already lost to me.

"Remember, God's already rejected you, so he's lost to you too."

She'd heard everything I'd thought. Her voice grew warm. Admiring, even. "We see you differently," she said. "We value you."

I'd been snared. Desire for all those gifts grew in my mind, dragging me toward the feet of Ariun Christian's prince. The promised prizes, already being enjoyed inside my mind, were too great to relinquish. I wondered if I could give the prince fake worship and still please Jesus.

Ariun shook a long reproving forefinger. "Don't even go there. The prince of the power of the air knows when you're truly his—and when you aren't."

Still I hesitated. Delayed. Muddled.

"God demonstrated his love for me when Jesus died for me, even when I was his enemy," I said. "Jesus will forgive and accept me when I obey him."

"You've brought shame to that name, so he's rejected you, remember. We offer you worldwide acceptance and adulation. More than you've ever gotten from God."

"I remember the shameful sins of my friends, but they showed me they were brought out of shame and back to

God through confession and repentance. I only wish I'd learned from them sooner."

She shrugged again and brushed her hair away from her face. Another shower of sparks flew up and drifted down from her fingertips. "Too late now for wishing. Time to pull up your socks and make up your mind. Who's it going to be? Us? Or *them*?"

I prayed for God's help, even as I wished for Ariun's gifts. At that moment, a calm, wise voice—the same voice that had led me to apologize to E.J.—spoke to my spirit in words from the Scriptures.

He was a murderer from the beginning, and does not stand in the truth because there is no truth in him. He is a liar and the father of lies.

Let not your heart be troubled; you believe in God, believe also in Me.

I am the way, the truth, and the life. If you ask anything in My name, I will do it.

I hesitated, because it meant giving up seemingly certain rewards in order to walk a path I couldn't clearly discern.

Finally making up my mind, I took a deep breath, looked Ariun in the face, and shook my head. "No. Not you."

"You're making the biggest mistake of your life," she said. "Those closest to you will die because of your foolishness."

I shook my head again. "No. Offer declined."

Ariun pounded the workbench with the mallet like a madwoman, one hard blow after another, until the workbench was scarred and dented. She stopped and stared at me.

"That's too bad. Means I'll have to finish the job my clumsy drunken servant started."

I stared at her, bewildered.

"Ubel. The fire Ubel set was meant for you." Her face contorted into something inhuman. Her eyes, shifting now from human to snake-like, swelled and threatened to burst in their sockets. "The fire was for *you*."

She hefted the mallet up, holding it above her shoulder. A hand saw appeared in her other hand, and she held it across her chest. "I'm going to beat your brains out. And then I'm going to cut off your head."

I couldn't get enough air. The acrid smell of smoke triggered my asthma. My heart hammered. I kept my eyes locked on the thing that had been Ariun as I backed away from the bench.

I grabbed the big crowbar from the pegboard and gripped it tight with both hands. I stood with it over my shoulder, as if to hit a baseball out of the park.

Ariun crept closer. "You think that's going to save you?"

"Why do you want me? What makes me so special?"

The thing stopped, doubled over, and howled with insane laughter. "Special? You're *not* special, Billy Goat." Her voice took on a darker, monstrous tone. "We fight like mad over every ... single ... human ... soul."

I gasped and took in air that had suddenly turned sulfurous and unbreathable. "But why me? Why now?"

"The battle's been going on since time began, so you aren't special. But you can thank Alexander for our entrance into your conscious life, after he revealed to you your true status with God. We got permission to respond to his action. Fair and equal representation for both sides, don't you know." She slid a step closer. "But the time for talk and bargaining has ended. As of *now*."

Ariun charged me with inhuman speed and knocked me down. My left hand folded underneath me against the crowbar, and pain shot up my arm and into my chest. In another moment, Ariun changed into the dark shrouded figure that had terrified me earlier. Now the figure stood over me, holding the mallet and the hand saw.

"Have mercy." I covered my face with my arm as the figure raised the mallet and the saw over its head.

"Your fear is pure pleasure to me," it growled. Unearthly peals of laughter issued from where the figure's face should have been. It hoisted the mallet and hand saw high in the air, hesitating for the space of a heartbeat. "So sorry, Billy. No mercy here."

The mallet and saw began their descent. I closed my eyes, and my mind shut down. The calm, wise voice returned, and time seemed to stop as the words floated quietly into my soul.

Do not let your heart be troubled.
Believe in God, believe also in Me.
If you ask anything in My name, I will do it.

I opened my mouth and shouted with all the energy I had left.

"I believe, Lord God! In the mighty name of your Son, Jesus, save me from this devil! I beg it in your Son, Jesus's holy name!"

The mallet and saw slammed into the concrete garage floor on either side of my head. The figure screamed a demonic laugh as it leaned over me, its dead reptilian eyes staring into mine. The demon's breath, hellish with sulfur, floated down over my face.

"For now, Billy Goat Billy, you are safe. Protected. But know you should have worshipped us when you had the chance. You will surely suffer for your choice."

The figure thumped me over the heart with the mallet. My shirt began to smoke. My chest burned. "Soon you'll be back on my side," the figure snarled, "without even knowing it."

In a flicker of shade, a shift of shadows, and one bright fiery flash, the figure vanished.

My heart had frozen, along with my breathing. I took in a long breath of clean, sweet air, and my heart learned all over again how to beat. I touched my head, face, and chest, and found no blood.

"Thank you, Lord. *Thank* you, Lord."

I made it to my car, with agony in my chest at every breath and my hand pulsing with pain. The ER doctor's diagnosis was two broken ribs and a broken left hand.

I arrived back at the Wilderness Hotel at one o'clock in the morning and immediately set my cell phone alarm for six-thirty. After all that had transpired this night, I could absolutely not be late for my baptism.

I resisted sleep for a long time, fearing the murderous demon disguised as Ariun would return through my dreams to finish its task. I prayed, thanking Jesus for his intervention, and finally God blessed me with a few hours of peace.

Perhaps all the craziness of the previous month was over. Maybe the angels and demons would do what they did out of my sight.

It didn't matter anymore. I was no longer afraid.

CHAPTER 35

The next morning I arrived at the church building where Ezriah worshipped at seven-forty- five, and strolled around outside in the already warm air. In front of the building at the edge of a bright green lawn stood a large sign with four lines of text. Purple and yellow flowers surrounded the sign, which read:

CHURCH OF CHRIST
WELCOME VISITORS
AND FAMILY MEMBERS.
JESUS LIVES!!!

Having lived the previous month obsessed with shame at being rejected by God, I focused on the word WELCOME, not as the church's reception but rather on the acceptance secured from the One who'd bought and paid in blood for the church—Jesus Christ. Traffic filled the street. Drivers whooshed and whizzed by to their vital appointments. Perhaps they didn't understand either their own status with God or the deeper message of hope the sign put forward.

The Son of God proved his identity by rising from the dead, and he'd been reaching out his hands to everyone ever since. But like I'd been for so long, passersby seemed to remain blind to the treasure offered to all. As one who'd devoted my life to teaching young adults hard mathematical concepts, my mind now focused to somehow do the same with the message of Christ.

"Billy, what are you doing?" Ezriah's hand on my shoulder startled me, interrupting my pondering. "I've been calling you. Let's go in."

We went into the hushed quietness of the church sanctuary where the minister, the church secretary, and a young man stood between the pulpit and the first pew. They greeted us, and then the minister signaled to Ezriah to take my confession of faith.

Ezriah said, "Billy, do you believe Jesus is the Son of God?"

"Yes, I do. I believe Jesus Christ is the Son of God."

"Upon your confession you are now to be baptized in the name of Jesus Christ for the forgiveness of your sins."

The three witnesses smiled, clapped, and said, "Amen."

Ezriah walked to a door at the right front of the sanctuary. The young man led me around to the left, and through the door on that side. He showed me to a changing room, like a large closet where long navy blue baptismal robes hung, and then he stepped out. I took off all of my clothing and the splint that covered my left arm and hand, and put on one of the thick cloth robes. The chill of the air conditioning raised goosebumps on my arms and legs. It felt strange to be naked except for the robe.

Before coming out of the little room, I took a deep breath. I was about to transition from death to life. My old life would be left buried in the baptismal pool. The water would serve as a tomb for the old man I'd been, and as a womb for me as a new creature—born again, as I rose up out of the water with my sins washed away by the blood of Jesus.

TRUE STATUS

Words of a praise hymn reached my ears. I opened the door and stepped out of the dressing room, and the young man led me up some stairs to the baptistry where the low whirl of a motor warmed and ciculated the water.

I looked down and saw Ezriah standing in the middle of the baptistry, fully dressed with dark green fishing waders protecting his clothes from the water that rose to just below his chest. A stairway of six or seven steps led down into the water. As I stepped down into the pool, I found the water surprisingly warm, and I stood there with Ezriah for a few moments.

Ezriah's voice boomed across the sanctuary.

"Billy, upon your confession that you believe Jesus is the Son of God, and having repented of your sins, you are now to be baptized in the name of Jesus Christ for the forgiveness of your sins. You will receive the gift of the Holy Spirit, and begin a new life."

I held my nose with my left hand and my right hand grasped my left wrist. I held both arms close to my chest, which still throbbed with pain. Ezriah grabbed my right wrist and put his other hand on my back, and he leaned me backward, immersing me completely under the water and then raising me up into the air.

I had just become part of the Lord's church, and partner of the bride of Christ.

That day I took part in my own funeral, birth, and wedding, and I was more thankful than anyone else could know. I dried off and began getting dressed, but before I put on my undershirt I stood in front of a mirror and trembled as I raised my left arm and looked at the same spot I had fretted over daily for the last month.

The 'rejected' tattoo was gone.

I continued to pull on my clothes, but as the immensity of the moment sank in I raised my hands above my head in a wordless gesture. Then I covered my mouth, closed my eyes, and sank to my knees as tears welled up behind my eyelids and ran down my face.

Several minutes later Ezriah tapped on the dressing room door.

"Billy? You okay?"

I opened the door, wiping the moisture from my face.

"The tattoo is gone. The 'rejected' tattoo is *gone*, Ezriah. I can hardly believe it." I almost fell to my knees again, but Ezriah caught me. "God has accepted me."

"Amen, brother. Amen. God is good." Ezriah hugged me, and my ribs ached. "You're no longer rejected—now you're redeemed. All you have to do now is obey the One who only wants our good."

"Redeemed," I breathed, echoing his words. "And I don't even deserve it."

When Ezriah and I returned to the sanctuary, I did a double-take at who was there.

"Congratulations. God bless you," said Lawrence Lessons, who grabbed me and gave me another painful hug. I tried not to wince too much. Even more shocking was the sight of Hugo Mason.

"Thank you so much. I'm amazed you guys made it."

Lawrence said, "When Ezriah told us you were going to be baptized, there was no way I was going to miss it."

"Congratulations, my friend." Hugo shook my hand.

"Thank you for coming, Hugo," I said. "But I have to admit, I'm surprised you would come to a Christian baptism. Are you ready to join us believers?"

"Not quite yet. I do value friendship, however, so I wanted to share your big moment."

Our cohort of four left the church building together, with Ezriah and Hugo up ahead and Lawrence and me following.

TRUE STATUS

I said to Lawrence, "How have you been, man?" I patted him on the back.

"I'm okay, but I've been better." Lawrence sighed and stared down at his hands.

"What's wrong?" We'd reached the parking lot, where we stopped and faced each other.

"My girlfriend broke up with me." That explained Lawrence's puffy face and his red eyes. "I really loved her."

"I'm sorry to hear that. What happened?"

"I decided our living together without being married was something I wasn't willing to do anymore. It was dishonoring God. I always knew it was a sin. I was taught better, but I didn't care for a while."

"Why not just get married?"

"That's what I asked her, but she said she wasn't ready for marriage."

"I know what that loss feels like. I guess we have to believe God has something better for us."

"I hope so. I feel like I've lost everything."

Lawrence and I shook hands and parted ways. I approached Ezriah and Hugo who stood nearby talking.

"I'm going to have to hit the road and see about my parents. They were in a car accident yesterday."

Hugo said, "I understand you have some broken bones. You shouldn't be driving any distance in that condition. I suggest you take a flight."

★★★

I took Hugo's advice, booked a flight to Chicago Midway, and proceeded to the Louisville airport. Before my departing flight left the airport in Louisville, I texted Angeline.

BILLY: Hi! Ezriah baptized me this morning. The tattoo is gone!!!!!!! I'm flying out today to see my parents. They were in a car accident yesterday.

I didn't receive Angeline's reply until I landed in Chicago at two-thirty in the afternoon.

ANGELINE: I saw your baptism. Thankful you're saved. Praying for you and parents.

I was shocked by that text and wondered if she'd hid somewhere in the sanctuary.

BILLY: How did you see it?

ANGELINE: The church posted it on their social media site. Sorry I couldn't be there.

That response made me breathe easier and gave me hope. At least she still cared enough to watch the video.

BILLY: I would like to see you when I get back.

ANGELINE: I would like that a lot. Maybe meet at the park and begin again.

BILLY: Great! I'll let you know when I'll be back.

The final text from Angeline came just as the flight crew released us and we began the slow slog to the front of the plane. A new me exited the jetway, based on the words of hope from both my baptism and the text messages. I wanted to sprint and shout, but instead I planted myself in one of the few available seats at the crowded gate and reread the texts. I laughed silently and leaned back in my chair and threw my arms up in a V for victory.

Then I read her text again, thinking maybe I'd misunderstood it. No, it was clear she wanted to see me, and she wanted us to renew our relationship. I began running in place as I sat there, but I was stopped by the pained smile of the elderly woman across from me. I tapped my phone and said, "It's good news. I just got good news."

"Wonderful," she said, eyeing me warily.

It had been the longest and strangest two days of my life, but what had it been like for Angeline?

What had changed for her? Was it my baptism? Had she had a passing anxiety attack?

Would this be a repeating pattern of craziness?

I'd find out in time. I wouldn't press her for explanations. I promised myself to become a student of Angeline, and with God's help, I'd love her and help her on her journey. My master plan included marriage and an arm-in-arm trek through life. How exciting it would be—after all, we were both new Christians with a lot to learn and much to give.

I sprang from my seat and maneuvered through the crowd to the baggage claim area. I'd arranged for a ride-share, and during the hour-long ride to Silver Cross Hospital in New Lenox, Illinois, I contemplated the threat Ariun had made toward my parents. She'd been wrong about Angeline.

I hoped she'd be wrong about my parents as well, but as we approached the hospital my sense of foreboding grew.

CHAPTER 36

Week 4—Thursday

My five siblings and their families still lived in the Chicagoland region, so the ICU waiting room teemed with nieces and nephews. I greeted them briefly before making my way to my mother. Dozens of gorgeous expressions of love adorned Mom's room—colorful arrangements and assortments of cards and balloons, with the younger grandchildren and great-grandchildren in the process of creating more. My sister and brother, Sabrina and Henry, sat talking quietly, and after I hugged them, I turned to Mom, who was sleeping.

I took Mom's hand and said softly, "Mom, it's Billy. I just got in from the airport."

Mom squeezed my hand, and without opening her eyes, she smiled.

"Hi, baby. I knew you would come." Mom loosened her grip and drifted back to sleep with labored breathing.

"Mom." I squeezed her hand to wake her. "I need to tell you something. I was baptized this morning. I'm saved." A weight lifted from my shoulders when I spoke the last two words. The faith that had eluded me for so long was finally mine.

Mom opened her eyes and focused on me. "That makes me happy, Son. An answer to many prayers ... thank God ...

I fretted over you a long time." Mom's words trailed off as her strength drained away.

"I'm going to check on Dad."

"Oh." Mom placed a hand over her heart. "How is my Lancaster?" I looked to Sabrina and Henry, since I hadn't seen Dad yet.

Henry said, "Mom, he had a stroke, but with rest he should be fine. He was asking about you."

Just like Mom's, cards and balloons decorated Dad's room two doors down from hers. When I entered, he was talking to my other siblings, Dolyana, Rueben, and Daphne. Dad seemed much stronger than Mom.

He said, "Well, look who's here." He held out his arms, and I gave him a hug.

"How're you feeling, Dad?"

"They tell me I had a stroke and a car accident. But I feel fine. Ready to go home." He moved his covers as if he was going to get up.

Daphne jumped up and gently pulled his covers back around him. "Daddy, you're not going anywhere. You were hurt bad. And you did have a stroke."

"How's your mother?" Dad closed his eyes for a moment. "I want to see my Junie."

"Mom's resting," I said. "Maybe you'll get to see her later." I fidgeted for a moment with the edge of his bedsheet. "I was baptized this morning, Dad."

A big grin spread across Dad's face. "Wonderful news, Son. Knowing that brings me great joy. Remember, I told you faith comes from hearing the word of God."

"Yes, I remember."

"This word is powerful." Dad reached for his Bible on the stand near his bed, but he was too weak to lift it, so I handed it to him. He fell back into the bed with the Bible on his chest.

"Reading it with … an open heart will change your life. I … I guess … I need a little rest." Soon, Dad was sleeping.

We all shuttled back and forth between Mom's and Dad's rooms, the waiting room, and the hospital cafeteria. We kept our vigil into the early hours of the next morning, when a nurse summoned us to our mother's bedside. The six of us together watched Mom's breaths become less frequent, until she took one last breath and passed on at seven minutes after two a.m.

We clung to our mother like six little lost children. I held one of Mom's hands, as did Henry. Dolyana kissed her cheek, Sabrina stroked her hair, Rueben and Daphne each held onto an arm, and we all wept. Gradually, we left our mother and gravitated to our father, gathering around his bed in silence.

Dad woke to see all of us there in his room.

"My Junie's gone home."

He spoke with certainty, though none of us had spoken about Mom's passing.

"I want to see my Junie."

Then, we watched our father weep as he had not wept since the day we buried his mother fifteen years earlier.

Dad rolled onto his side and drew his legs up toward his chest. During the next two hours, his vital signs declined rapidly, and hospital staff swarmed to revive him. We all watched in stunned disbelief, until at four fourteen a.m. he also departed this life, going home to join his Junie.

It was hard to believe anything could kill our father. The work accident did not, when he was crushed by thousands of pounds of goods and equipment. A stroke couldn't do it. Neither could the ensuing car crash.

All it took was a broken heart.

***

Their deaths were not fair or right.

Old anger and bitterness rose in me, until I remembered even death could not hurt my parents when they were on God's side. The grief remained, but for me the anger toward God subsided.

For Dolyana, it was not so. She threw herself into keeping up the house and the planning of our parents' home-going service, but her failing marriage and the traumatic loss of our parents was more than Dolyana could bear. She seemed to avoid thinking about the losses by keeping busy.

My siblings went to their homes in the area, while Dolyana and I returned to our parents' house, where I stayed for two weeks until the funeral. I spent time with Dolyana to comfort her and help with the arrangements, but mostly we grieved apart, each in our own way. Dolyana cooked, often asking me what I wanted to eat, but I ate little.

It comforted me to know my parents had learned of my salvation before they passed away. My time was spent roaming the house, mostly between Dad's office and Mom's craft room. I camped out often at Mom's white craft table. Smooth and cool to the touch, it held a white coffee mug on the right side, full of colored pencils and inscribed with Scripture in yellow letters, and a sharp pair of light-blue-handled sewing shears. She'd consumed many hours at the table preparing material for clothes, pillows, embroidery, and other creative endeavors. Flecks of purple and gold cloth—remnants of her ideas and dreams—remained on the table.

In the morning, beams of sunlight streamed through the craft room's glass doors leading to the garden patio, and they warmed me as I sat at the craft table. Near the doors, a bulletin board displayed artwork of many of my great-nieces and nephews. Several feet in front of the craft table, a white storage unit rose to the ceiling and spread across the room's width. It contained myriad labeled boxes of various supplies, fabrics, and tools. At the bottom of the storage unit, a built-in desk held my mother's prized sewing machine and a rack of sixty spools of colored thread.

The extreme organization of Mom's space contrasted with the clutter of Dad's office. Time was lost to me as I sat in their treasured spaces. Questions big and small came to my mind, things I wished I'd asked, just to hear their perspective on anything and everything. At times, I heard their footsteps right outside the room, and I expected them to fill the doorway and ask what was on my mind. Acute pain pierced me time after time, but it was always followed by the solace of gratitude that I'd had them as long as I did.

Gradually my thoughts turned to the future and Angeline. I'd bought her an engagement ring. She needed to know I wasn't fooling around, and how serious I felt about her, so I planned to propose marriage upon my return to Louisville. I also wanted to capture the life-altering truths from the book of Romans while the discovery experience was still fresh in my mind, so I began writing an essay a few days before returning home. I completed the first draft of the essay and emailed it to Angeline to review. The essay was meant for our future child when he or she became a young adult, but I purposely didn't tell Angeline that.

I was getting way ahead of myself. Ezriah would laugh at me, but time and life were uncertain. My learning had to be shared. Thinking of my yet-to-be child made it much more urgent, as tomorrow was not promised to me, as it never is to anyone.

Mr. Robert had called me a couple of days earlier and informed me Joseph Pullman had passed away, so there was more sorrow upon sorrow. Ariun had threatened me with suffering, and she'd certainly delivered on her threat, but at least I would see Angeline again soon. I hoped all would be well with us.

CHAPTER 37

Week 6—Saturday

After my parents' funeral and a total of two weeks in Illinois, I returned to Louisville on a Friday and met Angeline Saturday morning at nine o'clock at Pope Lick Park. She was already there when I arrived, standing by her car and basking in the warm sunlight of a cloudless day.

I parked and jumped out of my car.

"I really missed you." I gave her a hug and kissed her cheek.

"Missed you too. I'm sorry about your parents. How're you doing?"

"Okay, I guess. Being up there the last couple of weeks was good therapy for me."

"I'm sorry I wasn't there for you, and for the way I took off a few weeks ago." Angeline held her arms tight against herself and focused her eyes on the ground. "You're not like Junius, but … I … it's hard to explain how I—"

"Maybe you shouldn't try to explain right now." I took her hand and pulled her toward the walkway. "We'll have time for that later. I want to get your thoughts about the essay."

Angeline pointed to the splint on my left hand. "What happened to you?"

"Two weeks ago, before my parents passed away, I got into a fight with the devil. She broke my hand and two of my ribs."

Angeline stared at me before speaking.

"The devil is a woman? What were you doing hanging out with the devil?" She smiled slightly, as if suppressing laughter.

"You're making it sound funny, but I thought I was going to die. The devil was a woman named Ariun—at least, that was the disguise. For four weeks, I was in the middle of a fight between angelic forces, good and evil, that were battling for my soul." We resumed strolling down a paved walkway.

"Your life is like a horror movie. Every time I see you, there's some new thing. Where did you run into the devil?"

"She was a member of the night Bible class I was taking, and she appeared to be just another student. But she showed up at my garage workshop uninvited. That was scary."

Angeline grabbed my elbow. "What did she do?"

"At first she acted like a friend, and then she offered me everything I'd ever dreamed of. Women, success, wealth, fame, recovery for my parents."

"She tempted you with all those things? What did she want in exchange? Your soul?"

"All I had to do, she said, was fall down on my knees and adore and worship the prince of the power of the air— the god of this world." Joggers, walkers, and bicyclists went around us, since we would take a few steps and then stop and stare at each other while we talked.

Angeline shuddered and said, "Did you do that?"

"I wanted to get all those things, but I prayed. The prayer brought me to my senses, and I refused. She went nuts. Said she was going to kill me, but she didn't, because

I prayed that the Lord would save me from the devil, and he preserved my life. Ariun said she was going to make me suffer. But the good news is, the battle has returned to the realm of the unseen, so I won't be so aware of it."

"How do you know that?"

"Both Alexander and Ariun said something to the effect that their time with me was coming to an end, and nothing's happened in the last two weeks. I'm sure all the supernatural stuff is over. Let's find somewhere we can talk about the essay."

We picked up our pace and continued hand in hand.

"Okay," she said, "tell me. Who is Tenny?"

"Tenny is my child. My child of the future." I laughed at myself and the perplexed look on Angeline's face and added, "Not conceived yet. Definitely not conceived yet."

"And where is this child going to come from?"

I pointed back and forth from myself to Angeline. "Us. My plan is for Tenny to be our child. You do want children, right? I'd like two or three kids."

"I do, but I'd like one or two. At my age, I think two is the most my body could handle."

"Two would be great, but you know that means we've got to get started right away." I laughed, stepped in front of Angeline, grabbed her other hand and slowly walked backward facing her while holding both her hands. "We've got to get started soon. We're both so old." I stopped walking and leaned in for a kiss on the lips.

Angeline smiled and pushed me back gently.

"Wait a second, old man Yates. What do you think would have happened a couple of weeks ago when we got to your apartment, if not for the fire?"

"We would have been the fire. Smoldering between the sheets."

"Exactly. To honor Christ, we can't let that happen. You agree?"

"Yes, I'm willing to wait, but it felt so good at the festival. Seemed really right, didn't it?"

"That's the way God made men and women. That's why, if we keep dating and we aren't both in agreement—" She shook her head. "We would end up in bed together. Sexual intimacy is to unite husband and wife, and we ain't there yet."

"That's been my plan for you since day one. To make you my wife, that is." I stepped off the walkway into the grass. Angeline followed, and we stood in the grass facing each other.

"What are you doing? The pitch of her voice rose.

"I don't want to cause a collision with all these folks out enjoying nature." I got down on one knee and held out the engagement ring. "Angeline Otl, will you marry me?"

Angeline pulled me up and hugged me. "Oh, Billy, I do love you, but you've got to give me more time. We've only known each other four weeks."

I was numb to her hug, and as soon as she loosened her hold on me I began striding back to the parking lot. Angeline had to jog to keep up.

"Actually, we met about six weeks ago." I stuffed the ring back in my pocket. I wasn't surprised, but I was disappointed. "That's fine. It was quick, but I can wait." It wasn't really fine, and my mind closed to Angeline. My thoughts turned to my old college friend, Rose O'Leary. But she would never be to me what I wanted her to be.

Maybe Ariun was right about Angeline not coming back to me. Ariun had been right about Mom and Dad and Joseph. Maybe losing Angeline was part of Ariun's prophecy of suffering for me.

Angeline grabbed my hand and pulled me to a stop.

"I didn't say no. I did *not* say no. I just can't move so quickly. Don't be mad. I just need more time to be sure .... Let's focus on the essay. How did you come up with the name Tenny?"

I slowed and started walking again.

"My first name is Tennyson, so our Tenny could be a boy or a girl. I imagine by the teenage or young adult years, Tenny will be able to understand spiritual things and hopefully have a serious interest in them as well."

"We might have to make Tennyson a middle name. You know the mom does have some input on these things, right?"

"I'm open to that, but let's talk about the essay some other time. I need to get going." I didn't feel like talking about the essay when it seemed there was a strong likelihood there was never going to be any Tenny. "I'll call you later, okay?"

"Okay."

★★★

Sweat dripped from my cap by the time we reached the cars. I was anxious to be alone, so I jumped in my car and took off. Angeline waved meekly and watched me drive away. The cool air of the car soothed me and the short drive from the park to Wilderness Hotel was enough time for me to shove aside my rotten attitude.

It didn't matter whether Ariun's predictions proved true or false. My worries and fears didn't matter either, because in Christ, I already had everything I needed. As soon as my hotel door slammed shut, I fell to my knees and prayed.

"Dear God, help me to honor Christ in everything, and to love Angeline. Let me accept whatever happens and never forget all the good you have already given me. Oh, God, help me break this habit of harboring dark, brooding thoughts. Teach me to trust you and believe that all will be as you have planned for me. Amen."

CHAPTER 38

Spring and summer rolled by, and our romance flourished. In autumn, I resumed my teaching career as a member of the faculty of the Mathematics Department at the University of Louisville. On a Friday evening, we celebrated my new employment with dinner at Josh's Grotto, the Italian restaurant my friends and I had visited after class.

The place was packed, and after a twenty-minute wait we were seated in a booth. Our server was Amalea, the same server that the guys and I'd had back in the spring. She welcomed us and took our order, returning shortly with our appetizers of spinach artichoke dip and bruschetta. We gave thanks for the food, and started in on the appetizers.

"The answer to your question is yes," Angeline said.

"What question was that?"

"The one at the park. It was Saturday, May twenty-seventh, to be exact. I'll be your wife." Her faced beamed with confidence. "I will be so proud to be your wife. You're the finest man I've ever known."

My heart felt like it would explode. "Wow. Thank you, Jesus."

She'll be my wife? I'm the finest man she ever knew? It can't be true. Or can it?

This is the best day of my life.

I sprang from my seat and sat next to Angeline. "Now we really have something to celebrate." I leaned over and gave her a long kiss. Every bit of tension left my body, for I was finally at home with the love of my life.

"I love you, Billy. Thanks for being so patient with me. That day at the park, I thought I might never see you again. You were so mad."

"I thought you might never say yes, but I wasn't going to quit on you. You would've had to kick me out of your life for me to stop pursuing you."

Amalea brought our entrées. Before she left, she said, "Sir, didn't you and some of your friends come in here back in the spring, after a Bible study?"

"Yes, ma'am, we did. You have a good memory."

"I eavesdropped on your conversations. I got so interested about Jesus and the Old Testament prophecy, I enrolled in the same evening class. We just started a few weeks ago, and I'm really enjoying it. Thank you for coming in to eat today."

"That's good news. Thanks for telling me." I leaned toward Amalea and waved her closer. "I have some really great news too. You see this beautiful young lady here? We just got engaged."

"Congratulations. You make a lovely couple." She beamed at us. "Make sure you guys leave room for dessert, because it's going to be on the house. Enjoy your meal."

Angeline, with an expression of quiet amusement, watched Amalea as she left us to check on her other tables. "You and the fellows must have been behaving pretty well to have such a good influence on our server."

"Actually, we did a lot of debating. I guess you never know who's watching and listening."

When we had almost finished, I said, "You know we have to complete our assignment."

"What assignment is that, my dear professor?"

"We need to discuss the essay for our baby."

"Okay. I can still access it on my phone."

We both pulled out our cell phones.

Angeline said, "Let me go over the first paragraph. Why do you think you might not be alive long enough to see your child grow up? That's a little morbid."

"The devil did threaten to kill me. I don't really expect to die, but the recent deaths among my family and neighbors has made me conscious of how uncertain life is. I might die tonight."

"You better *not* die tonight." Angeline continued scrolling through the essay.

Amalea brought our desserts—strawberry cream cake for me and chocolate brownie lasagna for Angeline. Her dessert consisted of fudge brownie layers separated by layers of sweet cream cheese with chocolate shavings and drizzle. Mine was sponge cake with layers of vanilla cream, topped with strawberries. We reveled in the gorgeous presentation and the wonderful taste and textures of our gratis treats. We were distracted for several minutes before we returned to our labor for the one we would love.

"The part about 'a volcano of violent emotions' simmering in you is pretty scary to me."

Angeline was probably thinking about how Junius, her ex-husband, had attacked her.

"My point there was to acknowledge my need for a Savior, and that God is already changing me and taming my emotions."

We continued reading through the essay. There were a few things I needed to clean up.

Angeline said, "Overall, I really like it. I think one day Tenny will appreciate it and, Lord willing, we'll both get to hear Tenny's response together."

Angeline and I emerged from Josh's Grotto—after sitting side by side for three hours that felt like thirty minutes—ready to begin a new life together.

We would be prepared to face as one the battles waiting for us, against foes from within and without, both seen and unseen.

THE END

If you would like to read the text of Billy's letter to his unborn son, "An Essay for Tenny" begins on the next page.

AN ESSAY FOR TENNY

Dear Tenny,

Becoming a father is a life-long dream for me. The day of your birth will be the happiest day of my life, and being your dad will be my greatest honor. I'm writing to share things I've learned over the last month from the Bible's book of Romans while they are fresh in my mind, and with the knowledge I may not be there when you are old enough to understand this essay.

At the age of forty-two, I trusted in God's love. My heart had been hard, so hard it took supernatural events to open my eyes. On April 17, the miraculous interrupted my life and dragged me to the Bible, which led me to God. For much of my life, a volcano of violent emotions simmered beneath the surface, but God is working in me to tame my emotions. My prayer is that you will have a receptive heart and will trust God as a young person. Miracles are not necessary—only God's word is needed. You may or may not agree with my conclusions. Either way, my love for you will be the same.

Read the words of the apostle Paul in Romans 8:1–4. Verse three says the law was weak, because none of us, except Jesus, has had the ability to keep the law. Jesus became human and lived a sinless life and became the perfect sacrifice to pay the penalty for our sins. In Christ, there is no condemnation. Outside of Christ there *is* condemnation. We all have a desperate need for a savior, for eternity and for a better life now.

In Romans 1:18–23, Paul says the human rebellion began with the denial of God's nature. People worshipped created things, animals, people, and inanimate objects instead of God. After rejecting their creator, they rejected the design for which God created male and female. The design of human bodies as male and female shows husband and wife should be joined together both to satisfy sexual desires and for the propagation of the race. Tenny, I don't know why some people have same-sex attraction, but I hope you don't have this desire. If you do, I would ask you to pray God helps you live in a way pleasing to him.

The long list of sins Paul presents at the end of Romans 1 shows how we also rejected God's design for interpersonal relationships—we practiced unrighteousness, including greed, envy, and arrogance, all sins worthy of death. So, Paul argues, we became objects of God's wrath as law breakers. Some will say the penalty doesn't fit the crimes, but who gets to decide what is just and right? For a long time I thought I was qualified to make such a determination, but I was wrong. God, our designer and maker, is the only one qualified to determine what is right and wrong. Only God can say what is just. Tenny, if God is real, isn't it possible he could disagree with you about what is right and wrong? If so, will you yield to God? I hope you will. God allowed Jesus to take our punishment, and all he asks in return is that we honor and obey Jesus which means we have faith in Jesus.

Our sins make us enemies of God, but there is hope. Read Romans 3:21–24. Notice how the twenty-third and twenty-fourth verses merge a devastating indictment of humanity with the amazing demonstration of God's mercy. All have sinned, but all can be redeemed and justified through faith in Jesus Christ. There is no room for boasting, only for gratitude to God.

Romans 5:8–10 says Jesus died for us when we were his enemies. Tenny, you may commit some terrible sin, and ask, "Will God forgive me?" This passage answers that question in advance, since Jesus died for us when *all* of us were his enemies. God will surely forgive anyone who comes to him in the spirit of repentance. Never forget that, Tenny.

Tenny, Romans 6 says when we are baptized into Jesus we participate in the death of Christ. We are buried in the water and die to sin. When we rise from the water we share in Christ's resurrection to live a new life led by God. I just underwent this rebirth.

Tenny, Jesus offers a never-ending life with God. I hope you will receive this gift also.

Love,
Daddy
Your father,
Tennyson William Yates

ABOUT THE AUTHOR

Chuck Richardson was born and raised in Rome, New York. He always loved reading and writing and even considered majoring in English in college, but practicality won out, and he earned a BS in Mechanical Engineering and a Master of Education degree. Over the years, Chuck pursued his interest in writing as a freelance writer for a Black community newspaper and a local business newspaper, editing newsletters for a friends of the library group and for a professional association. Chuck considers himself to be an educator, so after fifteen years as an engineer for two large manufacturing companies, he changed careers to work as a quality management consultant and trainer for eighteen years.

Chuck now lives in Louisville, Kentucky, with Ruby, his wife of thirty-six years. They have two adult daughters, Brittany and Jillian. Chuck is a Curriculum Developer for a company that produces e-learning technical training materials in Southern Indiana. Chuck's position combines technical writing and being a subject matter expert.

Chuck has served as an elder, deacon, and teacher in the Church of Christ for more than thirty-five years. He is a passionate believer in Jesus Christ. Chuck enjoys teaching adult Bible classes and especially likes helping teachers become better teachers.

Chuck enjoys doing yard work, and before he began spending most of his free time reading and writing, he tried to complete one or two woodworking projects each year. He ran track and cross-country in high school and is still interested in sports, watching college and professional basketball and football games now and then.

Visit www.chuckrichardsonstories.com where Chuck blogs on various topics including the Bible, teaching, and writing stories as a tool to teach the Bible.

SCRIPTURE CROSS-REFERENCE

Dedication—John 5:24
Dedication—Matthew 7:13-14
Page 90—Matthew 13:47-50
Page 121—Proverbs 23:1-8 NIV
Page 136—Matthew 7:21-23
Page 176—Matthew 2:13-18
Page 190—Romans 1:18
Page 194—2 Peter 1:20-21
Page 194—Luke 24:25-27
Page 203—Romans 2:3
Page 210—Romans 3:21-25
Page 217—Romans 4:7-10
Page 227—Romans 5:8
Page 228—Romans 6:1-4
Page 259—Romans 8:28
Page 259—Romans 8:31-35
Page 259—Romans 8:37
Page 271—Psalm 23:4-5

All references NASB unless noted otherwise.